A Small Town Secret
Book 11: Love in Harmony Valley Series
Melinda Curtis

Franny Beth Books

This is a work of fiction. Names, characters, places, and incidents are products of the author's imagination or are used fictitiously and are not to be construed as real. Any resemblance to actual events, locales, organizations or persons, living or dead, is entirely coincidental.

First Edition: Copyright @2017 by Melinda Curtis

Second Edition: Copyright @2024 by Melinda Curtis

All rights reserved. No part of this book may be reproduced in any form or by any electronic or mechanical means, including information storage and retrieval systems, systems, without written permission from the author, except for the use of brief quotations in a book review.

Chapter One

"Tell me this isn't where we're going to live."

"What's wrong?" Mandy Zapien's heart had been clinging to a position in her throat for the last hour of the drive to Harmony Valley. It clawed a degree higher as she pushed past her teenage sister aside to get a good look inside the house they'd left seven years earlier.

Same dark chocolate shag. Same tan-and-navy plaid couch under the front picture window. Same oak side table with Grandma's sewing basket next to it and the fake Ficus in a colorful plastic planter Mandy had Bedazzled when she was ten. Nothing was new or out of place.

I'm home.

Mandy's heart slid back into her stress-strapped chest. "The house is perfect. Just the way we left it after Grandma died." Their grandparents had raised them.

"Seriously?" Olivia darted around Mandy, holding her cell phone and panning around the room, videotaping. "I opened the door and there was a nuclear explosion of dust." Her yellow flip-flops snapped as she made her way into the kitchen. Her pale bare legs looked long because her jean shorts were too short.

Mandy had considered asking Olivia to change this morning and throw away the shorts, or at the very least roll down the thin cuffs, but as the guardian of a seventeen-year-old, she had to pick her battles and not break eggs. Today, moving day, was not the time to upset her younger sister.

Mandy went to the fireplace, pressing her hand against the solid red brick. It was as sturdy as their grandparents had once been. Would they approve of what she was doing? They didn't have a legal right to be here. "I have good memories of this place."

"Really? I don't remember much." Olivia claimed not to recall the way the house looked or the tinsel-covered Christmas tree their grandparents put in the corner every year. Or the photos they'd staged of the two of them on the hearth on Christmas morning, wearing the annual holiday sweaters Grandma had knitted.

The doctor had told them memory loss was normal after chemotherapy, that Olivia might never remember the happy times here. But Mandy had hoped...

It doesn't matter.

Mandy breathed deeply. They were here, in the house and in the town where Mandy had felt safe during her childhood. Her teenage sister had a clean bill of health. Mandy had a promotion and was re-opening the post office. Things were looking up.

"Hey, the fridge is running," Olivia said from the kitchen.

"Is there..." Mandy's heart crept back into her throat. "Is there food inside?" *Has* she *been living here?* Mandy hurried into the kitchen in time to see Olivia pry the sticky refrigerator door open.

"Ew. That's disgusting." Olivia stopped filming and covered her nose.

Mandy peeked in. What once might have been a small basket of strawberries (based on the fermented smell) was now a glob of mold. That hadn't happened overnight. Mandy shut the door, more convinced than ever that their mother didn't call this home. With any luck, they'd be living elsewhere without her ever knowing they'd been here. All they needed was a few weeks to get back on their feet.

Olivia and her flip-flops snapped their way down the hall toward the bedrooms. "Hey, I recognize our room." She disappeared inside. "Why did we leave the bunk beds here?"

"Why?" Mandy leaned against the door frame, smiling fondly. There were more good memories in this room – bedtime stories read to Olivia, dreams made as Mandy fell asleep. "We left the bunk beds when we moved because I'd slept on the top bunk for ten years, and at twenty-five I wasn't going to do that anymore. Take whatever bunk you like. You're sleeping in here alone." She'd take her grandparents' room.

"I'm not arguing." Olivia actually smiled as she glanced around the room. "This room has the feeling of familiarity but…"

"Your memories will come," Mandy reassured her, wishing it was a true statement.

Olivia sighed.

"Do you remember this?" Mandy closed the bedroom door, shutting them inside the room they'd once shared. They had time for a little reminiscing before the day's summer heat made it too hot to unload her truck. "This is where Grandma tracked our height."

There was a narrow, framed mirror mounted on this side of the door. Their heights were marked on the frame with indelible ink. Mandy's in pink. Olivia's in purple.

"I don't remember…anything about this room," Olivia murmured, sounding sad.

"No matter." Mandy drew her sister close, and closer still, until they could see each other and their reflections.

Mandy, the tallest of the pair, looked too thin and too young with her slight smile and thick dark hair in messy ponytails beneath her ears. Her red tank was as baggy as the circles under her eyes. She'd been worried about her new job, about the move, about the bills, the house, Olivia, about…well…everything.

Olivia's frame was deceptively solid, a side-effect of her cancer treatment. To anyone who didn't know her history, the teen looked as if she'd put on extra weight preparing for a growth spurt. Her soft brown hair had finally grown back in an inch. The short style made Olivia's brown eyes and wide mouth seem more prominent.

"You were always taller than me." Olivia pointed out the two most recent pen marks on the mirror frame.

"And you were always prettier." Mandy nudged her scoffing little sister aside and opened the door, leading the way to the master bedroom. "You should feel lucky you didn't get my height *or* my shoe size."

Neither one of them opened the second bedroom door as they passed. That had been their mother's room. At least, she slept there on the rare occasions she'd visited.

Why did Grandpa leave her this house?

Mandy and Olivia stopped just inside the master bedroom.

The full-size bed was made with a pink chenille bedspread. There was a layer of cobwebs from the cherry headboard to the pillows. No one had slept there in a long time. Grandma's wide dresser sat in front of a wall with maroon-striped velvet wallpaper. The solid cherry dresser had a white marble top and a large, framed mirror attached to the back. Grandpa's taller, narrower dresser was made from the same cherry with a matching white marble top.

"After Grandma died and the post office in Harmony Valley closed, we moved to Santa Rosa." Mandy opened a top drawer of her grandmother's dresser. It was filled with colorful polyester scarves. "We didn't have the heart or the strength to go through Grandma's things and move the furniture." They'd furnished an apartment by shopping at thrift stores.

"I remember this room," Oliva murmured, frowning. "I remember you...taking care of Grandma."

"What else do you remember?" Mandy picked up a red, white, and blue scarf, shaking it out without really seeing it. "Do you remember Grandma's engagement ring?"

"Only because you told me it was made of brass." Olivia opened the closet. "Her clothes are still here. They smell of lavender." She moved clothes across the rod, scraping wire hangers over wood. "I thought you said you left Grandma's clothes. There aren't many in here."

"That can't be." Dismay made a special delivery to Mandy's gut with a one-two punch. She quickly folded the scarf, returned it to the pile and closed the drawer. When they'd moved, Grandma's side of the closet had been jammed full of pants, blouses and dresses, many with the tags still on.

But the clothes with price tags were gone. Mandy rummaged through the other dresser drawers. Except for Grandma's underthings, the other drawers were empty.

An old memory lurched from Mandy past, like a zombie coming to life after a long and restless sleep.

Grandma's voice, pitched low. "If you need money, Teri, ask. Don't go searching through my drawers."

"I was just admiring your scarves." Mandy's mother had slid the drawer closed, looking like a model in a short, clingy black cocktail dress and black heels more appropriate for a hotel bar than Harmony Valley. "They're so pretty."

Neither one of them had acknowledged eight-year-old Mandy lingering in the doorway, holding onto the hope that Mom would look her way and smile. That she'd stay this time and love her the way mothers should.

"Pretty?" Grandma scoffed. "Save those empty compliments for your father, Teri. You hate my scarves."

Mandy hadn't recognize her grandmother's voice. It wasn't sweet or patient. It didn't comfort or express love, not the way it did when Grandma talked to Mandy.

"Those scarves remind you of my cancer, Teri," Grandma went on. "They taunt you because I didn't die."

Horrified, Mandy had stumbled back in the hallway and then ran into her room. It wasn't until the door was closed and she'd burrowed under the covers that she'd realized her mother had been laughing.

"Do you think...?" In the here and now, Olivia came to stand near Mandy, unable to complete her question.

"That Mom was here?" Mandy asked.

Olivia nodded.

They both stared toward the bedroom they hadn't entered. Mandy imagined Olivia's thoughts were much different than their own.

Olivia's attitude toward their mother was as tentatively hopeful as Mandy's had been all those years ago. Despite the fact that Olivia had been shunned and disappointed by Mom, there was still a part of Olivia that wanted to believe every excuse their mother gave for her absence. That Mom loved her. Mandy held no such false hopes, not for either of them.

"Grandpa left Mom the house, but..." Mandy clasped Olivia's hand. "But if Mom lived here, it was a long time ago." The dust. The cobwebs. The strawberries fermenting in the fridge. "You know how Mom is. She comes for a very brief time and then goes away for a lot longer."

Still, neither one of them moved toward their mother's room. Neither one seemed to want to open the door and discover more clues as to how long it'd been since Teri Zapien had been here.

"I want to see her." Olivia's words sounded like they came from a young girl lost on a once-familiar playground.

"She might show up." Mandy hoped not.

Their mother was no good at keeping secrets, especially the ones Mandy kept from her sister.

"Kittens?" Captain Ben Libby drove Harmony Valley's fire truck around the corner toward the crowded town square. "We're taking the engine out for the first time for kittens?"

The adrenaline rushing through Ben's veins came to a crashing halt.

The fire department was just re-opening in Harmony Valley because the town had a need for emergency services. And although Ben was new to town, he'd never imagined their first call would be a kitten rescue.

"It's not just kittens stuck in a tree, son." From the passenger seat, fire chief Keith Libby, Ben's father, pointed to the large, sweeping oak tree in the middle of the square and the gathering crowd. "There's a boy up there, too."

Sure enough. There was a flash of red hair and knobby knees between the branches filled with large summer leaves.

Props to Dad.

His eyesight was still sharp even if the rest of his body wasn't in its prime.

"Kids seldom need rescuing from trees, Dad." Ben's godchild came to mind. He was guardian to seven-year-old, stoic Hannah. She'd probably never find herself in such a predicament.

"Give Harmony Valley a chance, son." Dad laid his hand on Ben's shoulder, choking back a concerning cough. "I know you didn't grow up here like I did, but I didn't ask you to come with me."

"No. That request came from Mom."

Because after decades of sleep-depriving forty-eight-hour shifts and the inhalation of too much toxic smoke in the busy Oakland, California, fire department had taken their toll on Ben's father. Dad's weakened heart and lungs made the fifty-five-year-old move like the seventy and eighty year-olds who made up the majority of Harmony Valley's population. Breathing had become a daily struggle. He'd be deadweight on a fire crew in a busy fire station, a danger to himself, those under his command, and those in need of rescue.

Ben had put his own firefighting career on hold to help his father reopen the rural fire department for the ten months his old man had left until retirement. Reaching full retirement meant a 25 percent bigger stipend each month for his parents. And despite his father missing out on much of Ben's childhood to pursue a career in fire—*cue resentment*—Ben couldn't live with himself if something happened to Dad.

"Let's finish this quick and move on to fire inspections," Ben said. There hadn't been any fires in Harmony Valley in more than five years, and Ben wanted to keep it that way.

He pulled to the curb and put the fire engine in Park. The engine shook, shuddered, and shot out a gasping blast of black smoke that drew everyone's attention in the square. Not exactly the entrance Ben had hoped for.

More like the worst-case scenario since this was the town's first impression of them. "I guess we need one more tune-up with Joe."

The town's mechanic had got the fire truck running after sitting for over ten years.

"Deploy the ladder," Dad said in his best *I'm-in-charge* voice, unbuckling his seat belt.

"Deploy the..." Ben clung to his seat belt with clenched fists. He'd known he'd need patience to work with Dad, just not this much. "We haven't had a chance to check the truck's hydraulics. The ladder might not work. Or it might stop working." Too many worst-case scenarios tumbled through his mind. Ben released the belt and unbuckled it. "Knowing that, are *you* going in the bucket?"

"I will. If you don't have the stomach for it." A challenge if there ever was one. Father versus son.

I won't worry about him being safe if you're here.

Mom's voice.

Her words helped Ben center himself.

"Stay in the truck." Ben had a take-charge voice of his own, one his father had been getting in larger doses since his arrival in town. "I'll get the kid and kittens down the old-fashioned way while you observe from here. There's a wildfire on the other side of the mountain and the smoke will aggravate your lungs."

"*Stay in the truck*," Dad grumbled, followed by a few deep coughs. "I'm the fire chief. And I say *we* deploy the ladder."

"Please, Dad," Ben added quickly, aware they had an audience in the square waiting to see heroics. The sky overhead was gray from all the smoke in the air. "What if you can't catch your breath out in front of all these people? Or worse, what if we deploy the ladder, you go up in it, get light-headed and tumble to the ground?"

What if the town realizes Dad's health isn't 100 percent and that I'm covering for him?

This last was almost as imperative as keeping Dad safe. If Ben's complicity was exposed and word spread, he'd find it hard to work as a firefighter again.

"I can handle this, Dad," Ben reassured him, hanging on to patience by a thin thread. "That's why I'm here."

"You and your mother..." Dad crossed his arms over his chest. "What do you propose I do while you go play hero?"

"Catch up on your phone calls. You said you had some neighboring fire departments to contact, alerting them to us re-opening." Ben hopped out of the truck without turnout gear or helmet and marched toward the oak tree.

There was a farmers market today, but the farm part was hard to see for all the other offerings—quilts, afghans, paintings, metal sculpture.

More than a decade ago, the grain mill—once the largest employer in town—had exploded and most people in the workforce had moved away, leaving the town more like a retirement community. But now there was a new employer in Harmony Valley, a winery, and businesses were sprouting up all over. Not only the fire department was being resurrected. He'd heard the post office was opening again.

Ben crossed onto the grass, working his way through a maze of folding tables. Sprinkled through the crowd of mostly elderly were a few babies, small children and people who looked to be about his age—early thirties.

"Look at that! A tall man in uniform." An elderly woman with short, purplish-gray curls waved at Ben as if he was a returning veteran in a homecoming parade. She stood out from the crowd in her Easter-egg pink tracksuit. "A fireman! And a handsome fireman to boot."

Ben gave her an indulgent smile. "Who called the fire department?"

"I did." The mayor separated himself from the crowd. He had a thin face made thinner by a long gray ponytail. The yellow-and-black tie-dyed T-shirt he wore over black khaki shorts made him look like an aging psychedelic bee. "Those kittens have been up there for a good thirty minutes. Breaks my heart." He leaned in closer to Ben and said in a low voice, "And I thought it'd be the perfect time to show the town we have emergency services again after so long going without." The mayor craned his neck to see around Ben. "Where's the chief?"

The truth pressed in on Ben. He couldn't quite meet the mayor's gaze. "He's returning department phone calls and waiting on my assessment of the scene."

Ben's grandfather stood beneath the oak tree next to a folding table stacked with cans of cat food.

"Granddad?" Ben gave the empty cat cage near his grandfather a disapproving look. The presence of kittens was solved, just not why they were in the tree. Ben moved closer to the tree.

"It's not my fault." His grandfather brushed white cat hair from his navy T-shirt and looked like he wanted to slink away with his empty cat cage. Felix Libby was the retired fire chief and just as thickly muscled as he'd been when he was on active duty. Now he ran a feline rescue. "Truman wanted a kitten, and he got the cage open before I could stop him."

There were two furry miscreants in the tree with the kid. One was black with white paws. The other was white with a black mask. They mewed from positions too far out on a branch to support a little boy and too far within the canopy for the ladder and bucket to be of any use.

"*Granddad*," Ben said again.

"It's not my fault," the retired fireman repeated.

Truman, aka the ginger-haired boy in the tree, grinned down at Ben in a way that made it hard to be annoyed at him. "Whichever kitten comes to me first is the one going home with me." His expression turned earnest. "Here, kitty-cat. Here, boy."

"Those kittens are girls," said a small, solemn voice at Ben's side.

Ben smiled down at his godchild. Her fine blond hair was windblown, and the ankles of her socks were dirt-rimmed. "What are you doing here, Han?"

Hannah didn't take her bespectacled blue eyes from the felines in the tree. "Granny Vanessa was cleaning, so I went for a bike ride."

"Please tell me you left Granny a note." Or Ben's mother was going to be calling him any minute, frantic with worry over where her small charge had gone to this time.

"Tru, come down." A petite redhead used her mom-voice and pointed to the ground.

Several spectators chuckled.

"But, Mom." Truman's wide grin was on a first-name basis with mischief. "I don't have a kitten yet."

"Truman..." Immune to the boy's charm, his mother was cranking up for a good lecture.

Ben tuned her out. In his experience, one of the two treed parties—kid or kittens—needed to come down to entice the other to the ground. Seeing as how Truman wasn't budging, that left two felines to convince.

Hannah had come to the same conclusion. She pushed her glasses firmly in place, opened a can of cat food on Granddad's table and called, "Here, *kitty-kitty-kitty.*"

Two small noses twitched. Two furry tails swished. Two pairs of innocent green eyes turned calculating.

"We need to ensure capture." Ben put the can of food Hannah had opened inside, and backed away.

"*Kitty-kitty-kitty,*" Hannah crooned.

The kittens leaped from one branch to the next, bounced to the ground and raced to the food.

Once they were inside, Hannah closed the door.

The crowd applauded.

"Way to go, peanut." Ben knelt and gave Hannah a quick hug.

Hannah didn't so much as crack a smile. She was a quiet child by nature, but since her firefighting mother, Ben's best friend Erica, had died three months ago and Ben had become the temporary guardian to Hannah, her smile had been as AWOL as the man listed as father on her birth certificate.

Ben hoped she'd smile freely when he found the man. He hoped by the time his own father retired that Hannah would be settled with her biological dad and Ben would be free to pursue a career in fire investigation.

"Well, now I don't know which one to pick." Truman reclined on his stomach on the thick branch, arms and legs hanging down as if he was a lion readying for a nap. "We'll have to take both."

Before Granddad could do more than perk up his silver eyebrows in glee, Truman's mother put the kibosh on that idea. "I don't think Ghost would appreciate you bringing home one kitten, let alone two. Old cats don't like to share their turf with other cats. Time to come down."

"Okay." Truman sounded disappointed, but he did as his mother asked. And he did a good job of it, too, moving quickly and with confidence.

Until his sneaker slipped and he fell, tumbling through the air in a slow-motion cartwheel that sent the crowd gasping.

Ben was ready. Arms outstretched, he was in the perfect position to catch the boy.

And a sneaker to the mouth.

Chapter Two

"It's not like the busy hub in Santa Rosa," Utley Rogers said in a voice thick with age and cigarette smoke. "But your grandfather and I loved the place."

Mandy clutched the Harmony Valley Post Office key ring tightly in her hand. This was the second homecoming of the day.

As a child, Mandy used to stop by the post office after school, grab a Popsicle from the freezer in the break room and sit on her knees at the interior window of Grandpa's office so she could watch Grandpa and Utley sort mail and work the counter. When she was in high school, she'd been hired to help during the holiday season, which turned into a full-time job after graduation.

Back then, everything about the post office was neat and tidy. The outside as well kept as the inside.

And today…

The paint on the gray wood siding was peeling, in desperate need of a fresh coat of paint. The white flagpole was speckled with rust. The lines of the parking spaces were barely visible on the asphalt. So why did the tire swing Grandpa had hung from the oak tree in back look like it was ready for a good spin?

"I always thought I'd be the next postmaster." Utley's expression wavered on the edge of tearful. He cleared his throat and settled a faded blue U.S. Postal Service cap more firmly on his thin white hair. His shoulders were stooped beneath his maroon Hawaiian shirt, as if still weighed down by a mailbag. "Are we going inside or what?"

Mandy forced herself to smile as she shook the key ring, trying to shake off the feeling that her life was being shaped by her past.

Inside, the lobby had the same white walls and scuffed gray linoleum she remembered. Everything else had changed. Dust motes drifted lazily in the sunlight. Cobwebs draped like valances over the grimy front windows and connected handles of the post office boxes like modern-day data network servers.

Instead of feeling comfortable with its vacant neglect as she had at the house, Mandy felt trepidation. The building and its operations were her responsibility now. There was a lot to be done before it was functional.

Utley rang the bell on the counter, but he didn't hit it squarely and the sound was off-key, jangling Mandy's already raw emotions.

After Grandma died and the post office closed, Grandpa had been offered a postmaster job in Santa Rosa, and he'd found a position for Mandy there, as well. For several years, they'd been happy. Maybe Grandpa was a bit grumpier and a bit more forgetful than when Grandma had been alive, and maybe when Olivia became a teenager her angst was drama-laden, and maybe Mandy had to sacrifice a social life and take on a bit more to keep their family together, but they had enough money to keep a roof over their heads and food on the table.

And then complications from Grandpa's diabetes forced him to retire. And the forgetfulness Mandy had once thought was endearing intensified until no one could deny he had dementia. It had all been downhill from there.

They'd buried Grandpa eighteen months ago. And during his last few weeks in hospice care, the former Santa Rosa postmaster had received visits from many work colleagues. He'd made it clear—in the moments when dementia allowed him to be clear—that his last wish was for Mandy to be postmaster in Harmony Valley. And every time he expressed the request, Mandy had smiled and patted his hand, certain it wasn't possible, certain no one would take his request seriously, certain she'd never return to Harmony Valley.

And yet, here she was.

Mandy unlocked the door to the back room, took in the state of things and sagged against the door frame. "I'm supposed to have this running in a week."

It would take at least two.

She'd expected the post office to be outdated, without a single modern feature or machine. She hadn't expected infestation. The place smelled musty, tinged with the aroma of dead things. The sides of the canvas mail carts had holes eaten through them on the bottom and would have to be replaced. Animal footprints (possum? raccoon?) ran across the long sorting counter.

Something scuttled in the corner and squeaked.

The sound had Utley lurching against the wall and Mandy shrieking.

"This isn't my finest hour," she said when she'd caught her breath.

"Ditto," Utley replied.

Responsibilities and deadlines loomed over Mandy like stacks of full mailbags the week before Christmas. Too many people had been passed over for this assignment. Mandy had a target on her back wider than a turkey platter.

"It can't be like this everywhere." Utley led Mandy to the back with shuffling steps that spoke of two knee surgeries without proper recovery. His leather sandals left footprints in the dust. "Let's give the postmaster's office a look-see."

Mandy didn't want to upset whatever beastie was living in the post office anymore, but Utley left her no choice. She couldn't let him go it alone.

Grandpa's office was next to the bathroom. It was impossible not to glance at the lavatory and gasp. Hard water had made dark rings around the toilet bowl. A tiny frog croaked and disappeared into the drain of the sink. The mirror had a jagged crack that split her reflection crosswise.

She'd been torn like that as a child. Heart ripped apart by a divorce that left her estranged from her father and with a mother who disappeared for months, or years, at a time. And those rare occasions when Mom had returned? Mandy had been torn between wanting to earn her mother's love and wanting to be loyal to her grandparents.

Utley entered Grandpa's office and pulled the chair from behind the desk. "It was George's proudest achievement, earning the title of postmaster." He brushed the dust and cobwebs from the chair, hesitating for a moment. And then sat down. "I look good here, don't I?"

Mandy let the slight pass, picturing her grandfather's round, patient face, remembered him sitting in that chair behind the metal desk with postmarks stamped on blotter. His booming laughter used to fill the air. Nearly every day, he'd tell Mandy that she was a big help to him—whether she was changing the date on the postmark stamp when she was ten or changing his adult diapers when she was thirty.

Mandy heaved a sigh, trying to feel proud for having earned a postmaster position before she turned thirty-five, trying not to think about what failure would mean. A demotion. A pay cut. Angrier debt collectors wanting her to make good on Olivia's medical bills.

Utley spun the chair from side-to-side. "When does the cleaning crew arrive?"

"She's already here." Mandy would need to add specific repairs to her to-do list. Dave, her superior in Santa Rosa, wasn't going to be pleased. He'd made it clear that reopening the office didn't mean it would stay open. She had to prove its profitability.

"You always were a hard worker." Utley opened drawers in the desk, poking around at their contents. "I can't wait to see how your newfangled equipment works. You know, I have a portable phone." He stopped rummaging in drawers and produced an old-fashioned flip phone from his maroon Hawaiian shirt pocket. "Now I understand why people send fewer letters. I can send mail from this here thing."

Mandy blinked. "You mean texts."

Utley blinked back. "Aren't texts and electronic mails the same?" He tucked his phone away, shrugging. "I never thought I'd see portable phones in my lifetime, much less all the fast, fancy stuff I expect you'll be bringing in here. A lot has changed since I retired."

"Equipment and supplies are coming next week." A credit card reader. A computer and scale to calculate postage. Stamps, shipping boxes, envelopes. The bare minimum to get the town's services up and running.

Utley gave Mandy a smile with wrinkles so like Grandpa's, she had to look away so she wouldn't cry. "They didn't call me out of retirement to run this place," Utley said. "You must've done something impressive to have been given the keys."

Mandy hadn't done anything impressive.

But Grandpa expected her to.

"Cheapest way to fight fires is to prevent fires." Winded and wheezy, Dad stood outside the Harmony Valley Post Office in his navy blue uniform, one sun-spotted hand on the wall. "Cheapest way," he repeated absently.

Ben didn't care about budgets. He cared about safety. He stopped next to his father, scoping the post office like a burglar about to do business. "The town council should have approved funding for a four-man crew. Imagine the two of us on scene for a fully committed blaze." Disastrous.

California's fire code required a minimum of four firemen on active fire calls, which left them dependent upon other nearby fire crews or trained volunteers. They had no trained volunteers yet, and Harmony Valley was in a far-flung corner of Sonoma County. Help wasn't going to be quick.

"You've driven around town." Dad sucked in a shallow breath, giving away the effect the smoky air had on his lung disease. "Our district constituents are old." *Suck-wheeze.* His face lost more color. "We'll be handling more medical calls than fire emergencies." *Suck-wheeze.* "Which is the way of the world now it seems."

Kitten and medical calls were turning out to be their charter. Once they put a volunteer program in place, they wouldn't have to rely on Cloverdale for backup if there was a fire.

Ben took Dad's arm. "Why don't you wait in the truck with an oxygen mask?"

Dad tugged his arm free. "Because I'm the one who signs off—" *gasp-wheeze* "—on inspections and citations."

Ben's jaw dropped. "You haven't issued any citations. Only warnings. Warnings don't bring buildings up to code as quickly as citations."

The post office was a plain, boxy gray building with an air of neglect. It looked in need of about ten citations. There was a small grove of trees behind it. Beyond the trees was a field with waist-high, dried-out wild grass. Beyond that was a two-story farmhouse that was more tear-down than fixer-upper.

"I'm almost sorry I raised you in the city," Dad said gruffly. "You don't understand the role of a small-town fireman. These people are our friends." Dad's expression was boss-man defiant.

Ben had a defiant expression of his own. Too bad Dad wasn't looking at him. "Friends don't let friends burn their businesses down. Issue some citations already."

"This round, a warning will suffice." His old man lumbered toward the post office door, his breath sounding like an out-of-tune accordion. "You'll understand someday."

"Maybe..." Ben chewed on the tether binding his sarcasm until it broke. "Maybe when I'm old and dotty, like you."

Dad mumbled something about ungrateful sons and fire captains who were wet behind the ears. In turn, Ben mumbled something about passing up a fire inspector promotion and fire chiefs who were softies.

And then, they both laughed, exchanging smiles before continuing toward the post office door. That rare moment of camaraderie gave Ben a warm, mushy feeling the likes of which he didn't associate with his father. He walked slowly.

"Walk with a purpose, son," Dad said as if Ben was twelve and lagging behind at the mall. "We have plenty more inspections to do."

"A list as long as my arm," Ben grumbled. After years without a fire department, father and son were playing catch-up on safety measures in Harmony Valley.

The outer post office door was unlocked. They entered the lobby, but the counter window was closed. Classic country music drifted out to them from the back.

Ben knocked on the door that said Employees Only.

There was no answer.

Dad leaned against the wall, frowning when he noticed Ben staring at him. "Yes, I'm out of shape. I'll get better."

Doubtful.

"Why don't you wait in the truck?" Ben repeated patiently.

"Because I'm the fire chief," Dad rasped, a welcome spark of energy in his blue eyes.

"At least use your inhaler." Ben pounded harder on the door while his father dug in his pocket for his medicine.

Again, no answer. The music was too darn loud. Playing music loud... It reminded Ben of Hannah's mom.

Erica had lived for the adrenaline rush—fast cars, base jumping, parachuting out of planes. She'd had a soundtrack for every experience, blaring it through booming speakers or her earbuds. If she'd lived to be eighty, she would've been deaf. He'd assumed little reserved Hannah would be the opposite of her mother. She wasn't. Erica's love of life had taken a different tangent with Hannah, a softer, quieter tangent.

What kind of person awaited them inside the post office.

Out of patience, Ben tried the door. It was unlocked. He opened it a few inches, but had to push aside a mail cart to get inside, and even then, there were boxes stacked in front of the cart. Talk about blocking safety entrances. Other than that, the mail room floor was relatively clear. There was a large rolling door in one wall that presumably opened to the parking lot for mail truck deliveries.

On the far side of the room a thin, tall woman was clad in postal service blue shorts and a baggy, blue-and-white striped shirt. Her dark brown hair was bound in messy ponytails that hung beneath each ear. Back to Ben, she mopped the floor, singing off-key to a tune about drinking too much.

Dad chuckled.

Ben found nothing funny about it. A fire to the rear of the building by the loading dock and this woman would be trapped.

"*Fire!*" Ben shouted.

The mop clattered to the floor. The woman whirled, sneakers slipping slightly on wet linoleum. Wide brown eyes landed on Ben with a gut-dropping thud.

She wasn't smiling, but she had the kind of face that carried a smile 99 percent of the time, the kind of face that aged gracefully with few lines because she never had a care. And Ben, who carried cares like other people lugged too much spare change, was struck with envy.

She switched off the music.

The sudden silence rang in Ben's ears as he breathed in cleanser fumes and waited to see if the woman had a frown in her arsenal, some hint that her life wasn't all rainbows and unicorns.

"I'm Mandy, the new postmaster." She blinked, and with that blink her expression seemed to reset. A small smile. A carefree tone of voice. A kick in Envious Ben's shin. "Where's the fire?"

"No fire. This is a fire inspection." Dad had drawn himself up to his full height. With Mandy in his sights, he wasn't wheezing or sagging. "Nothing for you to worry about."

Here we go again. Letting an offender off with a warning.

"Not so fast, chief." This one wasn't getting off the hook. This woman could use a care or two. Ben planted his feet more firmly on the floor. "Ma'am, did you realize you've blocked two of three primary exit routes?"

"Not permanently." Her smile never wavered. "Just while I'm cleaning."

"I mention this for your own safety." Ben surveyed the post office, counting more than five citations already. "If there was a fire at your loading dock, you'd be trapped."

Mandy gestured to the rolling overhead door that opened to the parking lot. "First off, there's nothing combustible back there. Second, those boxes before you are empty. And third, I could still get to the front counter if there was a fire."

Not an apology. Not an admission that she'd taken a safety risk, nor any assurance that it wouldn't happen again. Mandy was the only person to argue with them today. The only person to work her way sharply under Ben's skin.

He nudged the bottom box with his boot. The stack tumbled harmlessly to the ground. "I'll give you the boxes, ma'am, but if you aren't concerned about your own well-being, what about your employees?"

And there it was—her true expression. A smile so artless and wide it made Ben wonder what her laugh would sound like. "If there was a fire, that rat Riley can burn."

Ben exchanged a look with Dad that he hoped said: *Give her a citation. Please.* Message received. His old man shook his head.

"That was a joke." Mandy suddenly turned serious, not serious enough for her smile to be wiped off the face of the earth, but serious nonetheless. "Riley isn't technically a rat. I mean, he has four legs and a tail, sure. But he's a raccoon."

Dad chuckled, which morphed into a cough, and then gasps for air as he turned away from them.

Ben stayed on point. "The fact remains that—"

"Look, Officer..." She peered at his name tag. "Libby. Mr....Fireman...Libby..." She paused, seeming to collect herself and her awkwardness. "Are you related to Felix Libby?"

"We are." It would be just his luck that she'd fostered a kitten from Granddad and was in his grandfather's good graces. "I'm Ben, his grandson. And this is my dad, Keith."

"Oh. I can see the resemblance in your face." She waved her hand in a circle around her features. "If you come back in thirty minutes—" Mandy rushed on with her Mona Lisa smile "—the doorway will be clear and the rolltop counter open. No harm, no foul, right? Look, I'll even open the loading bay."

It was a good compromise.

Too bad it'd come too late. His pledge to safeguard the public made it hard to back off and apologize. Not that Ben wanted to back off or go soft on her. He was a firm believer in beginning as he meant to go on. Fire safety was important. Honesty was important.

Mandy pushed the button to open the rolling door.

There was a spark, a flash and then the sharp tang of electrical smoke.

Chapter Three

"Fire. That's a fire," Mandy said in disbelief at the same time that the seriously hunky fireman demanded, "Where's the fire extinguisher?"

The flames were about six feet off the ground, eight inches high and growing taller and wider by the second. They climbed up the wall bordering the dock's opening.

This is going to put me behind schedule.

It'd taken Mandy days to clear away the trash and outdated equipment enough to clean. And for what? A fire to turn her hard work to ash?

"Where..." Large hands took hold of Mandy's shoulders. "...is the fire extinguisher?"

In the face of his demand, Mandy had no time to register the strength of Ben's grip, the odd quirk to his mouth or the intensity of his blue eyes.

Where had she seen the fire extinguisher? Her mind flitted through a jumble of images, landing on one. "The bathroom."

Ben disappeared, leaving Mandy mesmerized by the ever-increasing flames. This was it. The end of her short stint as postmaster. Finding a territorial raccoon in the post office was inconvenient. Burning the place down was a firing offense. She'd be stuck in Harmony Valley without a job. Wouldn't her creditors love that?

While Ben searched, the fire chief walked with unhurried steps toward the loading dock. He and his son had the same broad shoulders, the same thick dark hair, the same confident stride and the same sharp blue eyes. Only the pallor of their skin was different. The older man's complexion was the pasty white of a ball of bread dough.

Keith swiped an old canvas mailbag from the stack in the corner and used it to smother the flames. By the time Ben returned with the fire extinguisher, the fire was out, leaving only a black shroud on the wall as evidence it'd occurred.

"Sometimes the simplest of techniques are the most effective, Ben." The fire chief coughed, turning away from the smoke. "Just like your kitten rescue earlier."

Mandy took a slow step back, and then another, hands shaking. She looked around, searching for reassurance.

It was going to be okay. No one was injured. The post office was still standing.

"Good job, Dad." There was compassion in Ben's voice, proving he was hunky but not a complete cranky pants. And then, he turned toward Mandy, expression darkening as he held the fire extinguisher aloft. "There's no pressure in this unit. It's useless. And even if it was working, it shouldn't be stored over the toilet. What would happen if there was a fire, and someone was using the bathroom?"

In the face of his blue-eyed intensity, Mandy couldn't find the words to defend herself. She stood the same way she had when the doctor delivered the news that Grandpa was dying—arms wrapped around her waist, a small, polite smile on her lips. The same position she'd taken when the doctor told her Olivia had cancer. "Um..."

Her reticence seemed to upset Ben all the more. He curled that odd-shaped lip of his. A fat lip, she realized.

Was this the man who'd rescued kittens and caught a falling child? The man the elderly visitors to the post office today called charming and heroic?

He wasn't likely to catch Mandy if she fell. He was more likely to sit on his hands and watch.

"Get out your citation book, Dad. We're going over this place inch by inch." Ben peered at the burnt, melted wires. "That wire was cut."

Mandy gasped, rushing forward for a better look. "How could that be?"

"Now, Ben," Keith said with the gravitas of an elder statesman. "A raccoon's been living here. Rodents and pests like snacking on wires."

"If we're not issuing citations, Dad, tell me what we are doing." Ben's voice was as hard as the look in his eyes. Intense. Intensely serious. Intensely handsome. Intensely annoyed at everyone in the room.

Not my type at all.

Mandy rolled her shoulders back. She didn't have time to have a type.

And Ben didn't seem to see anything in her but a fire hazard. "Dad, do you want to make a list and document the danger now? Or battle more flames with me when this place goes up in smoke because we went easy on her?"

Mandy's stomach turned. She raised her hand. "I vote for list-making. It's been more than a decade since this station was in service. If I promise to take care of things by, say, next week? Can we avoid citations?" It didn't matter that none of this was Mandy's fault; excessive paper trails would get her fired and the office closed.

Why couldn't Grandpa have wanted me to be the postmaster in Cloverdale?

Mr. Intensity stared at Mandy with angry eyes. When she'd first seen him, that anger had been like banked coals. That anger had been accented by the rigid set to his shoulders, the stiffness of his back, the determined set to his strong chin. Here was a man who was serious about his job and protecting others. He'd always fight for what he believed in. Passionately. In a loud voice. And with a fierce scowl.

She approached conflict the opposite way—calmly, softly, with a smile—because she'd learned nothing was solved with loud voices and lines of tears.

"Ben," his father said in a voice that soothed.

Ben's intensity faded. His fire banked. To a degree.

His jaw worked as he turned back to Mandy. "What's that noise?"

She glanced around, looking for a scuttling rat or raccoon. "I don't hear anything."

"Exactly. No fire alarm." Ben pointed to the ceiling and a round, age-yellowed fire alarm. "It should have gone off." He dragged a stool to the sorting counter. "Dad, sit down over here and get out your pen. We're making a list."

Mandy couldn't thank them quickly enough.

"No wedding ring," Keith noted, passing Mandy to sit on the stool.

"No husband," she replied without thinking.

"What's this?" Ben tilted the coffee tin on the counter, the one filled with matches.

"The guys who used to work here were heavy smokers." Utley and her grandfather. "I've been collecting their matchbooks for days so I can throw them out all at once." Filling the tin gave her a sense of accomplishment, something she needed given the overwhelming amount of work ahead of her.

"I'd feel better if we trashed them now." Ben arched a dark brow. His wasn't a suggestion.

"Fine." After this, she'd never get annoyed over Olivia's teenage drama episodes again.

Or at least, I'll think twice before letting my annoyance show.

"Don't let Ben rattle you." Keith settled on the stool. "My son is all about the unvarnished truth. It's why he's still single. But he's raising his godchild, which proves he has parenting potential."

"Thank you, oh, wise papa," Ben quipped. And then, his lips curled up in a lopsided, rueful smile that implied he'd be irresistible if he had a sense of humor and a heart. "He and my mother never let a chance with an attractive, single woman pass without letting her know that I'm single."

"And honest," Keith repeated, smiling. "Some folks don't like that much honesty."

"You, for example," Ben teased.

Mandy let their teasing surround her. It lifted her spirits, not to mention Ben had referenced her as attractive, which made her give the now-smiling fireman a second look.

Focus, girl. Focus. My career. Those bills. Olivia.

Mandy didn't have time to create a picture that smoothed over the faults of one too-blunt and tightly-wound fireman.

For the next fifteen minutes, Ben pointed out what needed fixing to bring the station up to code and why. New lighted Exit signs. New fire alarms. New extinguishers. New, new, new. As if the cost wasn't a consideration.

Mandy's head hurt.

Ben was so sure of himself. If Mandy was to succeed here, she'd need some of his confidence.

"The fire control panel should be outside." Ben led her down the outdoor concrete steps of the loading bay and across the graded space where mail trucks backed in so their beds were even with the loading dock. He walked the building's perimeter with long strides. Being a good six inches taller than she was, his legs ate up more distance than hers.

Mandy's mother would have said Ben had excellent posture. She would've said his attention to detail meant he was a good man. She would've said his thick dark hair was dreamy. Mandy's mother would've asked Ben out, offered to have his babies and then left those kids in the care of her oldest child.

Mandy sighed. She was getting as overly dramatic as Olivia.

She smiled harder, closing the distance between them. "I'm sorry. What did you say?"

"I can't find it." Ben halted his search, arms akimbo, frowning at Mandy, but not nearly as sharply as before. "And yet, you're smiling."

"I...uh..." Mandy had to stand up for herself if she was to succeed as postmaster. "I find a smile helps me through tough times. It keeps all the bad stuff at bay, you know?"

"Not really." His stare tried to pierce her words, but they were the truth and held up to his inspection. After a moment, Ben smiled enigmatically and turned his attention back to the gray, warped and peeling siding. "It should be right here." And then he stepped closer to the overgrown hedges bordering the wall, moving branches aside.

Mandy braced herself for Riley's now-familiar growl. The raccoon had been hunkering down in the bushes since she'd nailed a board over the hole he'd made in the siding.

But not even Riley was courageous enough to stand up to the ferocious Ben Libby.

"There it is." Ben angled so she could see the panel. He tapped the gauge. "See this? There's no water pressure. And when I open up the valve..." He turned the spigot.

Nothing happened.

Ben's gaze connected with hers the way a teachers did to a student's when waiting for an answer to an easy question.

"I'm assuming there's supposed to be water flowing somewhere?" she said tentatively.

"And an alarm going off." Ben shut the valve. "This needs to be fixed before you open. Priority one."

Such a long list. Mandy nodded numbly.

But she kept smiling.

"Is that..." Ben moved branches aside. "...cat food?"

"Yes." Mandy's cheeks bloomed with soft color. "I evicted Riley. I owed him something."

"Owed a raccoon?" Ben stood and studied Mandy once more. She didn't look as if she'd be full of surprises. This close, he could see the fabric of her striped postal shirt was worn at the collar, the thickness of her lashes, the weariness in her brown eyes. And yet, despite her fatigue and her smile, there was a determination to the set of her shoulders. She was a surprise, all right. "Won't free food keep him coming back?"

That smile of hers wavered, and she stared into his eyes as if he confounded her as much as she did him. "Have you ever wondered where you'll live?"

"No." His answer came too quickly. "Well, yes. Recently." After Erica died, he'd realized raising a little girl wouldn't work in his studio apartment. He'd sublet his unit and moved in with his parents. "It was unsettling."

"Then you understand," she said in a voice that said volumes about the uncertainties she'd faced in life. "Change is hard, even for a raccoon."

He owed her a smile. How could he not? They'd both ended up with more than they'd bargained for by coming to Harmony Valley. Suddenly, he was glad they weren't writing her citations. "My grandfather would approve of you. He rescues stray cats."

"Felix? I doubt he'd approve of me." She blinked, adding quickly, "I mean, who would?"

"I would. I do." The words spilled out, past the long list of safety regulations she was breaking and his professional standards. He wasn't here looking for her phone number. With all the balls he was juggling—Dad's health, launching the fire department, caring for Hannah while trying to find her real dad—he had no energy to put himself out there, no time for the slow ramp that led to friendship or perhaps something else. It was just... Mandy had a way of making his gaze linger.

Her gaze slid to the bushes, and the color in her cheeks deepened. She hadn't expected his endorsement, and given his intensity inside, he couldn't blame her.

"What's the word?" Dad called from inside the post office.

Thankfully, Dad couldn't see them from where he sat because Ben would never hear the end of it if Dad witnessed how near he stood to Mandy, how long he'd been staring at her, the near foolish tilt to his grin.

"It's as expected," Ben called back gruffly, feeling just the opposite. He took a step back. Straightened. Cleared his throat. "The fire panel is offline."

Offline. It was where he needed to store his unexpected fascination with Mandy.

That night, Mandy was too tired to cook.

Good thing it was Olivia's day to cook and do the dishes.

Mandy dropped her purse and shoes in the middle of the living room floor and collapsed into the recliner. She stared at the black screen of the small TV, too tired to get back up and look for the remote. Although perhaps not too tired to indulge in a brief fantasy where a well-built, blunt-speaking fireman retrieved it for her.

And, despite the hunky fireman of her dreams bearing some resemblance to Ben, the fireman in her imagination didn't lecture. He just smiled and looked gorgeous, as Ben had when they'd talked about her feeding Riley cat food. For a few minutes, she'd felt as if they were as comfortable with each other as a pair of well-worn sneakers. And a moment later, she'd felt as if she'd been caught wearing those sneakers on prom night when everyone else was in new, sparkly heels.

"I'm home," she called out for Olivia's benefit, spotting the remote across the room next to Grandma's sewing basket.

"I heard." Olivia drifted in, blowing on her painted fingernails. Except for her manicure, everything about Olivia was minimal—light makeup, bare feet, lemon-colored spaghetti-strap blouse and those dreadful short-shorts. "Look what I did. It's an American flag." She angled her hand so Mandy could see. There were red-and-white stripes on some fingernails and white glittery stars on blue backgrounds on her thumbs.

"Very nice." It was hard to deny her sister had talent when it came to nails, but, "How long did that take you?"

"All day." Olivia flopped onto the blue plaid couch. It said something to their cleaning skills that no dust billowed.

"I thought we agreed that you'd apply for work today," Mandy said carefully. That was the trick with teenagers. You had to walk on tiptoe when what you really wanted to do was screech about laziness and lost opportunities and, therefore, break some eggs. That's what Mandy called the loss of control over her emotions. Losing control meant a pile of eggshells.

Olivia's innocent brown eyes turned Mandy's way. "I couldn't go out without doing my nails."

Eggshells. Eggshells!

"You realize you have one more day to find a job and then you're coming to work for me." Mandy could use her help. Anticipating that need when she'd landed the job, she'd made Olivia take the postal employee test. "I don't like the idea of you being home alone." What she would have preferred to have said was Olivia needed to earn her own nail polish money. But that would have been unnecessarily mean.

Olivia admired her nails, as relaxed as Mandy was uptight. "I looked online and there were no job listings."

"Hence the obvious need to do your nails." Unable to filter a brief spurt of sarcasm, Mandy drew a deep breath, kept smiling, and tried again. "A town as small as Harmony Valley won't have jobs posted online."

"We might just as well have moved to the north pole." Olivia flopped back against the couch, resorting to her best defense—drama. "We're in the middle of nowhere. There's no mall or movie theater. What if there's an emergency? What if I get sick?" She was winding up like a pitcher about to throw a third strike. "What if—"

"We've been over this." Mandy was afraid her smile was slipping. "The nearest hospital is thirty minutes away. Plenty of time to seek care."

Olivia changed tactics as swiftly as a guppy changed course in a fishbowl. "I didn't want to move here."

"Harmony Valley isn't so bad." Mandy stared longingly at the remote, wondering how much longer her sister's energy for an argument would last.

"*Mandy.*" Olivia said her name as if Mandy was the one being unreasonable.

"What?" Mandy's battered patience felt as brittle and treacherous as a thin layer of ice on a blind curve. "I told you. We have bills." From Olivia's follow-up medical care, the extras Mandy's insurance hadn't covered. "And we need two months' rent saved to get a house." The town had only a few apartments available, and those were mostly studios above the old shops on Main Street.

The size of a place was a moot point. They didn't have the cash. End of story.

"We're squatting, Mandy," Olivia said in a judgy tone, sitting up. "Are postal workers supposed to break the law?"

"No one is supposed to break the law," Mandy said as stiffly as Ben had given his safety lecture earlier. "I'm the trustee of Grandpa's estate. I pay the bills that keep the lights on in this house. We can stay here temporarily." She should have stopped there. Instead, she added, "Mom won't mind."

Hey, lightning didn't strike.

Olivia's chin jutted at the mention of their wanderlusting mother. "If you wouldn't argue with Mom, she'd come by and see us."

Mandy refrained from asking where Mom had been during Olivia's long bout with cancer. She refrained from raising her voice or rolling her eyes or giving in to the urge to cry. She'd become quite good at soldiering on.

So, she swallowed annoyance, gulped back uncertainty and washed it all down with despair, dredging up her most chipper voice. "Do you remember how Grandma and Grandpa danced in the kitchen on New Year's Eve?" Remembering the good times was often the only thing that held Mandy and her smile together.

"No." Olivia sniffed and slid her thumbnail along her cuticle. "I don't remember stuff like that. I've got chemo brain."

Or she just didn't want to admit she remembered.

Someday Mandy was going to find a memory her sister recalled. And then they'd sit together fondly reminiscing over the best of times.

"Did you remember to cook dinner?" Mandy asked, knowing the answer because the house lacked the enticing smell of food in the oven.

"I was busy." Olivia hadn't taken her eyes off her nails.

"Brat." Mandy removed a band from one of her ponytails and shot it at her sister. It bounced harmlessly off her shoulder and to the brown shag carpet.

"Jailer." Olivia's lips twitched.

"Baby." Mandy's smile felt more real now.

Olivia grinned. "Old maid."

Before they could get in another round of good-natured insults, someone knocked on the door.

They stared at each other with wide eyes. Mom always knocked. Although per Grandpa's will, this was their mother's house. Not that it would be much longer. Grandpa's money was running out. And their mother couldn't or wouldn't pay for property taxes, insurance, and utilities for this place.

Mandy's lips stuck over her dry teeth in what was most certainly more grimace than smile. She wanted to ignore the summons and pretend they weren't home. Or better yet, escape out the back.

Responsible people don't run.

That's what Grandpa used to say.

Clearly, they didn't always rise to the occasion either, because Mandy didn't move from her seat.

Whoever was at the front door knocked again.

"Do you think it's the pizza delivery man?" Olivia stood, holding out a hand to help Mandy stand. "I was just wishing for a pizza."

Mandy couldn't be a coward in the face of her younger sister's bravery. Besides, for all Olivia's talk about wanting to see their mother, she wasn't rushing to the door to greet her.

She accepted Olivia's help to stand. "I think it's the man of my dreams, coming to take me away to his castle." And pay off her mountain of debt.

Olivia rolled her eyes and then reached over to remove Mandy's other ponytail band.

Mandy fluffed her hair, which she knew did little good to make her look presentable. Her hair fell like two stiff handlebars over her shoulders. "It's probably the neighbors." The house on one side was vacant, but the house on the corner next to them had lights on last night.

Mandy opened the door.

It wasn't the pizza delivery man or Prince Charming or their mother.

Three older women stood on the front stoop.

"Welcome to Harmony Valley." The first old woman at the door was pint-size with a pixie-cut hairstyle more silver than gray. "I'm Agnes."

"We brought broccoli casserole." The willowy woman behind Agnes had a ballerina's posture and a snow-white chignon. She held a square casserole dish. "I'm Rose."

"I brought cookies." A woman with white fluffy curls peered at Mandy through thick lenses. She pushed her walker forward, clutching a plastic bag full of chocolate chip cookies. "I'm Mildred."

"Oh, you shouldn't have." Mandy's stomach growled.

"That's not pizza." Behind Mandy, Olivia drew a deep breath. "But I'm not complaining."

Mandy's stomach growled again. She opened the door wider and stepped aside to let the welcome committee in.

Ballerina Rose glided past and delivered the casserole to the kitchen. "Oh," she said upon reaching the cluttered sink. She set the casserole on the counter and began to wash their dirty dishes.

Mandy hurried into the kitchen, hoping no one ventured into her bedroom and noticed the clothes she'd worn yesterday in a pile on the floor. "You don't have to do that, Rose."

I should have broken some eggshells. Maybe then Olivia would've completed her chores.

"I don't mind," Rose kindly said. "You look like doing dishes would do you in."

"Rose is right." Agnes drew Mandy back to the living room. "Sit down and have one of Mildred's cookies."

Cookies. Mandy's stomach growled a third time. She sat like a well-trained dog awaiting a deserved treat. Olivia did the same. In their love of chocolate, the sisters were united.

Mildred positioned her walker next to Mandy, flipped the seat down and sat on it. She handed Mandy the cookie bag. "Agnes, do you think these girls have low blood sugar? Diabetes ran in the Zapien family, and they look pale."

Olivia managed to bite her lip and frown at the same time.

"No. They're clear-eyed." Agnes pushed the top of Mandy's chair back, sending her into recline. "More likely they're just tired. Can you imagine moving here, and then cleaning out George and Utley's mess at the post office?"

"I can." Mildred patted Mandy's arm. "I've seen Utley's living room. You take it easy tonight, honey."

Mandy couldn't remember the last time someone had taken care of her. It gave her a warm feeling. She grabbed a cookie and took a big bite.

"Hey," Olivia protested, scurrying over to get one.

"That's it." Agnes patted Mandy's crown. "We need milk, Rose."

Luckily, they had some. Unluckily, to find it Rose had to open the refrigerator.

The sticky fridge door protested being opened, and Rose protested, too, opening it with a strangled noise.

Mandy's grandmother would be horrified that one of the neighbors had evidence Mandy wasn't Suzy Homemaker. Sadly, Mandy was her grandmother's kin. She didn't like the idea either.

That called for another bite of rich chocolate. "Remind me. How do I know you three?" They seemed so familiar and yet they were strangers, not to mention taking over the house. "Do you live next door?"

"No. We're the town council." Mildred's gaze floated in an unfocused manner over Mandy's face, blue eyes huge and distorted behind those thick lenses. "Been serving since you were... Well, we've been serving a long time." Despite the bug eyes, Mildred had a Mrs. Claus vibe that was oddly comforting, almost as good as chocolate.

Their faces—younger, yet not young—came back to Mandy. Growing up, she'd seen them at town festivals, at school events, at the ice cream parlor.

"One day you'll have to tell us about your grandfather," Agnes said in an I'm-so-sorry tone of voice, the kind that always brought tears to Mandy's eyes. "I always admired George and Blythe for taking you kids in when Teri was—"

"A flake." Rose returned to the living room with a glass of milk and indicated Mandy sit up. "Your mother is a flake."

Olivia stopped chewing.

Rose handed the milk to Mandy, paused, and then put together an apologetic smile. "No offense."

"None taken." Mandy bit into another cookie, making short work of the sweet treat. So much for casserole. "Have you seen my mother in town recently?"

"No." Rose returned from the kitchen almost immediately and handed Olivia a glass of milk. "You need some fresh baking soda in that fridge."

"Vinegar," Mildred said.

"It smells like there might be something dead underneath." Agnes leaned down to admire Olivia's nails. "Those are very pretty."

Her praise won Olivia over. She preened. "If you like that, look at my feet." She'd done her toenails yesterday.

Agnes bent over, hands on knees. "Are those fireworks or chrysanthemums?"

"Fireworks." Olivia wiggled her toes.

"Are you licensed?" Rose drifted closer to Olivia. "We've got a hairstylist in town, but not a nail lady."

"Not yet. I'm going to cosmetology school in a few months. My grandpa left me money, but said I have to wait until I'm eighteen to collect."

Mandy's feeling of comfort evaporated. She couldn't look at her sister.

"We heard your grandfather had dementia." Mildred's hand found Mandy's and squeezed. "Was it bad?"

"It was," Olivia said before Mandy could do more than nod.

"It was worse at the end," Mandy said in Grandpa's defense. As his kidneys failed and his organs shut down, his touch with reality hung by a thread. He hadn't slept more than an hour at a time. He'd wake up and sing at the top of his lungs, and not always with the right words.

Glory, glory hallelujah. Glory, glory with a poodle.

"Well..." Agnes tilted her head toward the door, perhaps noticing the mist in Mandy's eyes. "We won't take up any more of your time. Let us know if you need anything."

Now that Mandy was full of sugar and dinner was in the kitchen, her smile felt uncharacteristically carefree. "We're looking to rent a place." Too late,

Mandy realized that statement opened the door to unanswered questions about why they couldn't live in this house.

Other than a fleeting display of creased silver brows, the town council didn't seem to care.

"Oh." On her way out, Rose pivot-turned at the door. "There's a cute place around the corner that used to have a beauty salon in the garage. It might be the perfect place for a nail salon."

"We'll get you the owner's information," Agnes promised.

Olivia beamed, while Mandy wondered how much more expensive a home would be to rent with a salon inside.

After the town council left, Mandy and Olivia stared at each other.

"Just this once," Olivia said with a sly grin, "can we have cookies for dinner?"

"I hate that we think alike." But she loved that no eggshells had been broken between them.

They each ate three more cookies and drained their glasses of milk.

Chapter Four

"Hannah, that snake isn't coming inside." Ben's mother sounded flustered. She'd raised two boys and been around firemen all her life. Nothing ruffled her feathers.

Except, it seemed, a seven-year-old girl.

"But the snake is already inside." Hannah's calm voice, stating a fact.

Another crisis. Ben hurried to unlace his boots. Still in his navy blue uniform, he ran to the kitchen, assessing the situation as quickly as he would an emergency call.

Hannah held a slender gray snake that was about two feet long. Its small head rested between her thumb and forefinger. The rest of it was coiled around her forearm. Thankfully, it was only a garter snake.

Looking frazzled, his mother stood on sandaled tiptoe, backed into the corner of the dark kitchen cabinets. Her hands clutched her orange flowered tunic. Her short blond hair was uncharacteristically spiked up in front. If Hannah brought the snake any closer, she'd probably climb into the double metal sink. "Ben, thank heavens. Hannah slipped away again and she—"

"I didn't slip away." Hannah sounded weary of overprotective adults. Where Hannah used to deal with one parental unit, now she dealt with three. "You were taking a nap, so I went for a bike ride."

Ben bit back a smile.

"Fine. Yes. I took a nap. That's what grannies do because children are exhausting." There was a hysterical edge to his mother's voice. She gripped the counter so ferociously Ben was surprised she didn't embed a fake French nail in the butcher block. "But for once, honey, can you go on a bike ride and not bring home a critter?"

Hannah pushed her glasses up her nose with her free hand. Her knees were dirty, and her thin blond hair hung half out of its single braid. "I only bring home the lost and the injured."

Sensing an opportunity, Ben knelt next to Hannah. "That snake looks fine to me."

"He has a kink." Han gently pulled the snake's tail away from her arm so he could see.

"Take it out of the house, please." Mom shuddered. "I cook meals in this room."

"Hannah," Ben said in the easy-going voice he'd had to use a lot since he'd taken his godchild in. "That kink isn't something a stay in the infirmary can fix."

The infirmary. That's what Han called the wall of cages and terrariums in the garage. Mom hadn't wanted to keep animals in the house, period. But Hannah had insisted. It was the only time since her mother's death that the little girl had cried.

"But..." Hannah's eyes turned watery. "Iggy needs a friend. The other snakes make fun of him. He needs me."

Mom gave Ben a look that said: *You better set that kid straight.*

Ben stood and took Han's snakeless hand. "Little Iggy might have had friends back where you found him. They might have been better at hiding without a kinked tail."

"We have to take him back?" Han asked, lips drawing into a pout.

Ben would've relented, if not for Mom's vehement nod of the head.

"Come on, peanut," he said. "I'll drive you back where you found him." Which turned out to be an empty field near the river about a mile from the corner house his parents were renting.

On the return drive home, Hannah stared out the window, her forehead pressed to the glass. "I'm like Iggy. I don't have any friends. No parents. And now, no snake."

Ben tried to make light of the situation. "As your godfather, I'm crushed."

"You don't count." She turned those large, solemn blue eyes his way. "You don't want to keep me." Her voice was thin, but not whiny or accusatory. Just factual.

"That's not true." Her birth certificate said he wasn't her real father. His dedication to his profession said he wasn't the right person to raise her. He wanted to be a fire investigator. That involved long hours and unpredictable schedules, longer than a regular firefighter. Ben rejected the idea of having kids. Why repeat the pattern of neglect he'd grown up with? "I love you, peanut. Would I have taken you to Sylvia Steinway's princess-themed birthday party in Oakland if I didn't?"

She tilted her head and smirked at him. "Wearing princess dresses is stupid. I didn't want to go."

Ben didn't believe that for a moment. He'd caught Hannah gazing at her reflection in the mirror before they'd left for the party, fingers knotted in her poufy pink skirt. And she still kept her tiara on top of her dresser. But that wasn't the point. "Would I have taken you to see the latest Disney movie if I didn't love you? And don't forget I bought popcorn and Goobers."

Her smirk threatened to turn into a smile. She chewed on the inside of her cheek and looked away, such an old soul for being only seven. "And when my dad shows up? Will you want me then?"

"I'll want you always, peanut." Ben gently tugged what was left of her braid. "Just remember, dads have first dibs."

Later that night after Hannah had gone to bed, Mom pulled Ben into the garage. It was crowded with plastic storage tubs from the move except for the space they'd carved out along one wall for Hannah's infirmary. "I'm sorry Han got away from me again, Ben. I can't let my eyes off her even for a minute."

Dad sat in a burgundy camp chair next to the hot water heater, chewing on a cigar, which was the only vice left to him—chewing, not smoking. "You shouldn't worry so much, Vanessa. Harmony Valley isn't the Bermuda Triangle. Kids can safely roam free here."

"She isn't ours to let roam." Mom was wound up tighter than the snake had been around Hannah's arm. "What if she fell in the river? What if she got hit by a car? Her real father would have our hides. And who could blame him?"

"Time to face facts." Keith mouthed the cigar. "It's been three months. We may never find Han's dad."

"Don't say that." Ben had been searching since Erica died. A few weeks ago, he'd hired a private investigator to aid in the search. "Her father is out there."

Erica's parents couldn't take Hannah because her grandfather had Alzheimer's and her grandmother couldn't handle caring for a child on top of that. Nothing in Hannah's records—not even her birth certificate—said more than John Smith. There were thousands of John Smiths in California. And what if good ol' John had moved to another state?

Ben stared at the wall with cages. A rabbit with a broken leg. A guinea pig missing an ear. A bird with a broken wing. A baby possum that required bottle feedings. Hannah was a magnet for animals, especially those in need. Would her biological dad appreciate that?

"What Han needs are friends." It was too bad it was summer and school was out. "Let's ask around and see if we can't get her some playdates." Ones without princess dresses, at least at first.

"Fine." Mom slipped her arm around Ben's waist, smelling of the garlic she used in nearly everything she cooked. "But we need to start thinking about what we'll do with Hannah if you can't find her father."

"She's always got a home with the Libbys." Dad removed the cigar from his mouth and stared up at the ceiling, perhaps imagining he was blowing smoke rings.

Mom frowned.

Ben's lungs felt as if he was fighting a fully engaged house fire from the inside and had run out of oxygen in his tank. It was unfair to ask his mother to raise a child when she'd already raised two of her own. And firefighter hours? He couldn't walk away from a raging house fire if his shift was over. His father was the perfect example of absentee parenthood—gone for days at a time, never home when he promised, always rushing to pick up an extra shift or attend a union meeting. When other kids had dads in the stands for Little League or end-of-the-year school awards, Ben had had none. Those crazy hours? It was why Ben had been staying with his parents since Erica's death. It was why he'd moved in with them in Harmony Valley.

"All I'm asking is we think about it." Mom's frown disappeared. She gave him another squeeze. "You'll do the right thing, Ben. You always do."

Ben was doing the right thing. He was caring for another man's child. It blew his mind that he'd never met and couldn't find John Smith.

He'd formed many friendships at the fire academy, but none stuck like the connection between himself, Steven and Erica. They shared the same family lineage of firefighters and a drive to succeed. They'd all been hired by the Oakland Fire Department and assigned to the same busy, downtown station. And then one night Steven had been killed on-scene when a drunken driver plowed into the ambulance he'd been standing in front of. Ben had been the first to reach him.

That night, Ben had shown up at Erica's apartment with a six-pack. Six beers and several whiskey shots later, he woke up in her bed. They'd both been horrified. Erica had a boyfriend. They'd made a pact never to mention it again. And Ben hadn't until three months later when Erica announced she was pregnant. Ben had asked if it was his, because despite not wanting kids it'd been the right thing to do. When Erica denied it, Ben had been unable to hide his relief.

He wondered again for the umpteenth time... Was John Smith real?

If he wasn't real, that might mean...

Ben needed space to think. Space to stop himself from thinking. Space from Mom and Dad and even sleeping Hannah. Space from the nagging feeling that he'd been lying to himself for seven years. He and Erica had been friends. He should have met her boyfriend at least once.

Ben went outside and called the private investigator he'd hired to find Hannah's dad. His report? Still a dead end.

"But now that I have her laptop," Fenway said, referring to the computer Ben had given him last weekend, "I'm going through her pictures and reverting them back to the original photo. You'd be amazed what and who people crop out before posting to social media."

If John Smith existed, Hannah deserved to be with him. Being a fireman's kid wasn't a bowl of cherry-filled chocolates. There'd be missed meals, missed school events, missed ball games. Ben wouldn't wish a fireman's family on anyone.

He sat on top of the wooden picnic table in the backyard and stared at the sky. It was peaceful in Harmony Valley at night. There were no sirens. No gunshots. No road-raging shouts. Instead, there were wind-rustled leaves, curious owls and a singing cricket. It was peaceful, safe...boring. The kind of slow-paced place where a man had little to think of other than his own hard truths.

Am I Hannah's dad?

A branch snapped to his left.

"Ouch," a female voice said, sounding more annoyed than hurt.

The four-foot-tall shrubbery separating the Libby backyard from the rear neighbor shook. More branches protested a bodily intrusion.

"For the love of gardenias!" A figure moved beneath the shadows created by a large tree.

Ben hopped off the picnic table. "Need any help?"

The woman and the bushes stilled. "Um. No. I'm looking for... I'm trying to..." The woman huffed as if the weight of the world was too much for her patience. "I like to look at the moon, and this humongous tree is in my way."

Her hesitation and intensity gave her away. "Mandy?"

The very air seemed to go still. No crickets chirped. No owl hooted. Even the offending tree had gone still.

Ben peered into the shadows, trying to discern if Mandy was still there, imagining her holding on to that calm smile of hers. "Mandy from the post office?"

"It's Ben, isn't it?" She spoke as if this was the worst news of the evening. "How did I not know the fire marshal was my neighbor?"

He chalked up the defeat in her voice to the stress of his fire inspection. His opinion of the post office didn't reflect on her. She... He had to admit, she and her unflappable smile were more interesting than most things in Harmony

Valley. "We've both been busy working." And he went down Harrison to the firehouse, while she probably drove in the opposite direction to the post office.

"If our house looks vacant, it's because I park in the garage and walk to work," Mandy admitted. Gone was the postmaster with her defensive stubbornness. In her place was a neighbor shooting the breeze, one who fed displaced raccoons.

"Speaking of looking..." His lips turned upward for the first time that night. "I can see the moon clearly over here."

"Rub it in," she said, in a tone less pained than when she'd discovered he was on the other side of the hedge.

He was near enough now to see the outline of her face, although not a clear expression. Not her smile.

He wanted to see her smile.

Which was beyond ridiculous. A stranger's smile shouldn't matter.

Dad liked to say everything was different in Harmony Valley. If Dad were out here, he'd say Mandy wasn't a stranger. She was a neighbor. Practically a friend. Friends found solace in each other's smile.

"There used to be a fence here," she said from her backyard in a voice as neutral as Switzerland.

"You lived there before?" Ben moved closer until the thick hedge that separated them nearly touched his chest. He tried to take a bead on her feelings. Was she happy to be back?

"My grandparents raised me here. Back then the Morrettis lived in your place."

"My mom said a windstorm recently knocked down the fence and the Morrettis cleared out the debris, but didn't rebuild." He couldn't see Mandy's face in her shadowy backyard, couldn't fathom why she wanted to see the moon. He wasn't very patient or much good at beating around the bush. "Why do you want to look at the moon?"

More silence. He waited her out.

"I'm raising my sister," she said in a low voice he had to strain to hear. "She's seventeen going on thirty-seven."

"I'm raising my goddaughter," he said without thinking. "She's seven going on seventy."

Mandy chuckled. It was a warm sound that reached across the shrubs to ease the neck cramp he hadn't realized was there.

"You can see the moon over here," he repeated, adding quickly, "There's a break in the hedge toward the back of the yard." He'd discovered it when he'd checked the property to make sure it was safe for Hannah. He hadn't realized she'd use the front door and a bicycle to go exploring.

He and Mandy walked side by side to the opening.

Mandy entered his yard. The moon cast her in soft light, illuminating her gentle sanity-holding smile. She'd taken out her ponytails, and her hair hung loosely over her ears. She still wore her postal shorts and baggy shirt. She was comfortable in her own skin, disheveled as it was. Little about her should have been attractive or intriguing.

She intrigued him anyway. Opening a post office. Raising a sister. Giving him grief.

Mandy tilted her face to the heavens. "Hello, Mr. Moon."

She talks to the moon.

Ben bit back a grin. Of course, a woman who smiled through her troubles would talk to the moon.

Erica had been a firm believer in everything having energy and heart. She'd talked about cars and fires as if they were alive and had a personality. It was probably why Hannah projected personalities on every animal she came upon.

"Mr. Moon keeps all my secrets," Mandy whispered, bringing Ben back to the present.

He had the strongest urge to be pale and round and silent. He wanted to know the secrets Mandy told the moon, especially about her smile. He'd never been one to keep things inside. The few secrets he had, like the night he'd spent with Erica, were too personal to share with anyone.

Thinking better of his wish for Mandy's secrets, he took a step back.

Life was cruel. Bad things happened. People let you down. And it was best to scowl and go it alone, like the big full moon Mandy was sharing her secrets with. If only the moon were scowling and not smiling, like Mandy.

"Okay," she said with a burst of expelled air, the kind of breath that indicated she felt the awkwardness of the situation as palpably as he did. "Thanks for giving me my nightly sliver of sanity pie." She turned. There was no smile on her face.

No smile. None.

He couldn't believe it.

Ben almost reached for her, almost felt the impulse to cup her cheek with his palm. "Come back anytime," he said instead.

"Do you mean it?" She grinned a happy grin, one full of joy.

He grinned back. "I do."

"Thank you." She slipped through the hedge to her backyard. "The moon helps me deal with Olivia without breaking any eggshells." She turned back to him, everything but her voice lost in shadow. "That's what I call losing my temper. You know, because kids are fragile...and frustrating. And she's taken more hits than any kid deserves."

Like Hannah. "Wouldn't want to be Humpty Dumpty."

"No."

There was another awkward pause, awkward because Ben felt the need to fill it and couldn't find the right words. Mandy had her act together. He respected that. She had a way to deal with stress. He respected that. He was just worried that there were other things he liked about her that had to do with the distraction of an attractive, fascinating woman.

The last thing he needed in his life was a distraction.

"Good night," she said softly.

Her sneakered footfalls made soft noises in the darkness.

"Good night," he called after too long of a pause.

Ben waited until he heard Mandy's door latch, waited until Mandy and her secrets were locked safely inside. Only then did he turn back to the house.

Without looking up at Mr. Moon.

Chapter Five

"There it is," Dad said as he and Ben drove toward a small grass fire on a solitary stretch of two-lane highway on the outskirts of town.

It was their first fire operating as the Harmony Valley Fire Department. Ben was excited. Finally, the work he'd become a firefighter for had materialized. The peppery smoke was thick, the red-gold flames low, and a twenty-foot patch of ground blackened.

"You knock it down, son."

Ben stepped on the brakes too hard. "What about calling for backup?" They were only two men. "What about protocol?" A four-person crew.

"We can have this fire out long before the Cloverdale team gets here."

"Since when did you become a renegade?" His father had always played by the rules.

"Things are different in a small fire department." Dad grinned. "And I happen to be the fire chief."

No one would have their backs if things got out of hand. It would just be Ben and his father. It'd never been just Ben and his father, not even when he was a kid.

Ben leaned forward to study the fire again. It was a small fire, about the size of his parents' living room. The grass here was sparse, having survived several years of drought. Little fuel, little wind, little fire. Odds were in their favor.

"Okay, boss. We're saving Cloverdale Fire some gas." Ben would rather his father stay in the truck, but he needed a second pair of hands to run the system, monitor water pressure and occasionally help him with the hose.

With adrenaline-fueled speed, Ben hopped out and strapped on his breathing apparatus—his mask and a tank on his back. Then he pulled a hose free and connected it to the truck, while Dad readied the pump.

The fire crackled and popped as lazily as a ringed campfire. Ben wasn't fooled. One strong gust of wind and the flames would sprint to the hills and then the Mayacamas mountain range separating Sonoma County from Napa. The flames would feed on the sparse grass until it found something meatier, like an abandoned house or a grove of drought-thirsty trees.

Planting his feet firmly on the ground, Ben aimed the nozzle toward the fire. "Let's do this!"

Dad gave him juice, and soon water doused flames. The resulting steam sent a wave of heat rolling over Ben.

They were lucky. In no time, they were done. They'd caught the grass fire early. It died a quick death.

Goodbye, little fire.

Shades of Mandy, talking to inanimate objects.

Ben glanced skyward, where the moon made a daytime appearance.

A flash north of them caught Ben's eye. At the bend in the highway, a small gray car backfired as it pulled out from under the trees and drove away. It was too far off for Ben to make out the license plate or even discern the make.

"Shut it down," Ben called. When the water stopped, he removed his mask and pointed to the trees. "Did you see that car?"

"I was busy." Dad sank onto a bumper, gulping air. His mask-less face was ashen. "Watching you. And the gauges."

A rush of anger drowned Ben's adrenaline high. He stepped forward and clutched Dad's shoulder, giving it a shake. "Why didn't you wear a mask?"

Dad tugged off a glove and wiped his face. "I forgot."

"You don't forget. You *can't* forget. You're the fire chief." Ben bit back a rant that might break eggs.

"Well, I did." Dad produced his inhaler and took a hit. "What did you say before?" He drew in a labored breath that gave Ben sympathy gasps. "Something about a car?"

"I'm taking you to the doctor." Ben tried to help him up, tried to be patient, tried not to be mad toward or disappointed in or scared for his role model.

"No doctor." Dad shrugged him off. "Your mother will worry."

"As opposed to her grieving…" Ben began to shout. "…when you die!" He glanced down to count the eggshells he'd broken and stomped on the urge to break more. He couldn't let his father get to him.

"Don't be maudlin." The color was slowly returning to Dad's face. "Do you suspect arson?"

Ben fumed quietly for a moment, trying to decide if he should call Dad's doctor, or Mom, or no one at all. He made a choice. The choice to respect his father and his fire chief. "Doesn't it seem suspicious? A car left right after we put the fire out." Arsonists often stayed to watch the havoc.

"Maybe the driver was the one to call it in."

"Maybe." Ben's mind wouldn't let the idea of arson go. He'd studied to be a fire investigator for years. It was hard not to put any of that training into play.

Granted, the fire hadn't been fast burning, which seemed to rule out accelerant. And it was within cigarette flicking distance from the two-lane, which would lead him toward suspecting a careless driver. But their audience… It felt like someone was flaunting their dirty work.

The wind shifted, sending smoke in their faces.

Dad bent over, hacking deeply. Ben had to help him inside the truck, where the air was cool and filtered. After Dad was settled and breathing almost normally, Ben stowed the gear, keeping an eye on the blackened ground in case an ember flared to life again. Nothing did.

"Sorry I couldn't help with the cleanup," Dad said when Ben returned to the cab. His expression resembled that of a defeated old boxer who'd tried unsuccessfully to make a comeback.

"It's okay. I knew what I was getting into when I came here." Double duty. Hiding Dad's secret. Locking away his principles for the better part of a year.

Ben put the engine in gear and headed into town, letting his mind wander. It meandered to a tin of matchbooks he'd seen in the post office.

"I just didn't think I'd feel so worthless," Dad said, his voice barely audible above the engine.

If Dad had been among the new generation of firefighters, like Ben, he'd have worn a breathing apparatus at every fire—big or small. He wouldn't have developed heart and lung disease. He'd be finishing a long and illustrious career in Oakland. He'd be planning retirement and trips with Mom, making jokes about poor working stiffs.

And Ben would be switching gears, working as a fire investigator.

Those matchbooks...

He couldn't dismiss the thought. The...the...*implication*.

"Where are we going?" Dad asked when they missed the turn to the firehouse.

"I have a hunch." There was one person in town he knew of who'd started a fire and had been mesmerized. He hoped he was wrong. He hoped he was being paranoid, falling prey to a worst-case-scenario hypothesis. But being a worst-case-scenario thinker was a plus when it came to fire prevention, and Dad had just proved his judgment wasn't the greatest.

Ben pulled in front of the post office and wished he hadn't.

There was a small gray sedan parked in the lot.

Even with country music blaring from the radio in the post office, Mandy knew when the town's fire engine pulled up. The big engine rivaled the beat of the country song on the radio.

"I'm not ready for a fire inspection," Mandy muttered, turning the music down. It hadn't been a week since the first one.

What she really wasn't ready for was seeing Ben again. The past few nights, she'd stayed up late before going out to see the moon because their exchange had seemed too intimate. She'd told him about eggshells. She'd told him about sharing secrets with the moon. He must think she was an idiot!

Not that this was anything new when it came to Mandy and men.

Mandy didn't have her act together when it came to the opposite sex. And especially not when faced—literally—with a confident handsome man like Ben. He probably liked women who were petite and polished and wore heels the likes of which Mandy didn't have in her closet. She was launching a post office and raising a teenager. She didn't have time for pretty clothes, stylish hair or makeup. Who was she kidding? She didn't like clothes that showed how reed-thin her body was. She didn't like spending more than a minute on her hair. And makeup? It gave her acne.

On nervous legs, Mandy dodged the postal service maintenance crew, their ladder and the stack of boxes they'd brought containing fire alarms, extinguishers and lighted Exit signs. They'd claimed the sorting counter as their personal staging area, but they'd spread out like high tide on a flat marsh.

Utley sat in the sunshine on the loading dock in a webbed camp chair, a burning cigarette in his fingers. How long had he been sitting there? She hadn't noticed his arrival.

Mandy touched his shoulder as she passed.

The old man startled, dropping the cigarette on the concrete, barely missing the tin of matchbooks he'd saved from the trash several days ago.

She paused at the top of the stair. "Did I wake you?" It was hard to believe anyone could sleep through her music or the whine of drills installing new signage and fire alarms.

"No." Utley's eyes were heavy-lidded. "I was meditating." He lifted his fingers to his lips as if to take a drag from his cigarette, noticed his fingers were empty, and immediately brushed at his lap as if dozing and dropping cigarettes was a regular occurrence.

"It's on the ground," Mandy told him, hurrying down the concrete steps to meet Ben. "Don't light another." She'd already told him twice he couldn't smoke on the premises.

She'd received her first mail delivery this morning and wasn't sure how much of a stink Ben would put up about her operating without the fire control panel working. She didn't want to admit all her safety measures weren't in place, but she didn't want to disappoint her supervisor and delay mail delivery either.

She reached Ben in the middle of the parking lot.

He wore his turnout gear and smelled pleasantly like the wood fires her grandfather used to make when they went camping. She'd wondered about their next meeting. Would he be the rigid fireman or the compassionate neighbor?

Question answered. Ben wore his intimidating scowl, as if they'd never spoken in the darkness about eggshells or the moon.

The post office phone rang.

Mandy yelled to Olivia to take a message before turning to Ben with a smile she hoped didn't betray how nervous he made her feel. "Has it been a week already? It's been a challenge to pull work crews out here. But they're here today." She was babbling faster than a political talk show host. "And I'm checking things off my list." If she sounded any perkier, she might puke.

Ben stared at her as if he'd sat down at a poker table with people he suspected of cheating. And then his glance moved over the cars and trucks in the parking lot. "Have you been here long?"

"All morning. I just finished sanding the flagpole." She held up her red, raw hands, waving to Keith in the fire truck. The fact that the fire chief wasn't getting out had to mean this wasn't a fire inspection…she hoped. "I only went up about eight feet. I'm not very good on a ladder. I get vertigo."

"The flagpole out front?" Ben walked backward a few feet, every step magnetically drawing Mandy, too. He stopped where they could both see the front of the post office.

"Yes, the one and only flagpole." She'd left the ladder and supplies at its base. Was that a fire hazard? "Are you here for my inspection?" Or just to torture her?

"No one inside can see or hear you when you're out there," Ben noted, poker-faced. His lip was no longer fat, making the hard line of his mouth that much harder.

"It's a two-way street. I can't see or hear anyone inside either." Which was a blessing when Olivia was in drama mode. "Is there something wrong? I mean, I didn't dance naked out here. I was just sanding."

"It's hard work getting this place in shape." Utley shuffled up to them, adjusting his blue postal cap to shield his eyes from the sun. He always looked like he was on a tropical vacation. Today he wore a green Hawaiian shirt with white flowers over his khaki shorts. "Glad I could help."

If by helping, Utley meant lending moral support while he napped or reminisced about the old days, the retired postal worker was doing a bang-up job.

"Are you going to tell us about the fire?" The old man planted his sandals hip distance apart and rocked from side to side. "That's why you've got your gear on, isn't it?"

A flicker of fear for Ben skimmed Mandy's spine, so light she barely recognized it. But not so light that it didn't send heat into her cheeks. "Are you okay? Is Keith okay?"

"We're good. It was just a little grass fire," Ben said carefully, staring at her face. "It went down quickly."

"Oh, good. I'm glad." The heat in her cheeks changed to a prickle of discomfort at his continued scrutiny. Did she have something on her face? Ink? Rust? Cookie crumbs?

"Is that..." Ben leaned around Mandy, peering at the loading dock. "Is that the tin of matches I threw away?"

"It's my tin of matches." Utley patted his pockets as if searching for something. "I've been using them. I never let anything go to waste."

"I tried to stop him." Mandy brushed her fingers over her cheeks, wishing she could brush away her blush.

"You should have tried harder, Mandy." Ben and his hard-lining, code-adhering, firefighter voice. Added to the way he seemed larger than life in his uniform and...well...

I don't want to disappoint him.

But she was. No two ways about it.

Mandy glanced down at her tennis shoes and her blue work shorts and...sighed. Honestly, Ben was right about the matches. She was the postmaster. She shouldn't have let Utley keep the matches after the fire department wanted them removed. At the very least, she shouldn't have let Utley keep them here.

"Utley's having a hard time adjusting to me in charge." She continued to explain her case to Ben in a voice below Utley's hearing aid range. "He thought he'd be the next postmaster, and he's heartbroken. So, he nags, and he criticizes, but it doesn't mean much. The matches were a compromise."

A crease strobed between Ben's brows, and his lips twitched downward. She'd probably ruined her credibility by admitting she talked to the moon. She had to reestablish herself.

"Utley." Mandy turned to her grandfather's friend and coworker. "The matches will have to go home with you."

Utley stopped patting pockets and reached in one, most likely for a pack of cigarettes.

She laid her hand over Utley's arm, preventing him from taking whatever he'd been searching for out. "And you'll have to respect the no-smoking rule at this facility."

"So, that's how it is." Utley worked his wrinkles into a deeply lined frown that no longer reminded Mandy of her grandfather and happier times. "All those years of service and now I'm like a stack of unclaimed mail."

"Well, we never throw unclaimed mail away," Mandy said, trying to lighten the mood.

"It's not right." Utley turned and shuffled back toward the loading dock.

"About the cars back here," Ben began.

"Wait." Mandy snapped her fingers. "I almost forgot. I got a special shipment today. Keith has a package." She hurried past Utley and up the stairs. "It must have broken open during transit. Someone along the way resealed it." She picked up the white plastic bag, but something fell out. "Shoot." They hadn't resealed it very well.

A pill bottle rolled across the floor toward where Ben stood on the loading dock.

Mandy swooped it up and checked the name on the prescription to the address label. Satisfied they matched, she handed both the bag with several other prescriptions and the escaped pill bottle to Ben. "You might want to check the shipping manifest to make sure all the meds he needs are in there."

Ben stared at the bottles and then back at her.

What was he waiting for her to say? "I hope to be ready for inspection in a day or two. Shall we say Friday?"

"You want..." Ben moved out of the way of Utley, who was headed toward his chair and the tin of matches. "That's all you want. An inspection date?"

"Well, clearly, I want to pass." She forced out a laugh.

"We'll see." Ben left. It was hard to tell beneath his fireproof jacket, but Mandy felt as if she'd been given the cold shoulder.

Mandy glanced over to the maintenance crew in case they'd been doing something a fireman wouldn't approve of, but there was nothing suspect about them. Three were opening boxes and one was reading instructions.

"I'm tired of putting supplies away." Olivia wore blue jeans and one of Mandy's postal shirts. She had one of her wireless earbuds in one hand. "The caller asked for you but hung up when I said I'd have to put them on hold."

"It was probably Dave, calling to check up on my progress." Mandy hadn't reported in today, and probably wouldn't until later, after she'd delivered the mail.

Olivia shook her head. "It was a woman."

Mandy shrugged. If it was important, she'd call back, whoever she was. "I need to get the mail out." Thankfully, there wasn't much. Residents of Harmony Valley had been slow to change their post office boxes from Cloverdale.

Olivia's put-upon gaze landed on the departing fire truck. "Was there a fire?"

"Yep." Utley held up a matchbook and a cigarette, both of which he put in the matchbook tin under Mandy's stern glare. "Didn't you see him wearing his gear? Wish I'd been a firefighter."

"Aren't you missing out on the checkers game at Martin's Bakery?" Mandy asked innocently.

Utley lurched away, clutching the tin of matches. "I suppose I know when I'm not wanted."

Guilt tugged at Mandy's resolve. "See you tomorrow."

He waved a hand in the air as if to say he was done with her.

"Hey." Olivia touched Mandy's arm. "It's less than two weeks until my birthday."

Mandy hustled past Olivia toward her office. "What kind of cake do you want?"

"Let's talk dollar figures." Olivia trailed after her.

"We're not buying an expensive cake from the bakery." Mandy dodged trash. The work crew was worse than a child on Christmas morning. Boxes, plastic and Styrofoam pieces created an unnecessary obstacle course. "You'll get a homemade cake and twenty dollars in a card, just like always."

"I don't care about your gift." Olivia darted past Mandy and blocked her entrance into the office. "I want to know how much money Grandpa left me, so I know how much I need for cosmetology school."

This was it. The moment Mandy had been dreading. Grandpa had known for years how he wanted to divide his estate. But he'd told only Mandy.

Those years before Grandpa died had been a scary decline for him in many ways...

He'd been taking too many naps during the day, and when she'd asked him about it, he'd given her a weak excuse. "I'm not very good at managing my insulin." Which was true. But the naps were just the beginning of a long and drawn-out end.

His kidneys were failing, worn down by years of diabetic mismanagement. He had to quit work and seek dialysis. He didn't like needles to begin with. And now he felt his dignity was being robbed. He always seemed fatigued, short of breath, short on memory and, increasingly, short on patience and common sense.

When dialysis no longer worked, and they'd been discussing alternatives like home, hospital or hospice, Mom had shown up. They hadn't seen her for years, not since Grandma's funeral. Grandpa had taken thirty minutes to recognize her. And then he'd tottered to his bedroom alone.

A few minutes later, Grandpa had called Mandy into his room to help him dress. In a rare moment of clarity, he'd said, "I have a number for your mother in my phone. I check on her sometimes and tell her how you girls are doing." He'd handed Mandy a slip of paper. "Long ago, Blythe and I made you trustee of the estate. I've decided to leave everything to Teri."

To Mom? Mandy's knees buckled. Not that Grandpa had a lot to leave—a savings account and the house in Harmony Valley. She stared at the scribbled words, stating his intentions and ending with a signature. "Why would you leave her anything?"

"Why would I leave everything to Teri?" His eyes grew distant as if he couldn't remember. "Because...because... You and Olivia will be all right. You have the post office. Olivia can go to beauty school through the occupational program at high school for next to nothing. You'll be all right," he repeated, as if this phrase was well-rehearsed. "And Teri..." He choked up. "Teri needs a home base. You'll manage the finances for her so she always has a place to go."

Mandy wanted to say: *No.* She wanted to say: *Never.*

It's what Grandma would've said.

But Grandpa had raised Mandy as if he was her father. "If that's what you want. I'll do it." But she couldn't look him in the eye though.

Grandpa nodded.

Mandy thought about her grandparents taking her in, caring for her when they didn't have to. Never complaining. Giving her love. Grandpa had given her a job when Grandma's cancer returned and Mandy realized she couldn't go away to college and leave Olivia behind. He'd given them more than any house was worth. He'd given them love and a home.

Fifteen-year-old Olivia had entered to tell them Teri was restless.

Grandpa had reached for Olivia's hand. "I left you something at the bank. You can have it when you turn eighteen."

A year and a half later, Olivia was nearly eighteen. She stared at Mandy with glowing, trusting eyes. "Why wait to tell me? I'm nearly legal."

Because you won't like what he left you.

It'd been Mandy's responsibility as trustee to check the safe-deposit box contents after Grandpa died. There'd been no will inside just...

I need to tell her.

She opened her mouth, unsure how to spill this demoralizing secret to her hopeful sister.

"Hey, Mandy." Hank, the maintenance crew leader, saved her by his interruption. "Can I get a quick opinion on this?"

"We'll talk later," Mandy told Olivia. "After you put mail in PO boxes and I deliver the rest." She was required to deliver the mail she'd processed before her shift ended, which meant she had to leave in the next few minutes. She'd already loaded up the postal service Jeep.

"So, you'll tell me?" Olivia's eyes were bright with enthusiasm.

"We'll see."

Olivia frowned. She knew "*we'll see*" meant "*no*."

Chapter Six

"What was the rush to get to the post office?" Dad asked when Ben had the fire engine headed to the station.

Only Ben turned down a back road instead, needing time to think. And he thought best when he was in the shower or driving.

"Spit it out, son," Dad said impatiently.

"There've been no fires in Harmony Valley—not even a brushfire by the highway—for more than five years. New people come to town and now there's a fire?"

"I'm glad you didn't pursue a career as an investigative reporter," Dad deadpanned. "This is a nonstory."

"Did you see the gray sedan in the post office parking lot?"

"Yes. And I saw another one on the last corner. Don't jump to conclusions. If you're going to drive around, drive me to Martin's Bakery. I hear the coffee is outstanding." Dad had definitely recovered from the smoke he'd inhaled earlier. His feistiness had returned.

"Do you remember the way Mandy was enthralled by the electrical fire? She's new to town. And that car..."

"You suspect Mandy of setting the grass fire?" Dad guffawed, which caused a severe shortage of air in his lungs.

"Maybe you're right." Ben turned on a road that paralleled the Harmony Valley River, recalling Mandy's face as she gazed at the moon. She didn't fit the profile of an arsonist. She didn't feel like an arsonist. But she did feel like a woman with secrets. "I don't know what kind of car she drives. Plus she said she walks to work." But she might not have done so this morning.

"Common sense," Dad choked out. "Good."

"But she didn't want me going inside the post office today." She'd hurried outside to greet him. "And she gave me your medicine along with a request for a date to reinspect the post office."

"Those are your suspicions?" Dad sounded like a gunshot pipe organ, winded and off-key. "Were you really in the running for a fire inspector position? Because you're missing one thing."

"What's that?"

"Proof." Dad drank from a water bottle. His voice strengthened. "Something that's enough for a jury to convict. You've got nothing."

"She knows what meds you're taking," Ben said, unable to put his finger on what about Mandy didn't feel right. "She could tell everyone in town. You'd have to step down and there'd be no second chance at making full retirement." No reprieve for Ben either. "I'm just trying to figure her out."

"I'd say that sounds less like suspicion and more like attraction." Dad tried to chuckle, choked, and looked out the window instead.

"Attraction?" Ben scoffed. "Listen to yourself. Is it any wonder you need someone to watch your back?"

Dad sat up and put both hands on the window. "Slow down."

"I want to keep my eye on her," Ben said. "Purely for reasons associated with fire." Why didn't his words sound convincing?

"No, I mean literally. Slow down."

"I'm only going thirty-five." They had the country road to themselves, and the trees were far enough back from the pavement that the engine was clear of branches.

"Stop!" Dad twisted in his seat to look behind them. "Hannah's in that tree."

"Hannah?" Ben pulled over, bringing the rig to a jolting stop. They were near where Hannah had found Iggy. "She's this far from home?"

"Focus, Ben. She's in danger." Dad threw open the door and was climbing out before Ben turned off the ignition. "That branch she's on has cracked at the trunk and she's dangling over the river."

"Where?" Ben leaned forward to see.

Sure enough, Hannah was in a tree and in a predicament. She clung to a thin branch that hung at a forty-five-degree angle, the end submerged in the water.

Ben's heart banged in his chest. He jumped to the pavement, shucked out of his turnout gear and slipped into the black waterproof loafers he kept behind the seat. At a full run, he drew up to Dad, who was jogging slowly across the field, sucking in air like a clogged vacuum cleaner.

Ben darted in front of him, forcing the older man to stop. "If your heart gives out and you collapse, and Hannah falls in—"

Dad gulped air and nodded. "You'll save Hannah and let me die."

"That's right." Ben's pulse accelerated faster than his slowly measured words. He clasped a hand briefly on Dad's shoulder. "Don't make me choose."

Dad tilted his head in acknowledgment.

"Hang on, Hannah!" Ben shouted, spinning around and racing to the river.

Hannah let out a frail wail as if she was afraid anything louder would send her tumbling into the river.

Ben skidded down ten feet or so of steep bank to the water's edge and positioned himself downriver from the branch in case she fell in. The fifteen-foot limb swayed slightly in the water, like a broom being swept over the same spot repeatedly. How much longer would it hold?

He'd visited his grandfather enough times growing up to have gone tubing down the Harmony Valley River in spring and summer. This stretch was slow and deep, but just fifty feet away it twisted and turned, gaining speed and dodging some big rocks. Not exactly wild rapids, but a challenge for a little girl who'd had only one or two swimming lessons. If she fell in, she'd be scared, perhaps even panic.

His insides churned and his hands trembled. This was no welcome adrenaline rush on his way to a call. This was fear for Hannah, sweet, too-serious Hannah.

Blood relative or not, Hannah was a part of Ben. And she needed him to stay calm.

"Well, peanut." Ben schooled his features and his tone. "This is what Granny Vanessa would call a fine kettle of fish." Oh, those words cost him. His pulse increased. He wanted to be doing something. Scale the tree, climb to her, hold Hannah in his arms as he carried her to safety. But that route spelled disaster. The limb couldn't hold both of them.

Hannah's face was streaked with tears. "There was a baby bird…"

"Let's worry about you now, peanut," Ben said in that same casual tone, the one that was slowly killing him inside.

Dad reached the bank and choked on a bad word.

"Can you get me down?" Hannah hiccuped as if she'd already cried herself out. Her knobby arms and legs gripped the tree limb like a jockey did on a racehorse if his saddle swung underneath.

Dispatch squawked on the radios at Ben's and Dad's belts. Dad turned away to answer. Ben forced himself not to listen.

Hannah sniffed and hiccuped again. "Do you need to go rescue someone?"

Erica would be proud of her little girl. Of course, she'd have Ben's hide for allowing this to happen in the first place, but she'd be proud of her daughter nonetheless.

"We're not going anywhere, peanut. Not until we get you down." There were few options. One really. Ben had to wade in and Hannah had to jump. He took a few steps in the river. It was cold, the bottom rocky, the current more than a lazy pull, and the bank slanted steeply toward the middle of the river, making it a challenge to stay on his feet. "Do you trust me, peanut?"

"Ye-es."

"Atta girl." Ben lifted his arms, willing his hands not to tremble. He didn't want to telegraph to Hannah that he was afraid. "Do you remember how I caught Truman the other day?"

"He fell." Some of the stoic Hannah returned. She blinked at him from behind her smudged glasses.

Ben smiled, just the way Mandy smiled under pressure. She was right. It made him feel better, helped keep his fears at bay. "But I caught him."

"You almost didn't."

"I'll catch you, peanut." Ben shored up his footing and sent up a prayer. "Let go."

The river gurgled past his legs with a cold, insistent tug.

"I want the ladder." Hannah was a scared, stubborn thing, in need of enticement, like Truman's kittens.

Ben had nothing to entice her with. "The bucket can't reach over here. You're going to have to trust me, peanut."

"No." He'd never seen Hannah jut out her chin before.

"She learned that expression from you." Dad returned to the upper bank. "10-67 waiting."

10-67. Someone in Harmony Valley needed their help. Hannah was putting another life in jeopardy.

"Hannah Laurel Thompson." Ben abandoned patience and godfatherly tones in favor of breaking eggshells. "Get your butt down here. Now!"

"Don't let me die," Hannah sobbed, letting go and tumbling through the air with far less grace and control than Truman.

Ben caught her, but not without their heads connecting with a crack.

"Ow-wooo." Hannah began to cry.

He adjusted her in his arms, holding her close, never wanting to let her go.

"I'm sorry, peanut." Ben carried her out of the river and up the bank. His wet pants dragged, and his shoe soles quickly became caked with mud. None of it mattered. Hannah was safe.

In that moment, he needed to know the truth. Was she his biological daughter? Was she his responsibility? The weight of not knowing was greater than the weight of Hannah in his arms. It pressed the air from his lungs. It made his steps cumbersome. His purchase on the slope precarious. Was she a Libby? He vowed to find out.

Dad reached down, grabbed Ben's arm and pulled him the last few feet to the top.

"You hit…my head." Hannah was as out of breath as Dad normally was. Her palms covered her face.

"Let me see." Dad pried her hands away, revealing a red bump rising above her black glasses. "An ice pack will fix that right up."

"It won't." She buried her face in Ben's chest, glasses and all.

"It will." Ben's head throbbed, but he didn't care. He marched back across the grassy field. "Now, here's what we need to do, peanut. We're going to put you in the backseat with an ice pack and drive to our next call, where Granny Vanessa is going to meet us and take you home."

"You're punishing me!"

Dad chuckled, reaching the truck first. He dug in the first aid kit, found an instant ice pack and activated it.

"That's not funny, Grandpa," she said into Ben's shoulder. "Don't laugh."

But Ben imagined he could feel Hannah smile.

"I hear the siren, Elvira." Mandy held the older woman's cold hand. She'd heard Elvira's cries for help on the first street she'd tried to deliver mail to. "I'm going to flag them down. Stay here."

"As for that…" Elvira lay on her left side. She'd fallen on the lime-green linoleum beneath her kitchen table. "I'm something of a captive audience. I'll wait here."

Mandy stood and hurried to the front door through the large living room. Over rugs with frayed edges, circling antique armchairs and slipping past curio cabinets stuffed full of porcelain and china figurines of Victorian women in long flowing dresses. It was a wonder Elvira hadn't fallen in the front room.

Sparky, Elvira's small shaggy black-and-white dog, waddled after Mandy to greet the troops.

Ben was running around the front of the fire truck. "I can handle this, Dad. Stay with Hannah."

"It's a medic call." Hand to chest, Keith stepped down from the passenger seat like a man who'd had stitches recently. "Hannah is fine. And look. Here's your mother."

A frazzled-looking middle-age blonde pulled up in a gray sedan, followed by an old blue truck with a sheriff's star on it.

"I forgot," Keith said to Ben with a brief laugh that turned into a cough. "Your mother drives a gray car, too."

Ben mumbled something Mandy couldn't hear as he hurried around to a storage cubby in the fire truck and tugged out a first aid kit. His pants were wet to his knees, and his black shoes were caked in mud.

"Elvira fell and needs help getting up," Mandy said, stepping onto the front porch. "She's breathing easy and doesn't have any back, hip or neck pain."

Ben glanced up at her. There was a red lump on his temple that hadn't been there forty minutes ago. "What's the postman doing here?"

"I'm the one who called 911." Mandy commanded Sparky to stay (although that dog wasn't running away from his meal train) and held the door open for the rescue team. "I was delivering mail when I heard her." Elvira had been hoarse, having fallen at breakfast.

The tall man from the sheriff's truck ran past her. He wore blue jeans, a blue plaid button-down and a worried expression. "Elvira?"

"Nate? Did I disrupt your day?" Elvira said meekly. "I hate being a bother."

The frazzled blonde lifted a little girl from the backseat of the fire truck. The child also had a red lump on her forehead, similar to Ben's. Despite a pair of black rectangular glasses, the Libby-blue eyes shone bright.

"Madame Postmaster, you know first aid?" Ben lugged his equipment up the walk.

Mandy nodded. "I'm certified in CPR and first aid, plus I took care of my grandfather for years. I'm familiar with elderly emergencies, so hold on." She stood in the fireman's way, eliciting a glower. She lowered her voice. "Elvira's likely to have a heart attack if you enter her house with those muddy shoes."

"Get out of my way," Ben warned, leaning into her space. Earlier, he'd smelled of smoke. Now he also smelled of something green.

"My grandfather was more intimidating than you are." Louder, too. Mandy smiled harder. "Now, I've spent the last twenty minutes waiting for you with this woman. I got a lesson on the quality of rugs from Turkey. She's proud of her things, Ben. Please don't upset her."

Ben set his metal first aid kits on the ground like a weightlifter who'd just done a successful clean and jerk, efficiently, with no wasted movements. He removed his shoes and rolled his pant cuffs three times. His feet were larger than hers, a fact Mandy was embarrassed to appreciate.

He straightened, having rid himself of both shoes and frown. "Satisfied?"

"Surprised, maybe." She'd expected more of a fight. And a glower, not an almost-smile. Mandy moved aside to let him through.

"You can go now, Mandy," Ben said as he entered the house.

"Do not send away my savior." Elvira's voice unraveled for the first time since Mandy had arrived.

"I'm staying," Mandy called to her. The mail would just have to be late today. Mandy was sticking with Elvira as long as she needed her.

"She's stable," the sheriff said. He'd moved the heavy table back a few feet. "No neck, hip or back pain. Good job for getting her on her left side. Not everyone knows that. Mandy, is it?" The sheriff had a friendly, half smile. Ben could learn a lot from him about bedside manners.

Ben dropped to his knees next to Elvira, placing his equipment on the floor with more care than he'd shown outside. "Elvira, I'm Ben. I'm going to take your vitals."

"I'm single," Elvira said coquettishly, smiling the way Olivia did when she talked about her favorite male singer. "Is that vital enough for you?"

"I like a woman with spunk." Ben put a stethoscope in his ears. "If you like coffee, we'd be a match made in heaven. Breathe deep for me."

This was the man Mandy had spoken to beneath the stars. Deep inside her chest, her heart gave a little pang.

Sparky waddled around to Elvira's head and gave her forehead a little lick.

"I'm so embarrassed." Elvira's voice faded from sassy to vulnerable. "I leaned over to give Sparky a piece of bacon and just kept on going. Luckily, my front screen door was unlocked. Darn heat means I need to get some airflow until eleven. If not for the heat, I wouldn't have heard Mandy delivering the mail. Although I thought for a moment she was a burglar."

Elvira's chatter was charming. When Grandpa had fallen trying to get to the bathroom in the middle of the night, he'd been annoyed with himself, the world and with Mandy.

Elvira squirmed. The floor had to be uncomfortable. "Can we move me and this conversation to the living room?"

"Hold still," Ben said. "Do you hurt anywhere?" Despite being told twice that Elvira felt no pain, Ben ran his fingers beneath her head, along her neck and shoulders, and down to her hips. "Can you wiggle your toes?"

"My toes are curled." Despite her delicate features and delicate situation, Elvira was a pistol. "I can't complain about anything but the dirt on this floor. I never was good at housework."

"That's not what a man values in a woman." Without missing a beat, Ben put a blood pressure cuff on her arm. "Did you lose consciousness after you fell?"

"I was too busy yelling for help to pass out."

"Relax," Ben counseled, pumping the cuff.

"That's the trouble with elderly neighbors." Elvira's voice strained as the cuff grew tighter. "We're all deaf."

Ben silenced his patient by sliding a digital thermometer in her mouth.

Not to be sidelined, Elvira reached up and nearly touched the bump on Ben's forehead. Her gaze asked the question she couldn't: *What happened?*

"That's the price of being a hero." To his credit, Ben didn't draw back from her touch. In fact, he might have flashed a brief smile. "Or so I'm told. Fat lip one week. Knot on your head another."

The difficulty Mandy had fitting the different sides of Ben together suddenly locked in place. He cared about people. He cared so much that he dialed up the intensity to get through to people who wanted to make excuses for bending the fire safety rules. He cared so much that he was willing to risk his own safety for others. He was the fireman who'd be the first to break down a door to find those trapped in a burning building. Whoever cared about him would be right in worrying if he'd come home safely after a shift. And Mandy, who valued stability, felt a piercing shaft of fear for him once more.

"We've achieved silence in Harmony Valley." The sheriff glanced at Mandy in mock awe. "I need to carry a thermometer."

"Or show your bumps and bruises," Mandy offered, trying to shake off an unexpected impulse to touch Ben, to rub his back and reassure herself he was all right.

He was fine. Bruised, but fine.

"Ignore them, Elvira." Ben spared Mandy a curious glance before removing the thermometer and recording Elvira's vitals. "You're as healthy as I am."

"Like that's a surprise." Elvira was back to fighting form. "I may be weaker than a newborn, but I'm going the distance. I'm gonna live to be one hundred."

"The ambulance should be here in five," Keith said, coming up behind them. He was a bit out of breath, as if he'd run up the walk and front steps to update them.

"I hope you called it for yourself." Elvira squinted at Keith. "Because I'm fine. Just couldn't get up this time. But I'm ready to get up now."

"You had a fall." The sheriff sounded rueful. Given most of Harmony Valley's population was over age sixty-five, he probably dealt with falls and the fallout frequently. "You know protocol. We have to take you to the hospital and the doctor."

"That won't be necessary," Elvira said loftily from her prone position. "Besides—" Elvira gathered Sparky closer with one arm "—I can't go. Who will take care of Sparky while I'm in the hospital?"

Ben exchanged a glance with his father. "I have just the dog sitter for you. Her name is Hannah."

"Is that Felix's great-granddaughter?" Elvira perked up. "On Thursdays, Felix takes Sparky on a long walk. He says Sparky has a nose for charming kittens out of hiding."

Mandy suspected the little dog was better at charming treats out of the hands of those around him. But hey, what did she know?

Ben packed up his medical gear. "My only condition is Sparky has to come to our house for the night."

"Perfect," Keith said. "I'll go get the pet sitter before Vanessa takes her home."

"Sparky is persnickety when he's not with me," Elvira chattered on. "Why, one time, I left him with Agnes and the only thing she could get him to eat was salmon."

By the set of his mouth, Mandy knew Ben wasn't going to feed the little dog salmon.

A few minutes and several Sparky anecdotes later, the screen door squeaked open and then banged closed. As if sensing his new best friend had arrived, Sparky waddled to the door.

The bespectacled little blonde got to her knees to greet him. "Aren't you a pretty boy," she cooed. She seemed to know just how to pet a roly-poly little beast into submission.

Sparky collapsed on the floor and rolled onto his back for a belly rub.

Ben leaned down to whisper to Elvira. "Do you really think we'll need salmon?"

He may have been speaking to Elvira, but his gaze veered toward Hannah, shining with pride. And then it veered to Mandy, sharing his pride, his joy, his...

Her breath caught. Her stomach fluttered. She felt as if they stood together under the moon once more. Alone and sharing secrets without fear of breaking eggs.

She'd never believed in love at first sight or the fast connections of which her friends at the post office had spoken of when they'd slept with guys they'd just met in bars. She believed in slow courtships, feelings steadily built, common goals and a deep knowledge of someone else.

Oddly, she felt she knew Ben. Oh, certainly not anything concrete. He was a stickler for the rules. He had a dry sense of humor. He helped people. She'd known that much about other men and it hadn't caused her to linger, waiting for a moment to speak. "Thank you for being so good to Elvira." Mandy slung her mailbag to her shoulder as the old woman was loaded into an ambulance.

Hannah had long since disappeared with Sparky. The sheriff and Keith were talking to the ambulance driver, heedless of the hot afternoon sun.

Ben stowed his med kits in the fire truck. He leaned against the closed compartment and smiled ruefully, knocking dried mud from his soles on the curb. "Given how we met, you may not believe this, but I like people."

"Given how we met, you may not believe this, but I believe you."

He shifted that rueful grin her way.

That grin said he knew she felt stomach-fluttering excitement when their gazes connected. It apologized for being so gosh-darn charming.

Suddenly self-conscious, Mandy smoothed one of her two ponytails over one shoulder and turned her toes to the next house on her route. She shouldn't have said anything more. She did anyway, calling over her shoulder, "Besides, you have the endorsement of Mr. Moon." It sounded like she was flirting. She started walking. Fast.

Not fast enough.

Ben called after her, "Why do I feel like you'd leave a bowl of cat food outside for me?"

She turned, working hard to contain a smile that wanted to bloom into her being foolish. "You may not believe this, but I leave out food for all kinds of strays."

"I'm flattered," Ben said, no longer grinning.

"*Flattered?*" Mandy muttered, hurrying off, wishing she could disappear.

Flattered was man-code for: *thanks, but no thanks.* As in: *I'm not interested.* End of story.

Shut up, Mr. Moon.

Chapter Seven

"Hannah, no more television until you've taken your bath." Ben's mother was a strict disciplinarian.

Ben had rebelled mildly against that authority when he was a teen, but he could see the value of it from the other side now. And he was honest enough with himself to realize Mom's take-no-prisoners approach to running a household had influenced who he was as a firefighter.

Ben may be stubborn in fulfilling his duty, but Mandy had taken his intensity and diffused it with logic, a sly comment and a smile—at Elvira's, at the post office, on the sidewalk before she continued on her route. She was willing and able to stand up to him. Just thinking of her made him happy.

Hannah obediently got up from the floor where she'd been brushing Sparky's matted hair. If there was any positive from the river episode today, it'd been the change in Hannah's behavior. She hadn't wandered once. Not that Ben believed it would last.

"Before you do that, Hannah, I need you in the kitchen." Ben ignored his mother's curious look and led Hannah away. He retrieved a bag he'd put in the back of a tall cupboard before dinner, set it on the oak farm table and began opening its contents.

"What's that?" Hannah perched on her knees on a kitchen chair. Her pink T-shirt and jean shorts were just as dirty as they were every night. But her forearms and inner thighs bore scrapes from where she'd clung to the limb.

"Something I picked up this afternoon." On a special trip to Cloverdale, where the drugstore had a wider selection of merchandise than the small grocery in Harmony Valley. "We're going to play mad scientist."

"Do we need goggles and a white jacket?" Han sounded interested, but she kept her eye on Sparky, who flopped beneath her chair.

"What's that?" Mom carried her water glass to the sink.

Ben hesitated for a long moment, and then told her the truth. "It's a DNA kit." Since rescuing Hannah, he'd been unable to think of much else but the question of her parentage.

"Benjamin Edward Libby." Mom sank into a chair across from Hannah. "I thought you said..." She glanced at Hannah and started again. "I would've expected something like this from Mike."

"Mike has been happily married for years now." His younger brother was a fireman in Sacramento. Settled and nothing like the party animal of his youth.

"But you... This is not you," Mom said.

Ben knew what she meant. He'd been the careful child. The straightforward child. The child most likely to do his chores before being asked a second time. The exact opposite of his brother, Mike. "There's a one-time chance, Mom. I have to know."

"I'm glad your father is in his man cave." Meaning the garage. Mom turned her attention to Hannah, who'd been listening to their exchange with a curious tilt to her head. "What's the report from the infirmary? Any patients ready to be released?"

While Hannah talked about animals on the mend, Ben read the kit's instructions. He had to re-read them three times, and the process wasn't that complicated. But the feelings inside him were. The word *father* had been echoing in his head since he'd rescued Hannah from that tree.

"What's the holdup?" Mom's hands were clasped on the oak table, her knuckles white.

"I just want to get it right." If only Ben knew what right was. He should have asked Erica more questions when she made Hannah his godchild. He should have asked about John Smith.

"You mean you want to win. Isn't it a game?" Hannah asked, peering at him with an inquisitive expression reminiscent of her mother.

"It's more like playing doctor. There are no winners or losers." What a lie that was. If Hannah wasn't his, he'd feel like he lost. Ben held a swab up. "First me, then you." He swept the inside of his mouth and then sealed the sample.

"Let me do it." Hannah practically brushed her teeth with the swab before handing the stick back to Ben. "Now what?"

"Now we wait." Ben sealed her sample and then packaged the two swabs for shipping. No one would suspect the plain envelope held the balance of his life inside.

Except Mandy. She'd probably seen it all.

"Now we take a bath," Mom said, sounding confident of the order of things—dinner, bath, bed—which was a more comforting progression than Ben's order—kid, proof, fatherhood. "Let's roll." When the bath was running and Han in the tub, Mom returned to the kitchen. "She's seven, Ben. What's brought this on all of a sudden?"

"The fact that John Smith can't be found and might not exist."

"Oh, Ben." Mom hugged him. "If she's yours, what about your career dreams? You've always said you'd choose your career over the welfare of children."

"You didn't seem to worry about my dreams when you asked me to come here." Ben kept his tone in a place that didn't break eggs. He stuffed the empty DNA box back in the shopping bag and then shoved the shopping bag in the kitchen trash.

"And you didn't tell me the truth. Your own mother." Unexpectedly, she hugged Ben again. She smelled of flowers and garlic and acceptance. No matter what happened, no matter what the result, she'd love him. "What if she's ours? I'd feel like the wicked queen in an animated movie. Grandmothers are supposed to spoil grandkids and all I've done is—"

"Loved her." Ben placed his hands on his mother's shoulders and set her far enough away that he could look her in the eye. "You should feel like Hannah's fairy godmother. She needs a steady hand right now. You can spoil her when she's older."

"I always wanted a little girl." Mom's voice was wistful, a rare glimpse of her own dreams. She drifted toward the hallway. "I hope that test gives you the answer you're looking for, honey."

"That's just the trouble," Ben said morosely. "I don't know which answer would be best for Hannah."

Dinner was a frozen pan of lasagna Olivia had baked. She'd microwaved frozen broccoli with cheese sauce and buttered plain bread slices.

Mandy told herself she didn't care about carbs or salt. It was dinner and she hadn't had to make it. Yep, she was still stung by Ben's flattery comment.

What's wrong with me that Ben rejects the spark between us?

"I downloaded applications for cosmetology school today." Olivia picked up her plate and brought it to the sink where—*stop the presses*—she washed it. "The one I want to go to is the most expensive."

Mandy made a noncommittal noise.

"They use the high-end brands," Olivia went on, spooning the rest of the lasagna into a plastic storage container.

"I thought all nail tech schools were the same." Mandy mashed her broccoli flowerets with her fork.

"Everyone teaches the basics, but my favorite uses the latest techniques and has an extra two weeks focusing on small business accounting."

"Knowing how to handle money is important." Especially given Olivia couldn't manage her monthly allowance. Of course, the topic of money only made Mandy more exhausted. But she was as doggedly determined to find a shared memory of the past with Olivia, just as determined as Ben was to make the post office safe. "Do you remember how Grandma laughed every time she told the story about when Grandpa proposed?"

Olivia turned up her nose. "I don't care what you say, if a guy proposed to me with a brass ring, I'd turn him down."

"It was true love. And Grandpa had no money." Mandy's broccoli was mush, much like the mess Grandpa had left her in, legally bound to carry out his wishes.

"I'm not going to marry anyone who's poor either. I'm going to marry a movie star or a rock star or a..."

Mandy raised her head. "What was that last one?"

"Nothing." Olivia ran the garbage disposal.

Mandy must be dreaming. Olivia never ran the garbage disposal. "Come on, brat. Who is it you want to marry?"

Olivia turned and leaned her backside against the counter. She ran a hand over the growing cowlick at her crown. "I just realized how silly I sound when I may never live to marry anyone." The night's drama was beginning, releasing the stench of fear and uncertainty into the air between them. "I read about a woman who got married and two months later found out she had brain cancer."

"Technically, she did get married." Mandy had to be glib. This wasn't their first conversation about Olivia's length of life.

If Mandy didn't joke about this, they'd both collapse into sad, weepy messes. If Mandy didn't joke, fear would clog her throat and take the strength from her steps. If Mandy didn't joke, Olivia would know Mandy's deepest secret—that she feared Olivia would get cancer again and this time it'd kill her.

But there was a process to Olivia's worry. She had to play it out and Mandy had to listen. "And then there was this guy who found out he had stage four cancer. He married his fiancée in the hospital and a day later he was dead."

"It sounds like you shouldn't be surfing the internet." *Broken record, thy name is Mandy.* "These stories are sad, but—"

"They could just as easily be *my* story."

"But they aren't." Mandy brought her dishes to the sink and gave her sister a quick hug. "And they won't be."

"How do you know?" Olivia whispered, her brown eyes huge and haunted.

Mandy felt haunted, too. "Because you beat the crap out of cancer the first time." Mandy gently poked Olivia's shoulder. "Cancer is scared of you."

Olivia didn't look convinced. And when she spoke, it was in the hushed tones of the fearful. "Don't tell cancer, but I'm afraid of him."

"We have to face our fears, brat." Mandy glanced out the window toward the tree that blocked her view of the moon, willing fear to dissipate.

Fear ignored Mandy. It crowded her chest and made it hard to breathe.

"Do you know what I'm afraid of?" Mandy asked when she finally found some air.

Olivia shook her head.

"I'm afraid of what's in Mom's room." More precisely, she was afraid that Mom was hiding in the room, and they didn't know it. She was afraid that they'd open the door and Mom would be there with her selfish attitude and her selfish lifestyle and her cold, selfish heart.

Inwardly, Mandy cringed. She had to stop watching horror movies.

"Don't be afraid," Olivia whispered. She twined her fingers with Mandy's. Their hands were hospital cold. "We could go in there together. Mom would never hurt us."

"That's right," Mandy said, not wanting to go in at all. Not wanting to hear Olivia talk about mending fences with their mother even more. "Because we battled back cancer together. We're invincible." Who cared if invincibility was a lie? It was the right note to end on.

Drama done. A nightly session of mindless TV was called for.

But Olivia had other ideas. Without letting go, she tugged Mandy from the kitchen. "If we can face cancer, we can do anything." She turned down the hall, heading toward that closed door.

"Anything," Mandy echoed, her mouth dry. She'd rather talk about Grandma's ring or Olivia's inheritance than do this, than face this.

"We aren't going to find Mom in there." Olivia stopped in front of Mom's bedroom door and stared up at Mandy, suddenly uncertain. "Are we?"

"No." But Mandy was certain there was something unsettling inside that room. She could tell by the way her skin prickled and her legs twitched with the urge to bolt.

Neither one of them spoke. Neither one of them moved. Neither one of them wanted to admit that Mom scared them more than cancer.

Because cancer was about hate. It hurt and you had carte blanche to hate it back. You had methods to deal with it. You had options and support groups and people who knew what you'd gone through.

But Mom...

You were supposed to love your mom and moms were supposed to love you back. When they didn't, you had no options. You had no standard methods to deal. No pat emotions to reach for. A mom like theirs was like a California earthquake. She swooped in for unexpected visits. She shook things up. She left. And then you picked up what was broken—*mostly your heart*—and hoped to God it didn't happen again. But you knew you were kidding yourself. She'd be back. And you'd have to deal with her.

At least, Mandy had to deal with her, because that's what Grandpa wanted.

But Olivia—*dear, sweet Olivia*—shouldn't have to worry about Mom-quakes. She shouldn't have to worry about cancer-quakes. She should be allowed to live her life and plan her future as if the worst of life was behind her. But the only way Olivia could do that was if Mandy took the punches meant for her.

"I hate being a wuss." Mandy opened the door and flicked on the light. "Shoot." She hated being right.

There was an envelope on the bed. The words printed on it were easy to read. Black lettering. Block print.

For Olivia.

Mandy waited until it was very late to slip into the backyard and into the night.

She wanted to have a discussion with Mr. Moon, and she didn't want an audience.

Mr. Moon was still low in the sky. She'd tried walking around several blocks in the neighborhood, but the trees were either too large and blocked her view or she had to stand in the middle of the street to see him. She'd stood in the middle of Kennedy Avenue, and a nice little old man had come out on his porch and asked her if she was okay.

I'm not okay.

The note inside the envelope was chillingly brief: *If you stop by, sweet thing, wait for me.*

Olivia had been clutching Mandy's arm when she read the words aloud. And then, she'd laughed the way you did when something you'd long hoped for happened.

Mandy had wanted to pack up and leave. If not Harmony Valley, at least, this house.

We can't leave.

Oh, that was a lie. Olivia could leave if she could support herself, but Mandy... Mandy was stuck here. The debt she carried as Olivia's medical guardian was immense. Monthly-house-payment immense. Break-your-back immense. Make-you-stay-and-face-your-inner-demons immense.

Together, they'd been strong through the cancer. Mandy had refused to let worry over the cost to save Olivia's life drown her. Mandy had to refuse to let worry over what her mother would do if she showed up wash their futures away. So what if Mom knocked on the door? What was the worst thing that could happen?

I need to tell Olivia the truth about her inheritance.

Mandy broke out in a sweat at the thought.

She opened and closed the slider as quietly as possible and made her way across the grass to the break in the hedges at the back neighbor's fence. The moment she crossed into the Libbys' yard, something cold touched her ankle.

Mandy yelped and leaped back, tumbling into the bushes.

Strong hands closed on her arms and righted her.

"I had no idea Sparky was such a good watchdog," Ben said, smelling of clean clothes, clean man and control.

Mandy resented his control and his normalcy. He'd probably had a regular childhood with a stereotypical suburban soccer mom. He didn't need to sneak around and commune with the moon to settle the churn in his gut and the ragged rhythm of his breathing.

"Sparky caught me?" Mandy glanced down at Elvira's fur baby.

Hands still on her arms, Ben laughed.

Yes, he of the "flattered" turn-down was laughing.

It was the wrong time for laughter.

Flattered? I'll give you flattered.

Mandy shrugged off his hold and his mirth. "Were you waiting for me?"

"If I say yes—"

"I'll report you to the sheriff." Who seemed like a reasonable, even-tempered man, one who'd lock up stalkers.

"Then it was purely coincidence." Ben remained close enough to grab hold if Mandy fell into a gopher hole or fainted. "Sparky wanted out and I heard you skulking in the next yard."

"I don't skulk." Mandy turned her back on him and took a couple of steps forward, lifting her gaze to the sky. "I'll just be a minute." She needed a moment of peace. A small silent ritual. Was that too much to ask?

"You're still in uniform." Ben shadowed her, staying closer than he'd been the last time they'd watched the moon together.

Sparky stayed close, too. He sat on the toe of her sneaker.

"You're in uniform, too, Ben."

"I might get a call." She could feel the gentle curiosity in his words. "What's your excuse?"

"I hate doing laundry."

He chuckled softly, so close she imagined his breath passing over her hair.

Mandy had to remind herself she was here for some one-on-one time with the moon, not Ben.

"Excuse me. I need some space." She wasn't afraid of Ben. He just made her feel...like she could stay up all night staring at the ceiling and thinking about a future that might be possible, about white picket fences, shared lives and shared mortgages. She had debt and a sister she'd always watch out for. She shouldn't lose sleep over a man who was *flattered by her flirting*. He'd laid out a boundary. She was going to abide by it.

But Mandy was tense and out of sorts. She couldn't steady her breathing. There was the moon, and there was him.

A cricket burst into song close by, close enough that Sparky startled and sat farther on the top of her foot.

"Break any eggs tonight?" Ben's deep voice blended with the night, as if he fit and she was the intruder with Mr. Moon.

"Came close." Still might. "You?"

"Same." He stared up at the sky. High above them a few leaves murmured in her tree. "The smoke from the wildfires is still obscuring the stars."

"You can kind of see them." Barely. Mandy wasn't entirely sure the stars she saw weren't planes. "But it's the moon I'm interested in."

"Why?"

"Because I'm a nutty, unbalanced lady who likes to talk to something that orbits the earth?" Mandy tried to make her voice light when inside she felt anxious, even scared. Had Mom's note been there waiting for them all this time? Or had she been by and planted it? Was this the kind of mental game she'd played with Grandma?

"You're completely sane and balanced." Ben's voice was as soft and caring as it'd been with Elvira. "I've seen nutty. I've been off-balance."

She snorted at the idea of perfection having a flaw.

Sparky angled his furry head to look at her, before returning to his steady watch for the cricket.

"You don't believe me," Ben said.

Mandy could have used his teasing tone of voice earlier in Mom's room.

Heck, she could have used a voice, period. She'd been struck speechless.

"When I was a kid," Ben began, "I played baseball. I was an outfielder. And then one day, all three of our team's pitchers got injured and I was put on the mound. Me. The kid who was in left field because he could throw far, but not accurately." There was awe in his voice, as if being the one in control of the game had never been his role before. "But I surprised everyone, including myself. I struck out every batter. It was surreal."

"I'm happy for you, but..." Mandy crossed her arms over her chest, staring up at the sky, not at the attractive man next to her. "What does this have to do with Mr. Moon?"

"My mom had bought me new underwear." He paused, possibly weighing how much information was too much. "I wore a new pair that day. It was the only thing that was different."

"If you wore those shorts for every game..." She could tell where this was heading. "...please tell me you washed them under the light of the moon." Why else would he be telling her this story?

"Nope." There was childhood glee in his response. "I played dirty. And we won every game I pitched."

Mandy did look at him then. At the curve of Ben's smile and the corresponding laughter in his eyes. "So, no moon?"

His smile fell as he met her gaze, causing a corresponding drop in the pit of Mandy's stomach. "The point is that we both rely on ritual as a way to calm us," he said simply. "Those shorts kept me balanced and grounded. Like your Mr. Moon."

"I got that part," Mandy said, still slightly breathless from the impact of his gaze. "I was just waiting for a more solid connection between your story and my moon." Now she was sounding petty.

"We all need something, don't we?" Ben glanced up at the moon. Its light gleamed off his dark hair and softened the bruise on his temple.

"I hope you've moved on from dirty shorts." She couldn't resist the dig. She was in that kind of mood.

"I have. It's coffee." He faced her. "Every morning I cradle a cup in my hands. Those few moments of quiet keep me together." His head tilted to the side, and his gaze might or might not have dropped to her lips. It was hard to tell in the darkness. "What about you? Why is the moon so important to you? What does it give you that coffee doesn't?"

Mandy hugged herself tighter. Her smile felt carved into her cheeks. Was she really considering telling him why? She hadn't told anyone. Not Grandpa or Olivia. "I...um...I used to get up in the middle of the night when my mom left..."

"When she left for work?"

"No. When she left...for extended periods of time." Mandy glanced up at the moon. "She's never been someone who hangs around in one place for very long."

The cricket was done warming up and moved on to a concerto of chirps.

Ben glanced over Mandy's shoulder toward her house. "I'm sorry."

"I'm not telling you because..." She stopped that train to avoid breaking eggs. "You were asking about Mr. Moon."

"And I'm waiting patiently for an answer."

Mandy paused, testing his words for too much sympathy or too much sarcasm.

Finding none, she continued. "I couldn't see her leave from my bedroom, but I could hear doors open and close. I used to look out my window and imagine she was coming around the back to say goodbye." As if Mom knew Mandy was waiting and watching. As if Mom cared to say things like goodbye, take care, or I love you. "And while she was gone, every night before I went to bed, I'd look out my window and ask the moon to watch out for her." She gestured to the tree in her backyard. "That was before this tree grew into a behemoth."

"Do you still want the moon to watch out for your mother?"

"No." Mandy tensed. "I tell him my worries. I ask him to watch over Olivia." She drew a deep breath. "I feel less alone imagining someone is listening to me."

"Mr. Moon is a lucky guy." Ben's voice was much how she'd imagined Mr. Moon's—strong yet kind, patient yet able to see the little joys in life.

Still on her foot, Sparky belched, interrupting the cricket for only a bar or two.

Ben laughed.

Mandy wasn't sure who or what he was laughing at. "Are you making fun of me?"

"No." Ben knelt to rub Sparky's ears. His bare arm brushed Mandy's bare leg. She refrained from jumping back. She refrained from fainting. She even refrained from kneeling next to Ben and petting Sparky along with him. "You're not quite what I expected after my fire inspection."

"I realize I can be intense." Ben shrugged, standing. Standing too close. Their shoulders nearly touched. "But I want this town to be a safe place." He peered at her with a quirk in his dark brow. "That fire today…"

"The grass fire?"

He nodded. "I think someone set it deliberately."

Mandy gasped. "Who would do such a thing?"

He was quiet for too long. Then he raised his eyebrows.

A sickening suspicion took over her stomach. She did backpedal then, upending Sparky. "You think I'm an arsonist?" Someone had cranked up the volume on her voice. It boomed into the night loud enough to silence the cricket.

"Not really," Ben said casually.

"*Not really?*" Mandy's lungs expelled oxygen as if she'd been sucker punched. "*Not really?*"

Did suspects on an arson list with "not really" next to their name get hauled in for questioning? Arrested? Ruined?

"I suspect there's an arsonist," Ben continued as if unaware he'd not only pulled the rug out from under her but parked his fire engine on her chest for good measure. "Someone with a gray car."

"I drive a white pickup." Mandy sucked in air like a sprinter about to cross the finish line. Thank goodness she was in the clear. "Someone at the post office today drove a gray car. I have no idea who. But the work is finished. They aren't coming back."

The cricket had resumed its chirp. Sparky yawned and waddled toward Ben's back door.

Ben wasn't ready to leave, not her or the subject of arson. "Why did you stare at the flames the day we met? It was almost as if you were mesmerized."

"I was thinking..." She laughed self-consciously. "I was trying to figure out how long a fire would delay the opening of the post office, worried about the trouble it would cause me. Clearly, I think too much."

"Me, too." Ben took a lock of Mandy's hair and moved it over her shoulder, and then froze, as if he hadn't realized he'd touched her so intimately. "You didn't want me coming inside the post office today."

"You didn't want me coming inside Elvira's house either," she countered.

"I was protecting a patient's privacy."

"I thought you might get upset at how little progress I'd made on your fix-it list. That scowl of yours is like a weapon, and I didn't want it aimed at me." Mandy wished she hadn't admitted so much. She wished he hadn't admitted so much either. "How will you find this arsonist?"

"Well, there's the car and there are indicators." He ticked them off on his fingers. "Isolated. Stressed out. Angry. In need of an outlet."

"That describes half the freeway commuters I've met." No joke.

"And then there's opportunity." Ben stepped into her space, placed his fingers beneath her chin and tilted her face to the moon. "You're always smiling," Ben said, awe in his voice. "How do you keep it up?"

"Am I still smiling?" She was. "I..." It was easy talking to Ben in the darkness, easy to overshare. But he'd half thought she was an arsonist! He'd been flattered she'd leave out a bowl of food for him! She wanted to give him a generic answer. Instead, she blurted, "My smile... It's my only defense."

"You're incredibly honest."

"I'm not. I just... I have very little to hide." Only her feelings and her debt and the fact that she'd lied to Olivia about her inheritance and the reason their mother stayed away.

"I doubt that. Everyone has layers of secrets." Ben's head bent toward hers, almost as if he was going to kiss her. And then he pulled back, cocking his head to the side as if offering his ear for a whispered confidence.

The kiss impression was totally the moon's fault.

The moon was waning, appearing to turn half his face away and wink.

Stupid moon.

This was Mr. Moon's payback for not spending more time alone with him. Back in Santa Rosa their apartment had a south-facing balcony. Visiting the moon had been as easy as opening the curtains. And...

Ben hadn't moved.

Was he asking Mandy to bare her soul? No one wanted to hear about the bitter disappointment that was her childhood. Or the hardships she'd carried these last few years. It was almost as bad as telling someone woeful stories about your ex.

"I better go. I've got to be at the post office early." And the very act of standing this close to Ben made her feel like a romantic fool, waiting for a kiss and a ride on a white horse.

Ben backed up a step, staring after Sparky. "I hear the bakery opens at four thirty and has good coffee. Dad says they have a French press."

"Thanks for the tip." With one last glance at the moon, Mandy headed toward the break in the hedge.

"Don't forget about the other things."

She scootched through the hedge and turned toward home. "What other things?"

"My advice." He walked next to her on the other side of the shrubbery. "Never be ashamed of needing something, because we all do. And underwear. Dirty sometimes works. Especially if you don't like doing laundry."

She grinned. Unbelievable. Ben was infuriating and complicated and made her grin? "You should remember something, too. Next time a woman asks if you think she's an arsonist, don't say *not really*."

There was something wrong with Ben. He stood staring at the moon, the orb more visible tonight since the fire on the other side of the mountain had been contained.

He didn't pursue women with flowery words and poetry. He wasn't the master of smooth lines or smooth moves.

But he'd stood talking to Mandy in the moonlight about his lucky baseball talisman and the sensitivity of the moon. He'd looked into Mandy's eyes and wanted to kiss her.

Kiss her!

Harmony Valley was chipping away at his sanity.

It had to be because Ben was worried about being a dad. Or not being a dad. And worried about Hannah. And his own father. He was isolated, stressed out, occasionally angry and in need of an outlet.

Shoot. When I described myself like that, I could be the arsonist!

The screen door behind him slid open.

"I'm worried about your father." His mother came to sit on the picnic bench.

Ben took a seat across from her. "Dad keeps saying he's fine."

"We both know that's a lie." Mom pulled up the collar of her bathrobe against the evening chill and glanced up at Mandy's moon. "I can't wait for the end of fire season. The air quality is horrible. Your father shouldn't even be going outside."

The wildfire season in California had at least another ten full weeks. "He'd breathe easier with a cannula," Ben said, only half joking.

"Someone would notice him dragging around an oxygen tank," Mom said, only half-serious.

Had Dad been in on the conversation, he'd have been telling them he didn't appreciate their jokes. He'd puff up his chest and be the man showing no emotion.

"I'll encourage Dad to stay in the truck and wait for backup." And Ben would hope for no more brushfires.

"We'll keep trying alternative treatments to clear his airways and increase his blood flow." Mom stared up at the night sky. "Why haven't you put a volunteer program in motion?"

"Turf wars. The current and retired fire chiefs are arguing over who should recruit and train them." Meaning Dad and Granddad. "And I haven't pushed it because volunteers would notice Dad's health isn't what it should be."

Those in the tight-knit fire community might let Dad slide. He was well-known up and down Sonoma County, having served as the local union president in Oakland. But civilians? They'd wonder. And wonder led to talk. And talk would lead to questions from the mayor and the town council.

"Volunteers won't notice your father's health if *you* train them," Mom pointed out.

Another responsibility landed on Ben's shoulders.

"I appreciate your doing this." Mom's voice was transitioning in tone, from matter-of-fact to matters of the heart; shifting gears from business to family dysfunction. "I know you and your father haven't been close." Dad always favored his younger brother Mike. "And I know this is hard on you. It's hard on all of us."

"I get it." Ben knew in his head that he had to let go of past hurts. But it wasn't as easy as it sounded. "And if you twisted my arm, I'd admit that we're finding some common ground when we aren't fighting about issuing citations. Did he tell you what happened at the post office?"

Mom chuckled. "Your father told me about your fascination with the postmaster. Nice girl. And Dad said she's *not* an arsonist. You should bring her by sometime."

"I know Mandy's not an arsonist." The fires she lit inside of him was a different story. Ben drummed his palms on the table, managing a regretful smile. "Except...I wasn't exactly clear in my exoneration of Mandy to her face...so, inviting her to dinner isn't an option."

"Oh, Honest Abe. Not again!" Mom covered his hand with hers. "How many times do I have to tell you the correct answer to: *Do these jeans make my butt look big?* is always one hundred percent NO! Women don't want to hear the truth, especially not yours."

Her words stung. "You're saying I should lie to women? I should tell her I'm 95 percent certain she's not an arsonist?"

"No." Mom thunked the heel of her hand against her forehead. "I'm saying the truth sometimes hurts. Did you want to hurt the postmaster's feelings?"

"No. I just...maybe I wanted Mandy to be more careful. So, she doesn't look guilty the next time a fire starts."

"No one should live their lives trying *not to look guilty* of something they *aren't guilty of* in the first place." Mom sighed. "This is like the time you told my mother her Thanksgiving turkey was drier than beef jerky but not nearly as tasty."

"I was twelve." Ben tossed his hands. "And she asked me why I didn't clean my plate."

Mom reached for his hands again, capturing them with a firm grip. "If you can't say something nice..."

"If you can't stand to hear the truth..." he parroted back.

"I'm not giving up on you." Mom released him, getting to her feet. "Don't you worry about a thing. I'll fix it with the postmaster."

"Mother." His annoyance was a live thing, lifting him to his feet. "It doesn't need fixing."

But she didn't answer.

Chapter Eight

There was a man waiting for the bakery to open at 4:20 a.m. Mandy had been walking fast in her postal uniform and windbreaker, intent upon getting to the bakery when it opened at four thirty, but she slowed when she saw the man because it was still dark, and she was alone.

As she came closer, the light from the bakery window illuminated a man in uniform with a trim waist and broad shoulders. It was Ben, looking put-together and handsome. Mandy was certain she looked like she just woke up with her messy ponytails and no make-up on. It was a beastly hour of the morning and she felt beastly inside, still annoyed with the things he'd said to her last night.

Inside the bakery, a petite blonde scurried around a large set of glass cases. The rich smell of coffee drifted on the air, along with the warm smell of sweet treats.

"Good morning," he said. Despite the bruise on his forehead, he still looked handsome and dare she say kissable. Not that he'd kissed her. Not that he seemed to want to kiss potential arsonists. "You're a coffee person."

"I've been known to indulge." Hugging her windbreaker tight around her chest, Mandy sat on a wrought iron chair next to a small table and yawned. She hadn't slept well last night but she wasn't admitting he was part of the reason. "What do you need coffee for? You look wide awake."

Birds were singing in the town square; perky, predawn-loving birds that had more in common with Ben than with Mandy. She was always her worst in the morning.

"I just got off a call." Upon closer inspection, there were dark circles under his eyes. "But now I need caffeine."

"Shouldn't you just go back to bed?" Mandy would, if given the choice.

"I'm awake." He shrugged. "I'm a morning person. You?"

"Mornings are part of the job." She yawned again. "Of course, that makes my afternoons free for naps." Not that she ever had time for naps, but a girl could dream.

I used to dream of a taller-than-me, handsome man who could kiss my socks off.

Her traitorous eyes drifted to Ben's face.

"I can nap at the fire station all day as long as no one calls 911." His lips twitched.

Is he thinking about kissing an arsonist suspect?

She decided he was and tugged her windbreaker tighter across her chest. "What's the likelihood of no calls for you today?"

"Sadly, slim to none," he said ruefully.

That seemed to exhaust their small talk. They both stared at the blonde setting up the bakery for the day. The bird-song filled the silence. Mandy decided she'd rather hear Ben's voice than chirpy birds.

She racked her tired brain for a topic of conversation that wasn't related to fire or fire inspections. "How's your dad? He looked pale the other day?"

Ben shifted from friendly neighbor to fire inspector mode. "The chief's in better shape than your post office."

"Down, boy." She'd found a target, and she hadn't even taken aim. "You'd think I'd accused Keith of something like embezzlement...or *arson*."

"You're right." Ben held up both hands quicker than a bank teller at gunpoint. "Let's not toss accusations at each other."

The quick way Ben backed off gave Mandy pause. Was Keith seriously ill? It was more common nowadays for people to work while going through health challenges, like cancer.

Before she spent too long pondering the state of his father's health, Ben said, "I'd like to apologize. Consider the phrase *not really* retracted from our history of conversation."

Mandy sat back in her chair, taking stock of Ben.

Sincerity in his voice? Check.

Sincerity in his eyes? Check.

Mandy supposed this meant she'd have to be sincere in her reply. "Apology accepted. And I...I didn't mean to pry about your father's health. I've spent too much time in hospital and doctor's office waiting rooms over the past two years where I passed the time diagnosing others in the waiting room in my head."

Ben's posture eased. His expression softened. "Have you been sick?"

She shook her head. "If anything, I'm too healthy." And she felt guilty for it when Olivia had been through so much.

"Your grandfather then?" Ben stared at her compassionately, ready to listen to whatever she had to say, like she imagined Mr. Moon was. "I'd heard your grandfather passed."

Mandy hesitated before answering, trying to decide how much to say about Olivia, who valued her privacy. "My grandfather had dementia, which required a lot of care, and my—"

The bakery door opened. The perky blonde welcomed them with a sweeping gesture. "Hey, peeps. I'm Tracy. Are you..." She took in their uniforms and grinned. "Are you going to be...early-morning regulars?"

"Definitely." Mandy entered first at Ben's urging. "My shift starts at five. I had no idea you opened this early until Ben told me."

"Signage," Tracy murmured with a shake of her head. "I'll put that...on my list. Wait a minute." She scurried in front of Mandy. "I know you. Mandy Zapien! I'm Will Jackson's kid sister."

"I remember you." The class sizes at Harmony Valley High had been very low when Mandy had attended. Everyone knew everyone. "And Will, of course." She'd gotten into a spot of trouble at school with Will.

"Madame Postmaster." Tracy dipped her head as if Mandy were royalty. "We'll catch up soon. With Will and Emma, too. They got married. First baby due any day." She grinned at Ben. "Fireman Ben, isn't it?"

"Yes." Ben tapped Mandy's shoulder, and then pointed at Tracy. "*She* passed her inspection."

"Jessica, you mean," Tracy corrected him. "The owner."

Mandy frowned at him. "I'm working on it."

"And I appreciate you for it." Ben smiled.

And that smile... "You make it hard for me to resent you."

Ben leaned closer to Mandy. "That's the plan."

Don't grin like an idiot. Don't grin like... Don't grin...

Too late.

I'll regret this later.

But for now, Mandy couldn't seem to stop smiling.

"I'll be a regular whenever you're open, Tracy," Ben said cheerfully, beaming at Mandy. "My shifts go for twenty-four hours but mornings make the most sense."

"We close at four. We'll offer dinner someday." Tracy was a chatterbox, with an infectious smile, the same as she'd been in school. She moved behind the counter, apparently unaware of the smiley exchanges Mandy and Ben were exchanging. "A few more residents. A few more workers. It'll happen."

Ben and Mandy each ordered dark roast, black coffee. Tracy pushed for a purchase of a horseradish-lemon scone, but Mandy resisted (*I mean, horseradish!*). Instead, she selected a sugar cookie shaped and frosted like a mermaid.

While Ben fiddled with the lid on his coffee cup and Tracy bagged her cookie, Mandy drank deeply from her cup of coffee and contemplated her day. More clean up. More organizing. More equipment put in place. She was in a race against the clock.

"Here you go." Tracy handed Mandy a small bag with her sugar fix.

"See you tomorrow." Mandy headed out.

"*And my...*" Ben followed Mandy through the door carrying his large coffee that she doubted would let him nap during the day.

"And my what?" Mandy took another sip of coffee. It was strong, but she'd need a few more minutes for the cobwebs to clear completely.

"Before we came inside..." Ben cupped his palm over her shoulder and then ran it down her arm, cupping her elbow before dropping away.

He... Was that a caress?

Mandy couldn't breathe.

"...you mentioned your grandfather," Ben continued as if he hadn't thrown Mandy off balance with his touch. "And you implied someone else was in the hospital."

"Yes, I..." *Stop.* Mandy paused to sip her coffee, wondering what it was about Ben that picked the lock on all her secrets. She stared at his face, wondering why it felt as if they shouldn't have any secrets between them.

"You don't have to tell me." But Ben didn't budge.

"Right after Grandpa died," Mandy began slowly, "Olivia was diagnosed with cancer. She's cancer-free now, but if you ask her to her face how she's doing, I'll deny I ever mentioned it to you. She's seventeen and doesn't want people to treat her like she's sick or recognize that she's different in any way."

"Can't blame her." Ben sipped his coffee and stared toward the town square, not in a hurry to leave. "It's hard enough being a teen without adding a life-threatening illness to the mix."

Where is this going?

"That's it, isn't it?" Ben said slowly as if having an epiphany. "We all just want to be treated as if we aren't different. Not of weak health or emotionally a wreck." His gaze drifted to Mandy the way a kayak comes leisurely around a gentle river bend. "The inside and outside aren't mirror reflections. But people expect what they see on the outside to be what's going on inside. So, we all wear a mask. Or try to."

"Yes. That's exactly..." *How I feel.* Cracked inside, held together by duct tape, but able to go on as if it was any other day if she smiled and kept it all in.

In that moment, in the gray light of dawn, on an empty sidewalk, with those darn birds singing like this was going to be the best day on the planet...Mandy felt less alone, less jaded, less guarded, less held together by duct tape and the occasional prayer.

Mandy nodded, smiled, considered hugging him. Not a brief, friendly hug, but an all-out bear hug that conveyed a personal connection that might lead to

"That's exactly what Olivia is going through," Ben said, in that same *aha* tone of voice, shattering the connection Mandy had been building between them. "I won't say anything to your sister that gives away I know what she's been through."

Mandy's mouth hung open.

Oh, this man is dangerous to me.

"Thank you," she managed to say.

Thank you for putting me in my place. The flattered for the flirting, but you're officially in the friend zone.

Life is supposed to be good.

Olivia Zapien wasn't convinced.

At seventeen, she was supposed to be part of a loving family with a caring, hovering mother. She was supposed to have marched across the stage for her high school graduation. She was supposed to have her act together as she embarked upon this grand adventure called life.

She'd had an adventure, all right. And her tour guide for the last eighteen months had been called Cancer.

Yep, Mom had listened to Olivia's diagnosis—anaplastic large T-cell non-Hodgkin lymphoma—blinked and asked in a startled voice, *"What?"*

"Cancer," Mandy had said with a grim smile, her arms wrapped around her waist.

Mom hadn't spoken another word. Not on the car ride home. Not during dinner. Not when Mandy sat in the Grumpster's recliner with Olivia in her lap as if she was six, not sixteen. The next morning Mom was gone, and neither Olivia nor Mandy had heard a word from her since. Not until that note.

It was Mandy who'd helped Olivia through chemo—*twice*. It was Mandy who bought Olivia a floppy yellow hat, a bright blue wig and a box of nail polish. It was Mandy who held Olivia's hand through the discomfort of stem cell harvesting and later the stem cell transplant. It was Mandy who had cried along with Olivia when Dr. Abadie said she was cancer-free. She'd taken Olivia for ice cream afterward.

Whereas Mom had no words, Mandy had lots. Mandy used words like: *think positive, be brave, when you're recovered* and now that *you're a survivor.*

Survivor? Olivia wasn't sure she deserved that label. What if the cancer came back? Dr. Abadie wanted her to return for testing every six months. Olivia wanted to be tested every day. Really. Every day. She shaved her legs every day. Why not check for cancer with the same frequency?

When she'd mentioned it to Dr. Abadie, he'd exchanged a look with Mandy that said daily testing wasn't an option. Mandy hadn't fought him on it.

And Mom... Mom loves me.

Olivia knew that was true. She doted on Olivia when she was around. Mom would have told Dr. Abadie that Olivia's mental health required more frequent testing. Mom would have fought for Olivia's rights. If Mom was around...

Olivia hadn't seen Mom since that first diagnosis. She was probably scared. Mom and Mandy didn't get along. So, if Mom was scared, she couldn't lean on Mandy the way Olivia did. It was hard to face your fears alone.

Mom loves me...but she's kind of a chicken.

Olivia huffed, disapproving of her own thoughts.

She sat in a chair at Mandy's desk in the post office enjoying a short break.

Bent over the blotter, Olivia painted a dog's face on her thumbnail with a toothpick. She didn't like working at the post office. It wreaked havoc with her nails, and the uniforms might just as well have been paper bags. So not stylish. Plus, Mandy liked to leave the rolling door open at the loading dock, which meant she didn't run the air conditioner, which meant it was hot, which meant Mandy's loud country music was more annoying than usual.

"*Ha-looo.*" A man's voice rose above a country song about a cheating woman.

Olivia's head came up.

Because that voice...

It wasn't a gravelly, old man's voice like Utley's. It was strong and clear and deep. And it was coming from the customer counter.

Mandy was stacking tubs of mail on a dolly in the truck. She didn't seem to hear anything, but then again, she had the music on loud.

"Anybody home? *Alguien en casa?*" The man's voice again.

Olivia crossed the room and peeked around the corner.

It was a dude. A tall dude with wind-tousled dark hair and scruffy whiskers on his chin. He looked like a broke college student. His arms were tan, and his grin made up for his stained T-shirt with the Harmony Valley Vineyards logo on the front.

In this town full of old people and little kids, he was the first person she'd seen who was about her age. And he was *cute*.

Olivia realized she was a hot, sweaty mess wearing a too-large postal shirt.

"Hey," the dude said to her, still grinning.

"Hey," Olivia replied, striving for cool, but sounding like a water-deprived bullfrog.

He waved an envelope. "I need stamps."

"Just a minute." Olivia pulled back around the corner and pressed her back to the glass partition, heart pounding.

Mandy wheeled the dolly across the loading dock and inside, spotting her. "What's wrong?"

Customer, Olivia mouthed, pointing behind her.

Mandy turned her music off, hurried into the customer service area and sold Mr. Tall-and-Cute a book of stamps. She was all cool and stuff, but it was her job to be nice to people.

Over at the ramp, the delivery driver closed and locked the back of the truck and took off.

"Hey, uh." The dude lowered his voice, but not enough that Olivia couldn't hear him. "I hope I didn't say anything to hurt her feelings."

Mortified, Olivia sank to the floor, covering her mouth.

"Who? Olivia?" Mandy gave a fake chuckle. "She's just shy." And then she thanked him for coming in, stepped back into the mail room, and helped Olivia to her feet.

"I'm shy?" Olivia said angrily. "Why did you say that?"

"I could have said you were crushing on him." Mandy grinned.

Olivia rolled her eyes. "Anything but that."

"Anything but that and *she's shy*." Mandy took a plastic tub from the dolly and set it on the counter. "What should I have said?"

"She's busy or she had a phone call or—"

"You're not busy, and you weren't on the phone. A cute guy came in and you panicked. Get over it. There are a lot of cute guys in the world."

"But not in Harmony Valley." Olivia closed her eyes and did the slow, deep breathing she'd been taught to use when she was stressed or scared or wanted to shout at someone who didn't understand. "At least tell me his name."

"I don't know his name." Mandy laughed.

Olivia tossed her hands, belatedly noticing she'd smudged the dog she'd painted on her thumb. "What happened to small towns and everybody knowing everyone else's name?"

"I was too busy trying not to laugh because my sister was hiding behind a glass wall." She tapped the glass with her knuckle. "He could see you standing there."

Olivia knew better than to wish she could die. But she wished life didn't suck so much.

"Next time, pick a better hiding place, Olivia." Mandy set about sorting mail.

A little blonde girl with black rectangular glasses rode up to the loading dock on a pink bike with purple tassels hanging from the handlebars. A small pink shoe bag hung from her shoulders by black corded straps. "I'm looking for a raccoon." She didn't look big enough to tangle with a kitten, much less a raccoon. But she did have a bruise on her forehead and some scabs on the inside of her knees, indicating she was no fussy princess. "My grandpa said you have one."

"Just a minute, Hannah." Mandy leaned into whisper, "I recognize this kid. I've got stuff to do before the electrician gets here. Why don't you entertain our guest and keep her away from Riley." Not a question. And her sister didn't wait for an answer. Mandy went back to work.

Olivia approached the edge of the dock, standing in the sun where it was hot. "What do you need a raccoon for?"

"I don't *need* him." She scowled from three feet beneath her. "*He* needs *me*."

"Hannah!" A woman with blond hair and mom jean shorts pedaled a bike around the corner. "There you are. Wait for me."

"Oh, man." Hannah scuffed her sneaker on the concrete. "Granny found me."

Olivia hopped to the pavement next to Hannah, ready to take hold of the handlebars if necessary to stop the little girl from fleeing her grandmother. "Are you running away from home?"

"No." Hannah pushed her glasses up her nose. "I'm rescuing animals."

"Hannah." Hannah's grandmother pumped her way into the parking lot and stopped, panting. She was the put-together, defy-my-age type of grandmother. She didn't have gray hair. She wore conservative, skillfully applied makeup, and had flat-ironed her short blond hair. "What did we talk about? No sneaking off when I'm taking a nap." She smiled at Olivia, an expression as worn out as her coral lipstick. "I heard the screen latch and came after Hannah, but she's too quick. I had to stop twice and ask if anyone had seen her."

The little girl sighed. "There was an emergency situation. I left you a note."

"This note?" Hannah's grandmother pulled a crumpled scrap of paper from inside her bra. "It says, I'm gone. Don't worry." She waved the note in the air. "Gone where? Doing what? I've ridden all over town, and all I've done is worry. The last time you snuck out you nearly drowned in the river."

"But I didn't drown. Ben caught me." Hannah gazed up at Olivia, seeking someone on her side. "I left her a note."

"As a runner myself..." Olivia had gone through a phase where she couldn't stand to be at home. Although she could always be found at the corner coffee shop. "...you have to write better notes and be clear about where you're going if you don't want people to panic."

"Forget notes. You need to wake me up and ask permission." Hannah's grandmother finally seemed to have caught her breath and her composure. "I'm Vanessa. Are you the postmaster? I was expecting someone older."

"No. That's my sister, Mandy." Olivia tugged on her blue striped postal shirt. "I'm the part-time help."

"Part-time." Vanessa grinned like she'd just won the lottery. "Would you like to earn extra money and babysit for me? Are you available in the afternoons?"

Olivia was being offered a job where no uniform was required?

She bobbed her head. "I'd love to hang out with Hannah." They could listen to music while Olivia did Hannah's nails. "Would you like that?" she asked the little girl.

After looking Olivia up and down, Hannah grumbled, "Okay. But only if we can continue my work."

"Your work?" Caution slowed Olivia's words.

"My work." Hannah nodded, as solemn as Dr. Abadie when he'd refused daily testing. "Rescuing animals." She slung her pink shoe bag off her shoulder and dug inside, producing a small tissue. "Here. I think you're getting a nosebleed."

Olivia touched her nostrils with tentative fingers. Her thumb came away bloody. Panic pulsed through Olivia's veins like a fast dance beat at a late-night rave. She grabbed Hannah's tissue and squeezed her nose with it. *"Mandy?"* This was how they'd found out she had cancer in the first place. Frequent nosebleeds that wouldn't stop. *"Mandy?"*

Mandy appeared above her on the dock and quickly took stock of the situation. "Oh, sweetie. Slow breaths. Sit on the steps. I'll get you another tissue."

Olivia perched on a middle step. The sun-warmed concrete was almost butt-burning. "Call Dr. Abadie."

"Are you dying?" Hannah asked.

"She's not dying," Mandy yelled before Olivia could answer. "Nosebleeds can be caused by hot dry air or growth spurts."

Vanessa had moved closer to the steps, but not to look at Olivia. She watched Mandy.

Meanwhile, Hannah had moved into Olivia's space and gawked at her face. "You look like you're dying."

"She's not dying," Mandy yelled again.

I am dying.

The nosebleed proved it. Olivia wanted to release her nose and check how much blood was on the tissue, but Mandy was a mind reader.

"It's too early to check your nose," her sister said, returning to the dock with a tissue and a bottle of water. "Be patient. Pinch-pinch-pinch. Panic never did anyone any good."

"Maybe she's right." Hannah laid her little hand on Olivia's knee. "Maybe you're not going to die. Today anyway."

Chapter Nine

The trouble with having an epiphany was knowing what to do with it. While talking to Mandy in the wee hours of the morning, Ben had realized his father didn't want to be babied or fussed over the same way Olivia didn't want to be. But how could Ben not baby him? The man operated on 100 percent mode when in fact he was closer to 50 percent functionality with a risk of system failure.

"Excuse me."

Ben looked down from the ladder controls on the rear of the fire engine. He'd been testing the hydraulics on the bucket.

The elderly woman with short purplish-gray hair who'd greeted him effusively at the town square kitten rescue waved. "Could you help me?"

"Sure." Ben climbed down.

"I'm Eunice." She was wearing that neon pink tracksuit again and lime-green sneakers. "I'm stuck. I've tried everything." She batted eyelashes thick with mascara.

Ben headed inside. "I'll get the first aid kit for some eyewash." Because she wouldn't be making googly eyes if she didn't have something stuck in one.

"That's interesting." Eunice kept up with him. "I didn't realize eyewash could be used on splinters."

Ben led her to the common area, which had a small L-shaped kitchen, an old blue recliner, a pea-green microfiber couch and a card table surrounded by four brown metal folding chairs. "Eyewash works on anything stuck in your eye. Have a seat at the table." He opened the med kit in the pantry.

"Ah." Eunice sat on a folding chair, which made the usual folding chair creaky complaints and tinny noises. "I have no need for eyewash. The sliver is in my hand."

Ben turned to look at her. She was still sending Morse code with her eyelids. "Nothing's in your eye?"

"Can't you tell?" She swiveled one shoulder forward and tilted her chin over it. "My eyes are perfect." *Blink-blink-blink.*

In his dozen years as a firefighter, Ben had seen his share of characters. None had left him speechless. But this woman...

He put the eyewash back in the pantry med kit and went to a smaller first aid kit he kept stored over the sink. And then he sat next to Eunice at the table with a pair of tweezers and a bandage.

"Normally, I'd ask Duffy or Jessica to tend to my mishaps." She gave him her hand. She had a small red bump on her finger with a short black sliver visible beneath the skin. "But they're at work and you were just down the block." Her flowery perfume was too strong, but he supposed it was balanced by all that mascara. "Word on the street says you're single."

Ben hadn't been born yesterday. There was more than medical care being sought here. "This is going to pinch."

"I'm made of tough stuff." But she looked away with less blinking and steadied her breathing. "Have at it."

"How did you get this?"

"I'm cutting back bougainvillea. Darn thorns cut right through my gloves." She drew a sharp intake of breath when he pinched her skin. "Is your father here? Is he down with the flu? I saw him leaning against a building before he inspected Mae's Pretty Things. I thought he might lose his cookies. There's a bug going around."

Ben mumbled something about bad sushi, resenting the fact that he had to lie.

It took some digging, but Ben got the sliver out. He wrapped her finger in a small bandage. "All done."

"My hero." She patted his cheek. "I'll bring you a casserole later. My specialty. Ham, hollandaise and banana."

"Oh." Ben's eyes opened as wide as Eunice's. He got to his feet, realizing he might have hurt her feelings. "I mean... Oh. Don't go to any trouble. I'm eating at my mother's place."

"Oh." Eunice stood, making the chair protest once more. "Is that wise? For a bachelor, I mean. I'd heard men living with their mothers was a deal breaker for single women." She stared up at him expectantly, as if waiting for him to defend his manliness.

Ben took her by the arm and steered her toward the street. "You may have heard that I moved to town with my goddaughter. My mom helps watch her when I'm on call. It's the best arrangement for Hannah."

"That's an excellent answer." Eunice smiled and batted her eyes. "That should be one of your early talking points on a first-meet."

"*A...a what?*"

"You know." Eunice nudged him with her elbow, which was small and bony and slid into a tickle point at his ribs. "When you meet a woman and you're telling her about yourself. Start with fireman, because that's got huge appeal. Talk about your godchild, because parenting skills are a bonus. And then maybe just stop talking and look... I don't know." She studied his face.

He was trying not to scowl and not succeeding.

"Yes, look brooding. Like that!" She waved and went on her way.

Ben swept the driveway, stewing over the bad advice Eunice had offered. He wouldn't be interested in any woman who was looking to marry a fireman. And since he wasn't interested in having kids, the parenting angle seemed like false advertising. And the brooding? Few women wanted to deal with his intensity level.

It didn't faze Mandy.

Mandy was a different breed of woman. He suspected her patience came from a natural tendency to nurture—her grandfather, her sister, Elvira. Her lack of makeup and casual ponytails suggested she might be a wallflower, not strong enough to speak her mind. But she had no such hang-up. In fact, she was grittier and more talkative in the morning before her first cup of coffee than she was at night under the full moon.

Thinking of Mandy reminded him about his epiphany and the need to talk to his father about more realistic expectations of his job performance. He locked up the fire station and made the short walk to the house.

It took him a few minutes to locate any family member. No one seemed to be home, until he got to the garage and found Dad.

His old man was dozing in an anti-gravity chair. He wore an oxygen mask. Except instead of being connected to an oxygen tank, the mask was connected to some kind of humidifier and the room smelled like minty eucalyptus.

"What's all this?" It didn't look like Dad was on call.

His father pushed himself upright and pulled the mask away from his face. "It's a new breathing treatment your mother wants me to try," he said, half yawning.

With his mask off, the smell of mint increased, as did the humidity level in the room.

"How long do you need to sit there?" His wearing a mask didn't seem conducive to Ben's planned father-son chat.

"An hour. Longer if we don't have a call." Dad checked his watch. "Forty-five more minutes. Thought I'd watch Mike's softball game. Lisa taped it."

Ben's jaw worked as he struggled not to break eggs. In addition to being a fine firefighter, his brother Mike was also an outstanding athlete. Dad enjoyed watching him play when he was a teen.

It was close to noon, which must mean Dad had slept all morning and hadn't checked on Ben. Not exactly the best sign for an active-duty fireman, much less a fire chief.

Ben took off his firefighter hat and put on his doting-son helmet. "Is the treatment working?" Might be wishful thinking on Ben's part, but Dad sounded more robust. Robust was good.

"I'm not coughing." In fact, Dad wasn't even wheezing. "I'll finish my hour and head over to the fire station." He fitted the clear mask over his nose and mouth, only to remove it again. "Did you need something?"

"No." Their talk could wait. Who knew how long they had before their next call?

Ben left the garage and entered the house via the kitchen. He paused in the foyer. The fire chief sat in the garage while his pager and cell phone sat on the hall table. Firefighters on call didn't leave their devices farther than an arm's reach away.

Dad might want to be treated as if he was able-bodied, but his actions said something else entirely.

Ben ground his teeth, took two steps back to the garage, and then returned to the hall table, staring down at his reality.

This was what he'd signed up for.

He could only hope Dad grew stronger and time flew by.

"Mandy?" The woman with Hannah looked less harried than she had outside Elvira's house the day before. She stood at the top of the loading dock stairs.

"That's me." Mandy had been alternating between answering email and searching for large rubber bands while Olivia tried to stop her nosebleed. She rubber-banded a handful of mail destined for Main Street, the last bundle before she started the delivery. "Can I help you?"

"I'm Vanessa Libby. Ben's mother." She catalogued Mandy like a multipack in a big-box store, looking for appeal or value or counting the options with raisins.

Personally, Mandy liked raisins, but multipacks were always a gamble, and when it came down to it, Mandy didn't much care what Ben's mother thought of her.

Vanessa must have found something to like about Mandy because she added, "My son shared something that he said to you, and I just wanted to explain that Ben—"

Mandy kept her gaze carefully on Vanessa's blue eyes, although the image of Mrs. Libby's face was fading into an annoyed haze of red and her ears were ringing fire alarms.

What had Ben told his mother?

"—is honest to a fault. And I mean fault."

"Um," Mandy said intelligently, wishing she was somewhere else. Like in a Siberian blizzard or on the path of a charging rhino or at a café with her crazy ex-boyfriend, the one who used to stiff every waiter, no matter how good the service.

"Are you apologizing for something stupid your son did?" Olivia wasn't helping. In fact, in Mandy's mind, Olivia took her place in front of the stampeding rhino. "Is Ben, like, twelve?"

Mandy's face felt as if it'd been sunburned. Vanessa must have felt the same. Her cheeks were red, too.

"Ben isn't twelve." Hannah's bright eyes flashed behind her glasses. And then she looked sheepishly at Vanessa and whispered loud enough for them all to hear, "Did Ben do something bad?"

Vanessa tucked the slight girl in the shelter of her arm. "Ben accused Mandy of—"

"Let's not go there." Mandy grabbed the keys to the Jeep. She was late doing the mail run. What else was new? "In the scheme of things, it wasn't really anything."

"You're right," Vanessa said with a sly expression that made Mandy nervous. Increasingly, she was sounding like the kind of mother who decided whom her son should marry and then devoted all her free time to making it happen. "We shouldn't use the word accuse."

"What did he accuse you of?" Olivia asked Mandy in a whisper just as loud as Hannah's.

"There were no formal accusations," Vanessa said crisply. "There were thoughts. Ben had thoughts." If the calculating look in Vanessa's eye was any indication, Ben's mother considered Mandy's verbal dance around the truth a plus. "Ben had thoughts. About an arson-suspect list."

"Thoughtless thoughts." It was too late in the conversation for Mandy to play dumb.

"I'm having thoughts," Olivia said slyly. It was clear her thoughts were aligning with the matchmaking Mrs. Libby's. "How about you, Hannah?"

The little girl tossed her hands. "I have no idea what anyone is talking about!"

Mandy might have laughed along with Vanessa and Olivia if she hadn't felt she was being outmaneuvered.

"I think your granny is trying to get my sister to go out with your godfather." Olivia's grin practically filled her entire face.

It'd been too long since Mandy had seen such glee from Olivia. It almost made it worth the embarrassment and suffering. Almost.

Hannah gave Mandy an inspection just as thorough as Vanessa's had been.

"She cleans up well." Olivia was doing an inspection of her own, adding, "When she cleans up, which is admittedly almost never."

"All right." Mandy pocketed the Jeep keys and picked up a plastic tub of mail. "You've had your fun." She met Vanessa's gaze squarely. "Your son is intense." He'd stood in the post office arguing for her safety when admittedly she was more interested in productivity. "And he's also caring." He'd been adorable with Elvira. "But he and I...we're like..."

"Sunlight and moonbeams?" Olivia guessed.

"Raccoons?" Hannah guessed.

"Peas and carrots?" Vanessa guessed.

None of the guesses were right because none of them had seen her and Ben together when they weren't talking fire safety.

What were they? Not coffee buddies. Not moon aficionados. They were... It was easier to avoid the speculation. "We're not meant for each other." Besides being honest to a fault, Ben was a master at sending mixed signals.

Mandy's statement silenced the peanut gallery. But it didn't stop Vanessa and Olivia from exchanging knowing grins.

Mandy had a feeling those three weren't done talking or guessing about what she and Ben would be like together. So, she left them and went on her mail run.

Chapter Ten

Ben was cleaning the fire truck when a call came in, setting the station's alarm clanging and his pager vibrating.

A small brushfire on Parish Hill.

So much for the theory that one of Mandy's maintenance crew was an arsonist. They weren't working in Harmony Valley today.

Ben called Dad on his cell and got no answer. He was probably still in the garage dozing and taking his breathing treatment.

Ben could see the house from the fire station. He jumped into his turnout gear, expecting to see Dad emerge at any moment.

He didn't.

Mom and Hannah must still be out somewhere.

By the time Ben had dressed in his turnout gear, he'd convinced himself he could handle a small fire on his own. He pulled the wet, soapy rig out of the station's driveway, fully aware that he was breaking protocol. If it was larger than the highway grass fire, he'd make an immediate call for backup.

He flipped on the lights and siren, picking up speed. If that didn't wake Dad, he didn't know what would.

Ben made the turn onto the road leading up to Parish Hill and navigated the switchbacks toward the top, looking right and left for the fire. On the third switchback, he spotted it a few feet away from the road. Luck wasn't with him. Ten-foot-tall flames converged on an oak tree on the slope above.

Ben called for backup. It'd be at least thirty minutes for Cloverdale Fire to reach him. By then, the flames could be racing the wind up the hill, over homes and through vineyards. In theory, he could operate the truck solo, but at the very least, he'd feel better if someone had eyes on him.

A white Jeep with red-and-blue stripes approached from higher up the hill. A woman with ponytails beneath each ear was at the wheel.

He flagged Mandy down. "I need your help."

Mandy didn't hesitate. She parked the Jeep across the road. "Where's your dad?"

"I can't wait for him. I need you to keep watch." Ben handed her the radio. "Press this button if anything happens to me and tell dispatch what happened. They know where we are."

"Okay, now you're scaring me." She touched his arm the way kids touched wax statues to see if they were real. One-fingered. Decidedly brief. "Are you sure you can put that out alone?"

"No." He primed the pump and drew out the hose. He was sweating in his turnout gear. The sun was hot, and the flames were hotter. All conditions he was used to. And yet, he hesitated to go against the fireman code and fight the fire alone. He had more than his own safety to think about now. He had Hannah. He'd mailed the DNA test in. He'd requested the results through the mail. It would take longer, but he preferred an official, printed document.

He hated the urge to hesitate. He hated the loss of single-minded focus. He hated that his heart pounded with something other than adrenaline.

Right here, in this moment, he should only be thinking about the fire.

"Where is your dad?" Mandy asked again.

As if on cue, Dad screeched his truck to a halt behind the fire engine. "You're fired." His face was beet red, and he walked to the side of the truck with a purposeful stride and barely a gasp of breath. "You know how dangerous this can be without a full crew."

Ben exploded with anger. "You want me to treat you like the fire chief? Show up for work! Wear your pager! And now that you're here, wear a mask!"

They glared at each other.

"I feel as if I'm interrupting." Mandy's smile was more like a grimace. She held out the radio. "And there's a fire. Up there." She pointed in case they'd forgotten.

"My dear," Dad said, taking the handheld from her, "can you wait in the cab of the engine where it's safe?" He led her to the front seat. Once she was inside, he handed her the radio again. "On the off chance that anything bad happens—"

"I know. Press the button." Mandy met Ben's gaze. "Be careful."

Dad put on his turnout gear and breathing apparatus with the speed of a veteran, and they went to work. Ben on the hose. Dad on the pump and gauges.

Just as the fire gasped its last breath, a crew from Cloverdale pulled up. The driver grinned out the open window. "What? You didn't leave us any?"

"Sorry, Matt." Dad climbed on their running board and greeted the rest of the crew. He coughed, but not nearly as long as he had after the other fire.

Mandy got out of the fire truck. "You guys were amazingly efficient and emotionally dysfunctional, all at the same time."

"That's all on me." Ben tapped his chest and lowered his voice. "You saw some of Dad's meds. He shouldn't be out here right now." *He shouldn't be out here ever.*

"That explains your epiphany this morning." Mandy gave his father a speculative look. "I thought... Never mind what I thought."

"I'm sorry for the mixed signals. I'm not very good at communicating when I have a lot on my mind." Ben stared at Mandy, committing the image of her cool composure to memory. He had no idea why he felt compelled to do so. "And I have the annoying habit of blurting the truth."

"That you do. But speaking of truths, I have to ask. Do you think I set this fire?" The way Mandy stared at him—with a glint of challenge and that emotion-cloaking smile—did something odd inside his chest.

"No." He'd seen her drive the Jeep up the back side of Parish Hill earlier. About the time the fire began, she'd been on the other side of the summit.

"I expected you to say *not really*." Mandy grinned, and her eyes sparkled with amusement. All that joy. All that easygoing camaraderie. She was beautiful, inside and out.

This. This is why I'm drawn to her.

For the second time that day, Ben froze. It was one thing to enjoy Mandy's company and maybe feel some attraction in the moonlight. It was another to be slayed by the feeling that Mandy was the kind of special that came along only during a leap year or a solar eclipse.

"You're silent. You've been coached by your mom," Mandy was saying, still grinning in that way he enjoyed. "And now you're trying not to blurt some uncomfortable truth to me."

Ben was still thinking about her natural beauty and depth of personality when the meaning of Mandy's words sank in. He groaned. "Every bachelor's worst nightmare—*a meddlesome mother.*"

"Come on. You gave up your right to privacy when you decided to live with your parents." Mandy backed toward the Jeep, still beautiful, still grinning, still stealing his breath.

Ben struggled to participate in the conversation. What had she just said? Oh, yeah. The parents dig. "You know, I just received advice on how to deal with women like you."

Who knew Eunice's words of wisdom would come in handy?

Mandy stopped backtracking and fiddled with the set of her postal shirt on her shoulders. "Women like me?"

"Women who question my masculinity because I live with my parents." He forgot about his hesitation to fight the fire and the attraction he had to her, and grinned. "First, I tell you I'm a fireman." He struck a pose, hands on hips, doing his best not to laugh along with her. "Then I tell you I'm raising my goddaughter, which makes me good husband material."

Mandy rolled her eyes.

"And then I give you a brooding look." Ben did his best, but he kept laughing because Mandy was laughing, too.

He couldn't remember the last time he'd had so much fun with a woman. He wished he could extend this moment, analyze it, rationalize it. Find its truth.

Mandy took a step closer to the Jeep. "I bet whoever gave you that advice was single."

"And seventy." If she was a day.

Mandy got behind the wheel. "Don't try that on women you're seriously thinking about picking up."

The moment called for exaggeration. Ben pressed his hands to his chest and took a couple of swaggering steps. "I'm wounded that you'd think I wasn't serious about you."

"Goodbye, Fireman Libby." The Jeep rumbled to life.

"You can rib me more tonight. Under the moon." That was smooth. And totally unlike him.

"We'll see." The Mona Lisa smile was back as Mandy drove away.

With a loud blast of horn, the Cloverdale Fire truck drove away up the hill. There wasn't enough space to turn the rig around on the narrow road. Ben would have to do the same.

Dad bid them farewell and then approached their rig. "You overstepped your bounds." He grabbed on to a handle on the fire truck as if he needed it for balance. "I'm suspending you."

"You can't suspend me." Ben stood in the middle of the narrow mountain road, once more itching for a fight. "I'm the only able-bodied fireman you've got."

"Without pay!" His father's cheeks were florid. He sucked in air. If he wasn't hamstrung by a shortage of oxygen, he'd probably be on a long-winded rant.

But he was air-deprived, and Ben wasn't the only one in the wrong. He used Mandy and her unflappable smile as a role model. "Dad, I realize this is hard to hear, but you haven't been acting like a fire chief. You didn't wear your mask the other day. You didn't have your pager or cell phone on you while you were taking eucalyptus hits."

Suck-wheeze. "You have no idea what a fire chief does." Dad spit the words out in one strained breath.

"Maybe because you haven't shown me." It was important to remember eggshells. Ben took his tone down another notch. "Regardless, something has to change. I can't do this for nine months."

"Son, if we don't work together, we won't make it another nine hours." The fight left his father. His entire body sagged as if the weight of his gear and his hopes were too much. "You have no idea what it's like to lose your vitality and your self-worth."

Ben toned it down. "You looked pretty darn strong on this fire." And he had. With barely a cough.

"Don't be a suck-up." Dad walked to his truck, head high.

"I'm not here to suck up," Ben called after him. "I'm here to protect you."

Without another word, Dad got in his truck, executed a three-point turn and headed downhill, hopefully back to his eucalyptus treatment.

Nine months. Ben shook his head.

So much for telling Mom things were better between them.

The good news was that Ben had gone from considering Mandy not really an arsonist to not an arsonist at all.

Mandy scoffed to herself.

The bad news was she and Ben had something in common—at least temporarily, until Keith was healthy again. They both were watching after the health of a loved one. Olivia looked better every day. Keith had looked healthier today. More able to catch his breath. More color in his cheeks. More authority in his tone.

And Ben? There was something that unsettled Mandy when their gazes connected, something that caught in her throat and wouldn't let go. Something that fluttered in her chest and made her steps light.

Friendship, she decided. Because she'd opened up about things she'd never told anyone else.

Romance, a little voice inside whispered.

She ignored that idea.

Mandy hustled through her mail delivery route, trying to make up time. Fortunately, there were fewer than 200 residents in Harmony Valley, many of whom still had their mail delivered to the post office in Cloverdale. Unfortunately, there were a lot of empty and abandoned houses. Her deliveries were spread throughout town, and many expecting mail were retirees. Retirees liked to talk.

"The mail!" an elderly woman with a bright blue streak in her waist-length gray hair called out. She wielded a wooden walking staff to the end of her driveway. She wore a faded jean skirt, a black peasant blouse and Birkenstock sandals—a true California hippie. "I've been waiting for you, Mandy. It's Mrs. Stephens, your high school science teacher. One of them anyway. Do you remember me?" She was close enough to clasp Mandy's hand.

"Yes." She'd nurtured Mandy's love of science. She still watched shows about black holes and nebulas, programs Olivia found boring.

"I always expected you to be an astronaut. How far did you make it?"

"To Santa Rosa." Forty-five miles away. Mandy tried to sound cheerful. If nothing else, she'd gotten her fill of medical science as Olivia's guardian. "Life doesn't always work out the way we plan."

"But it tends to work out the way it's supposed to be." Mrs. Stephens waggled Mandy's hand as if trying to shake some happiness in her. "You're back. And you're a regular bigwig. *Postmaster*. I'm just as proud of you as I'd be if you landed on the moon."

That was a big overstatement. Mandy thanked Mrs. Stephens and tried to extricate her hand.

The retired science teacher wasn't done yet. "Have you seen Joe Torino? Or Will Jackson? They're back, too."

"Not yet." And she'd never deliver their mail if she didn't get moving. "I've really got to be going." She managed to free her hand.

"I'll see you tomorrow." Mrs. Stephens beamed as if Mandy's mail delivery was the highlight of her day. "Same time?"

"More or less."

"This is going to be my daily exercise—walking out to meet you." She did a penguin turn, rocking back and forth.

Mandy couldn't stand the thought of the older woman falling. "I'll help you back to your house." At a snail's pace, but Mrs. Stephens was so grateful, Mandy didn't mind.

A few blocks over, Mandy was accosted again at a small bungalow.

"I made you some fudge." Dee Adams held a red plastic plate covered with aluminum foil. She wore a tank top with an orange tabby on it that showed surgical scars at her shoulder and elbow. Her gray hair was in tight pin curls. "It's a recipe I got from your grandmother, and it's better than any fudge Mary Stephens makes at Christmas."

Mandy had to admit, the fudge was worth a few minutes of her time. And it made her think fondly of the way Grandma used to bake.

Around the corner, Agnes was waiting in her driveway. She handed Mandy a bottle of water. "We made a phone chain to monitor your progress," she explained. "The post office reopening is another sign the town is coming back to life. We want you to feel welcome."

Mandy felt welcome. And appreciated. If only she wasn't so far behind time-wise.

Utley stood at the end of the block, his baseball cap pulled as low as his bushy gray brows. "You're late."

"First week on the route," she said cheerfully instead of snapping, determined not to be derailed.

Olivia called her cell as Mandy hurried toward the next set of deliveries. "The electrician is here. He says he can't start work without someone over the age of eighteen on the premises."

"Tell him I'm on my way." He'd never wait until she finished. She had at least thirty minutes left of mail deliver, and there was a woman with purplish-gray hair and a pink tracksuit waiting for her ahead. "Tell him... Tell him I have homemade fudge if he waits."

Olivia gasped. "Is there enough for both of us?"

The fire engine's siren cut through the quiet of Harmony Valley like sharp scissors through crisp Christmas wrapping paper.

"I knew that place was trouble." Ben steered the truck around the corner and gunned it up the street toward the smoking post office.

"Put me out of my misery." Dad took a hit from his inhaler. The eucalyptus treatment or his anger with Ben seemed to have helped his lung function today. "Just ask the girl out. You need to relax. Maybe then you wouldn't go rogue and disrespect your boss."

Ben scowled. "I'm stressed out because of you, old man, not because I'm single." And attracted to the postmaster. Going solo to the fire had been a mistake, and Dad was still fuming about it.

"A good firefighter lives a balanced life, because he could go at any time." Said the man most likely to kick the bucket at any time.

A shaft of fear at the thought of Dad dying pierced Ben's armor. Jokes and jabs aside, working with his father brought home that reality.

It took Ben more than a moment to reply. "A good firefighter needs to focus so he lives a long life. Families—*and fathers near retirement*—are a dangerous distraction." Just look at what had happened to Ben today at the Parish Hill fire. He'd hesitated while thinking about Hannah. He'd flirted with Mandy instead of putting away the equipment.

As if proving his theory, Ben accidentally hit the curb with his tire. All because he wasn't focused on the task at hand.

Dad grabbed the engine's cheater bar. "I did not make you do that."

"I'll give you that one," Ben muttered. He needed to get his act together.

He parked behind a white van with *Perry the Electrician Is on the Job!* painted on the side.

"Dad, what would you say if I asked you to stay in the truck?" It looked like things were under control. Smoke billowed a soft, slow gray, rather than a fast, angry black.

"I'd demote you." The color was high in Dad's cheeks. There was no hitch to his speech. And he shot a glare sharp enough to wound. "I'd demote you to errand boy."

Ben got out, smiling. Maybe this call was just what the doctor ordered.

Mandy met them on the open loading dock, fire extinguisher in hand. Her brown eyes had a wild look to them, and her ponytails looked more disheveled than normal. "I think we have it under control. Perry is shutting down the circuit breakers."

"What happened?" Dad took a wide-legged commanding stance beneath her on the asphalt. He looked full-strength and capable, until he coughed.

"I flipped on a light fixture, and everything just went...*poof*." Mandy wouldn't look at Ben. She paced the width of the dock.

Ben noted the scorch marks in the wall and ceiling above a ladder, the drip of extinguisher foam and her bleak smile. "That's two fires in less than two weeks."

"Oh, son." Dad shook his head. "When will you learn?" He slowly climbed the loading dock steps.

Mandy's eyes narrowed on Ben. "They were accidents."

"The wrong-wattage bulb was in the wall fixture." A man Ben assumed was Perry the Electrician spoke from the side yard where he crouched near the fire control panel. "A costly mistake in these old buildings but not Mandy's fault."

Inside the mail room, Dad climbed the ladder, heedless of the slight wobble, and inspected the damage.

A stitch of tension drew tight between Ben's shoulder blades. "Did you see the fire start?"

"No fudge for the firefighter." Mandy crossed her arms over her chest.

"Don't include me in that ban," Dad said, knowing full well fudge wasn't on his approved diet.

Ben steadied the ladder.

"I was working on the panel out here." Perry stood, hitching up his blue work trousers in back, leaving his belly hanging over his belt in front. "I heard the pop but didn't see it happen. And just let me say—" he pointed at Ben "—big mistake on not earning fudge."

A pale teenager stood in the office doorway wearing jean capris, an overly long postal service shirt and the curious contempt teens learned by osmosis. She had short, mousy brown hair, Mandy's soft brown eyes and a deep frown that probably wasn't in Mandy's expressive repertoire.

That must be Olivia, Mandy's sister and the babysitter Mom had texted him about.

"I heard a pop and a scream," Olivia said. "Which means Mandy was surprised and it was accidental. *Not* arson."

Ben sent Mandy a what-the-heck frown, express delivery.

"Don't look at me." Mandy tightened the cross of her arms. "Your mom told her."

"Your mom and I are tight," Olivia said mutinously to Ben with a slicing hand gesture more appropriate for the streets than the post office. "And look. I ruined a nail jumping up to watch Mandy run around with the fire extinguisher." Olivia held up one finger with blurred colors on the fingernail as if it was proof of Mandy's innocence. "My sister isn't an arsonist. She doesn't break the law." And then she gave Mandy the oddest of looks, as if that last statement wasn't quite true.

Ben's investigative instincts flared down his spine. Arsonist or not, Mandy had a secret, one he intended to find. Currently, Mandy's smile didn't crack under his scrutiny.

But it might under the moon.

"For the record..." Dad climbed back down the ladder, pausing at the bottom to catch his breath. "...I don't suspect anyone here of arson. And I'm the fire chief." He drew himself up on willpower and a feed-me smile. "Now, where's that fudge?"

Mandy pointed to the counter in the back. She may have been annoyed with Ben, but she still looked rattled from the fire. She moved her feet every few seconds, and her hands were clenched beneath her crossed elbows.

"It's okay. The fire is out." Ben put his palm on her shoulder and ran it down to her elbow, where skin met skin. Without thinking, he'd touched her like that this morning outside the bakery, but she'd been wearing a windbreaker. And although he'd touched her, he hadn't touched *her*.

Mandy's skin was soft. Their eyes met and held. He saw something in her gaze he couldn't name. A feeling he had no words for.

Color bloomed in her cheeks, but she didn't look away. Was she searching to identify this feeling, too?

"Oh, man," Dad said. "This fudge is fantastic."

Ben's hand fell away. He took a step back.

Confusion bent Mandy's brows.

"FYI," Ben said, trying to lighten the moment. "I can't be bought by fudge." He went to see what Perry was doing to the control panel by the bushes.

A loud growl came from the shrubs as he approached.

"Move slow," Perry cautioned, holding his ground at the panel. "Or you'll upset Riley."

"The raccoon?" Ben bent and peered at the bushes, spotting a masked face, pointy nose and sharp teeth. "Now, there's one angry, stressed-out dude."

Mandy laughed. "Sounds like he could be your arsonist."

Chapter Eleven

Ben only meant to comfort.

That's what Mandy told herself as she and Olivia walked home that afternoon after work.

Ben had only meant to comfort, a friendly touch to her shoulder, a steadying hand on her elbow.

I didn't feel comforted.

Their eyes had met, and Mandy's world had tilted. The man before her came into focus. Those slashing dark brows over thick black lashes. The strong lines of his cheek and jaw, softened by the upturn of his lips. The brawn of his shoulders that carried the weight and responsibility of others without bending.

The man came into focus, not the firefighter, not the fire inspector. Not even the first responder who was kind to old women who'd fallen.

Her body had been chilled, an aftereffect of adrenaline from putting out the ceiling fire. But as she fell into the depths of Ben's blue gaze, she'd felt as if she'd stepped into a warm ray of sunlight; she'd felt as if his strength was hers to borrow.

"I can see why you have a thing for Ben." Olivia walked beside her down the cobbled sidewalk of Main Street, knotting the tails of her borrowed postal service shirt at her waist. "He's hot."

Denial was automatic. "I don't have a thing for—"

"Shut the door. You do! I saw the way you two looked at each other." Olivia tilted her head and fluttered her eyelashes. "It was cute. You'd make a cute couple. You'll have these tall kids who'll play basketball or volleyball. And I'll be like, yeah, I'm the cool aunt who was there when your parents met. Sparks were flying."

"You weren't there when we met." In theory, sparks had flown, although they'd been induced by a cut wire, not personal chemistry.

"Look at how adorable that is." Distracted, Olivia had a squirrel moment and paused at the window of Mae's Pretty Things to admire a white crocheted top. She sidestepped until her reflection lined up with the blouse as if she'd tried it on. "I could totally rock this look." And then her gaze landed on her short brown hair. "If I had better hair." She plucked the cowlick with her fingers.

Mandy moved to stand behind her, a full head taller. She placed her hands on Olivia's shoulders. "Your hair is adorable, just like you."

"I wanted to die when my hair fell out." Olivia's eyes filled with tears. "and now, I've got this moon face and chunk body." Her nose and mouth scrunched as if fighting the urge to cry. "I want my body back, not just my life."

"It'll come."

Olivia sniffed, slipping a hand up to cover Mandy's on her shoulder. "I'm going to buy that top. I have money coming to me. Can I get an advance from my paycheck?"

"No." Mandy's hands dropped away. She turned toward home.

"Why not?" Olivia trotted alongside her.

"That's not the way the adult world works. Besides, you need to save money for cosmetology school. There'll be expenses, ones whatever Grandpa left you won't cover." Mandy cringed. Why had she implied he'd left her money? What Grandpa had left Olivia wouldn't cover anything.

"I don't think my birthday money will buy that blouse." Olivia slowed down.

Mandy stopped. "What's wrong?"

"I wish Mom would come for my birthday."

Mandy wished Olivia would stop obsessing about their mother. "You know how Mom is." Mandy picked up the pace again, trying to outrun secrets. "Don't get your hopes up."

"It would be nice after all this if we could have a dinner together." Olivia was on a roll now. "Maybe some holidays, too. I'd like to meet my father. Family is important." She cast Mandy a measuring look. "You've met your father."

"The last time I saw him, I was four." Mandy's dad had no interest in a relationship with her.

They crossed the street near the town square and El Rosal.

"It's been a long time since we've gone out to dinner," Olivia said. "Can we go tonight?"

Mandy had been watching every penny they spent. She walked to work to save on gas. What harm was there in one dinner? "Okay." Mandy turned toward El Rosal.

"We can't go like this." Olivia tugged her toward home. "We have to clean up."

Clean up? Wasn't that what Olivia had said to Ben's mother earlier?

"What are you up to? This better not be a blind date." A small thrill went down Mandy's spine at the thought.

"Would I do that to you?" Olivia's smile split her cheeks.

"Yes."

Olivia laughed and kept leading her home.

"Tell me who passed their fire inspection." Granddad sat to Ben's right at the bar at El Rosal, the Mexican restaurant on the town square. Other than his gray hair and a couple of sunspots on his burly arms, he looked healthier than Dad. "I'm assuming El Rosal did, since we're here."

The red, blue and green color scheme in the restaurant was as vibrant and lively as the Spanish pop blaring through the speakers overhead. Mom had suggested the restaurant's happy hour as a place to discuss the volunteer fire program between the current and former fire chiefs.

"You want to know what passed?" Ben loaded a chip with salsa, glancing up at the baseball game on the television mounted above the back bar. One out. One on base. "This place, the Italian café and the bakery."

"There were other places," Dad groused from Ben's left. There was still tension between them after Ben tried to take on the Parish Hill fire alone. He was drinking fresh-brewed iced tea instead of beer and hadn't touched one chip. Not that he wasn't eyeing Ben's beer and the chip bowl in a way that said his vow to eat better wouldn't last through the inning. "The sheriff's office and the winery's storage facility downtown passed."

"Basically..." Ben reached for another chip, elbowing Dad's hand farther away from the bowl. "Everything that had been updated recently passed. And the rest—"

"Man, I don't envy you two the paperwork from all those citations." Granddad cut Ben off.

"There is no paperwork." Ben was willing to give up all his father's flaws. "Dad gave them warnings and said we'd be back. Even at the post office, where we witnessed an electrical fire."

"A warning is fair." Dad leaned toward the salsa bowl.

The batter hit a foul ball.

Ben drew the bowl away. "You're soft, Dad."

"I'm allowed to be soft." Dad picked up a chip, inspected the salsa bowl and then set the chip on his drink napkin. "I'm close to retirement."

The base runner tried to steal third on a wild pitch and was thrown out. Two down.

"I'd rather you were curmudgeonly." Ben moved both bowls closer to Granddad.

"That'll be you." His father's gaze remained on the chips. "You'll be the lonely old man yelling at kids to get off your lawn."

"So true." With a hearty guffaw, Granddad slapped Ben on the back. "You're wound a little too tight."

The next pitch went wide.

Ben bristled, thinking of Mandy and her smile. "I'm not curmudgeonly. I'm meticulous and honest."

Dad swung around to face Ben. "You're meticulous, cranky and single. All of which prime you for mistakes, like that stunt you pulled today."

"You keep bringing up my marital status." He'd done so with every woman in town, be she married or available, thirty-five or sixty-five. And Dad was continuously harping on him about dating Mandy.

Ben wasn't one to rush into things.

Dad narrowed his eyes. "After retirement, I'd like to have grandchildren to spoil. Other than Hannah."

"Are you adopting Hannah?" Granddad asked gleefully. "That kid's got a good heart. And she wants a kitten."

"If John Smith shows up," Dad said in a way that let Ben know Mom hadn't clued him in on the DNA test, "I'll need grandkids more than ever."

"Why don't you hound Mike and Lisa to pop out some babies?" His brother was married and deserving some grandchild pressure.

"I will." Dad broke the chip on his napkin into little pieces. "The next time I see them."

Ben glanced at the television. Another foul ball. "Can we talk business for a minute?" He needed to change the subject from marriage and babies. "How can we recruit volunteer firemen? A crew of two is too small."

"Leave recruitment to me," Granddad said confidently.

"Watch out, world." Dad rolled his eyes, looking more like himself than he had lately. "I bet Granddad wants to give a kitten to each recruit. We'll handle it old man."

"Don't joke." Granddad puffed out his round, reddening cheeks. "Harmony Valley should pass a law—every new citizen needs to adopt a cat." He gestured to Ben with his beer. "Starting with you, Mr. Meticulous."

"No go." Ben gently pushed Granddad's beer back into his space, struck with an idea. "Once Hannah's gone, I'm living in the firehouse full-time." Ben drew a breath, ready to continue with the jokes, until he realized the results of the

DNA test might mean he'd never move into the firehouse and never pursue a career in fire investigation.

"You can't bring a woman home to the firehouse," Dad said with a twinkle in his eye.

"And we're back to my relationship status." Ben was glad Mandy wasn't in the room.

"Or lack thereof." Granddad clinked his beer bottle against Ben's. "Wouldn't mind seeing the next generation of Libby firemen before I go."

"Go where?" Ben watched the batter connect with a pitch, sending it sailing over the right field fence.

"Go kicking the bucket." Granddad turned serious. "I'm two years shy of eighty. My ticker could go. I could get the Big C. Or I could—"

"Live to see ninety." Dad glanced at the chip crumbs on his napkin morosely. "You're as healthy as that batter."

That was true. And why wouldn't he be? Granddad had spent the majority of his fire career in Harmony Valley. They averaged less than fifty major calls a year.

"I'll handle recruitment," Dad said firmly. "I'm the fire chief. End of discussion."

"Hey." Granddad perked up. "There's some potential recruits right there." He nodded toward the rainbow-colored lobby where two women stood waiting for a table. "And at least one looks of legal firefighting age."

Mandy followed the host to a table. Instead of postal service blue, she wore a green flowered blouse, form-fitting blue jeans and flat sandals. Her usually messy ponytails had been tamed into a sleek, thick braid. Olivia wore a teenage girl's summer uniform—a yellow tank top, jean shorts and yellow flip-flops.

"Let's not ask Mandy." The last thing Ben needed was his kryptonite on his fire crew.

"Mandy?" Granddad frowned. "Mandy Zapien?"

"Yeah. So?"

"She was one of the kids who accidentally started a fire at the high school years ago. Practically burned down the gym before we got there. I could never prove she was there, but I suspected…"

While Granddad prattled on, Ben exchanged a look with his father.

Dad's seemed to say: *Don't believe it.*

Ben's said: *There are too many coincidences here.*

But he didn't believe it either.

"I'll have the steak and shrimp fajitas." Olivia ordered the most expensive item on the menu.

"No. She'll have two chicken tacos. À la carte," Mandy corrected, choosing the cheapest item. "And so will I." She waited until the waiter left to lean closer to Olivia. "You knew Ben would be here."

Before Olivia could protest, Ben's father approached their table. "Ladies." Keith leaned on a chair back, sagging like he needed the support. "We're filling a roster of volunteer firemen. Firehouse meeting. Seven thirty tomorrow night."

Olivia beamed at Mandy. "Can I?"

"Are you eighteen?" Ben appeared next to his father, clapping a hand on Keith's shoulder.

"I'll be eighteen soon." Olivia slumped. "But since I'm going away to cosmetology school after that, I shouldn't promise anything."

Mandy was simultaneously bursting with pride that her sister realized she couldn't commit to something she was interested in and deflating inside because Olivia's dream was going to be harder to achieve than she expected it to be.

"Oh, say. Are you the nail girl Agnes told me about?" An elderly woman with purplish-gray hair at a table several feet away beckoned. Mandy thought her name might be Eunice, only because she'd delivered her mail. The hair was hard to forget. "My cuticles are horrible."

Olivia went eagerly to give the old woman advice. Keith moved toward the door, leaving Mandy and Ben alone.

"Truthfully," Ben said in a low voice meant only for her, "I don't think you'd do well in the program. That first fire…"

"Call it first-timer shock." Mandy wasn't sure why she was defending herself and a right to a volunteer position. She had no time or energy for anything other than the post office. "Besides, I didn't run away when you asked me to be your safety net on Parish Hill. And I put out a fire at the post office today."

Ben's gaze delved into hers but didn't stay long. "My Granddad seems to think your first time seeing a fire was in the high school."

Mandy's smile fell. And not a little fall either. It plunged past her stomach to the tile floor. "That was an accident."

"A secret you told Mr. Moon?" Ben leaned down until his face was near her ear.

If she turned her head, she could kiss him.

And make a complete fool of myself.

"I'd like to know that secret," Ben whispered. "And if you tell me, I'll let you be a volunteer fireman."

Mandy swallowed thickly. "Aren't you afraid if I tell you, you won't want me to volunteer?"

"I'm actually feeling it'll be the opposite." Ben angled his face toward hers, a hint of amusement in his blue eyed gaze. "But I know you and secrets. You'd rather keep them to yourself. So it's a safe bet."

Oh, how Mandy hated a dare.

"What's Hannah doing outside?" Ben's father pointed out the restaurant window when Ben joined him in the lobby. "Did she run away again?"

The appearance of Hannah left Ben no time to gloat over the corner he'd backed Mandy into or to be relieved that there had been no more deep confusing glances.

Hannah's pink bike was leaning against the restaurant window. Her blond pigtails were askew. She crouched in front of the window holding a small jar with holes punched in the top.

Ben hurried outside and knelt beside her. "Whatcha doin', peanut?"

"Truman told me the best place to find crickets is in the cracks on Main Street." Her little brow was furrowed over the top of her black glasses. Her pink zippered sweatshirt hung almost off her shoulders.

Ben was afraid to ask. "Why do you need crickets?"

"I found a lost spider earlier. It needs to eat." She wiped at her nose. "Can you be quiet? I haven't heard a cricket since you came out here."

"It's time for dinner." Ben realized he should be calling Mom to let her know Hannah was all right. A glance inside the restaurant showed Dad on the phone.

He mouthed, *Mom.*

"*Dinner?*" Hannah stood. She looked like she'd done the army crawl through a mud field. "So soon? Did you ask Mandy out? Is that what you were doing here?"

"No... I... Who told you that?" Ben didn't need her answer. His mother was on the case to solve his bachelorhood. He wished he could put his parents in time-out. He glanced back inside at Mandy, feeling both annoyed and guilty. "Was that why Mandy dressed up? Did someone tell her I was here?"

Hannah shrugged. "Getting her here was Olivia's job." She pressed her nose against the window. "She does clean up nice. At least her braid stays." Hannah's never did.

Mandy noticed Hannah's scrutiny and waved. Olivia returned to their table, saw who Mandy was waving at, and waved, too.

"Do you know who else cleans up nice?" Ben asked, righting Hannah's bike.

"Who?"

"You." Ben wheeled Hannah's bike to his truck and loaded it in the back, hoping there was time before dinner to get her in the bath. "I'll give you a ride home. Grandpa Felix and Grandpa Keith drove separately."

He and Hannah got into the truck.

"Do you know that Great-Grandpa Felix rescued a Mau the other day?" Hannah said when she'd buckled herself in. "Mau sounds like meow."

Ben backed out. "I take it a Mau is a cat."

"A gray-and-black tabby, except instead of stripes everywhere, she has stripes on her legs and dots on the rest of her body. And she sounds like this." Hannah yowled and meowed and made a noise that sounded like a purr. "Do you think I can adopt her?"

Ben was going to kill his grandfather. Was there anyone not on his family hit list? "We talked about this, Han. No more pets—"

"Until we find my dad." She slumped in her seat. "That's taking forever."

Maybe not as long as she feared. The DNA test was due next week.

A crane flew in front of them and landed on the bank of the Harmony Valley River.

"Look! Look!" Hannah pressed her nose to the window. "Isn't he pretty? Did you know that cranes eat frogs and…small snakes." She turned in her seat, eyes large behind her lenses. "We have to go find Iggy. With his crooked tail, he won't be able to get away from that crane."

"Circle of life, Han." She had to be more realistic.

Hannah sucked in a horrified breath. "You'd let Iggy die?"

"You'd let the crane starve?" Ben teased.

"That crane doesn't have a name!" Hannah sat rigidly. "Iggy has a name. And he loves me."

And no matter what Ben said, Hannah was determined to worry about that snake. Finally, Ben turned around and drove back just in time to see the crane take to flight. "Look, the crane has a frog in his mouth."

"Iggy's safe." Hannah relaxed in her seat.

When they got home, Ben phone chimed with a text. While Hannah went inside to wash up for dinner, Ben checked his phone.

It was the private investigator: *I found John Smith. I'll call you tomorrow.*

Tomorrow? Ben had questions now. He wanted answers now.

Was John aware he had a child? Was John interested in raising his child? Was John an upstanding guy or just some loser who shouldn't be raising a puppy, much less a little girl?

Ben called Fenway back. The private investigator didn't answer his phone.

"You're late," his mother scolded upon his entrance into the kitchen and the small nook where they took most of their meals. "This is family time."

Dad had beat him home and was already eating.

"Sorry," Ben managed to say. He glanced at Hannah. He'd nearly convinced himself that John Smith was a figment of Erica's imagination.

He'd told Fenway to find John and send him to Harmony Valley. For all he knew, John Smith could show up tomorrow. He could take Hannah away. And there was nothing Ben could do about it.

Before Erica died, Ben had loved Hannah. He'd loved her like a favorite uncle who took her out once a month and spoiled her a little. For the past few months, he'd had a say in how Hannah was raised, how she was fed, how she was disciplined (okay, maybe the last part had been led by his mother). The appearance of John Smith meant Ben had no more say in Hannah's welfare at all.

Unless the DNA test proves I'm her father.

Even if John Smith hadn't been a sham name Erica had written on the birth certificate, there was still that chance.

A feeling of helplessness welled in his throat. He should have requested the electronic DNA results.

"By the way, Ben," his mother said as she cleared her dishes from the kitchen table. "I approve of Mandy. I talked to her today."

"So I heard." Ben huffed, digging into his vegetables. "It's like I'm in middle school again and you're arranging for me to take Lori Caldwell to the Sadie Hawkins Dance." He frown at his mother. "News flash—the Sadie Hawkins Dance is where *girls* ask the boys."

Mom tsked. "Lori Caldwell was a sweet, shy girl who needed a boost in confidence."

"She thought I liked her." She'd tried to stick her tongue down Ben's throat at the after-dance party. That was Ben's first kiss. Talk about shock and ew.

"I wonder if Lori is single," Mom said with an evil glint in her eye. "I could call her mother."

"Please don't." Ben frowned. "Forget the please. Just don't."

"Or you could ask Mandy out." Mom came to stand behind Hannah, who nodded in agreement. "I could cut some roses from the yard. Women like to receive flowers."

"Granny is the evil queen," Ben told Hannah with a straight face. "If she offers you an apple, watch out."

Hannah's eyes widened.

"Ben!" Mom swatted him in the shoulder with her dish towel.

"You need help with your personal life, son." Dad winked at Hannah, who was still sulking about Iggy and the crane. "Marriage is like being on a team. And you know that everything is better when you're on a team."

Ben rolled his eyes.

"Am I on a team?" Hannah seemed to think the answer would be no. She stared at her brown rice as if it was an animal she'd named and couldn't bring herself to eat.

"Of course, you're on a team." Dad ruffled her hair. "The Libby team."

Hannah smiled at them all. She rarely smiled. "With you and Granny and Ben? Forever and ever?"

Yes.

But Ben had no right to make promises.

Chapter Twelve

"You made two nail appointments tonight," Mandy said with genuine enthusiasm. "That's awesome."

They crossed the freshly mowed grass on the town square as the sun was setting.

"I know, right? Everything's going my way." Olivia skipped a few steps ahead, threw out her arms and spun around. "As soon as I graduate, I'll be my own boss. I could set up shop at that house the town council told us about if you rent it. And when Mom comes back—"

"If *I* rent it?" Mandy felt a niggle of impatience that threatened eggshells. "Once you start working, you'll need to pitch in on things like rent, utilities and food, especially if you're operating a salon there."

Olivia slowed down. "But…"

"You're about to become an adult." Mandy wasn't sure Olivia was ready to be one. And some of the blame fell on her. "You'll be free to do what you want, but you'll also have to pay your way." When Olivia said nothing, Mandy couldn't stop herself from pointing out the hardships of self-employment. "Are you sure you want to be a nail technician? There's not much future in it. You won't get a cost-of-living increase every year or retirement."

"I want to follow my passion," Olivia said with all the gusto of the naive. She held out her hands so Mandy could admire them. "I don't care about things like raises or—"

"Health insurance?" Mandy's voice was suddenly raw. Her sister needed a reality check. She was a cancer survivor. She needed the best health insurance out there. "Are you ready to pay for your own health care?"

Olivia glared at her. "You don't understand. All you've ever wanted to do is work at the post office. You achieved your dream."

"That's not true." Why did it feel like she'd swallowed broken glass? "I was like you when I was eighteen. I had dreams. I wanted to go to college. I wanted to be an astronomer." Each statement rose higher into the sunset as if giving voice to her dilapidated dreams made them important again. "I wanted to work for NASA."

"What happened?" Olivia's gaze turned butter soft. She was a bleeding heart when it came to personal stories. It was why she was in danger around their mother.

"Grandma got sick." *Cancer.* How Mandy hated what that disease had done to their family. "She couldn't take care of you." Mandy tried to look Olivia in the eye, but the long-buried resentment welled up in her eyes, and she was afraid her sister would see it. "If I went off to college, I couldn't take care of either one of you."

"But the Grumpster—"

"Don't call him that. *Grandpa* had to earn a paycheck for all of us. He had to make sure we had health care." Mandy waited for the sheriff to drive by in his truck before crossing the street. "He offered me a job when I turned eighteen. And I had to be an adult and take it."

"You could go to school now," Olivia said in that bright, innocent tone.

"I can't go back until I retire." In eight more years. Where had the time gone? "By then I'll be too old to be a college student."

"You can go back to school at any age. When you're forty." Olivia was behind Mandy, but she was grinning. Mandy could tell from her cheerful voice. "When you're seventy."

"But I won't want to." Now that their grandparents were gone and Olivia was healthy, it was time to make some new dreams. Ben's face drifted into her mind.

She quickly shoved it out again. "Maybe I'll babysit your kids when I retire. I'll knit sweaters and bake pies and they'll call me Auntie Maddy."

"Old maid."

Her term of endearment didn't seem so dear this time. And Mandy didn't have the heart to call her a brat.

"Grandpa used to say dreams were for the young and foolish." The words came out of Mandy with the deliberate pace of the disillusioned. "He used to say you found one thing that made you happy and that's what kept you going."

"What was his one thing?" Olivia asked breathlessly.

"Grandma."

They reached their street. Their steps slowed, until they stopped at the edge of their driveway. The house had once been a cheery blue with white trim. The door was yellow. A welcome yellow, Grandma used to say.

Staring at the faded paint colors on the house, Mandy didn't feel welcome.

"The front door is open," Olivia said, stating the obvious. "Didn't we close it when we left for dinner?"

"I thought we did." Despite Harmony Valley being one of those small towns where you didn't need to lock the door, Mandy considered turning and running after the sheriff.

Responsible people don't run.

Mandy didn't budge. Not an inch. Not forward or back.

"Ladies." The masculine voice leaped out of the dusk and made them both jump. It was Ben.

"Our door's open," Mandy choked out before he could say much else, hanging on to Olivia's hand, wishing she could hang on to his, too. And then she looked at him, really looked at him, and registered the expression on his face.

Ben was upset. Not annoyed to the point of anger as he'd been with her the day they'd met. Not frustrated to the point of anger as he'd been with his father at the fire today. Not even exasperated by his flighty neighbors. No. The color had leached from his face. His brows were low and his chin was high. He was tense-eyed, trying-to-keep-the-emotion-from-spilling-out upset.

Mandy recognized that look from too much time spent in hospitals and doctors' offices. When someone got that look, they got reckless.

Mandy released Olivia's hand and grabbed hold of Ben's arm as he walked toward their door, trying to stop him. "We can handle this."

"What?" Olivia squeaked. "Without Ben?"

"It's nothing. Probably our mom stopped by to visit." Mandy tried to give Olivia the head-jerking high sign that something wasn't right with Ben, but Olivia continued to stare at Mandy as if she'd lost her mind. All the while, she was holding on to Ben's sturdy biceps and digging in her sandaled heels. Not that it did any good. He was determined to take action.

"Would your mom leave the door open?" Ben charged forward.

"Well, no." That was the rub. Mandy leaned closer, although nothing short of a breathy whisper would escape Olivia's hearing. "But you're upset about..." At his frown, she quickly backpedaled. "I don't know what you're upset about, and I don't want to bother you. We can deal with this alone."

Ben covered her hands with his. "I'm not the kind of man who lets women walk into the unknown."

When they'd first met, she'd doubted Ben would ever rush to her rescue; but here he was, proving her wrong. Proving what kind of man he was and maybe how he felt about her.

A feeling took hold. Warm and knee-weakening. Almost the same feeling she'd had when the town council had spoiled her with cookies and milk. Almost. No one spoiled Mandy. Or at least, she hadn't been spoiled or taken care of in a long, long time. Not that Ben was spoiling her. But he was watching out for her safety, for her well-being, for her.

She breathed deeply, trying to hold on to the feeling, knowing it was fleeting. Because this was...they were...he was...

My hero.

Mandy jolted back to reality. To Ben staring into her eyes.

A different kind of warmth took hold, spreading through her cheeks. Embarrassment. She released his arm, sliding her fingers from beneath his.

"Do you really think Mom's inside?" Olivia's tone held out hope, while her expression remained doubtful.

Mandy couldn't bring herself to say yes. She was still half-lost in the fantasy that Ben was her knight in shining armor.

Speaking of Ben, he was still moving. And he wasn't moving down the sidewalk on his way elsewhere. He was heading to their front door. "I'll clear the house for you on one condition."

"What's that?" Mandy hurried to catch up.

"I get a piece of that fudge."

Ben had wanted a distraction from his problems. He'd found one next door.

He couldn't convince the Zapien women to wait outside while he checked their home for burglars. Mandy followed closely, the palm of her hand on his shoulder blade.

"Mom?" Olivia called out, close on Mandy's heels.

Mandy said nothing, but her fingers curled into Ben's shoulder as if she needed to hold on to something sturdy at the mention of her mother.

Their living room was practically bare, more like a typical bachelor pad. There was a television, an outdated blue plaid loveseat and a blue recliner. Nothing hung on the walls. The kitchen was lived-in. Dirty dishes were stacked in the sink. No pots or pans, just dishes. A portable microwave sat on the counter next to the plate of fudge.

The rear slider and garage door were locked. Ben turned on the porch light and looked into the backyard. Nothing seemed out of place. He opened the garage door next, beginning to think their front door had blown open and that the house was safe.

Mandy peered over his shoulder. She was one of the few women he knew who was tall enough to do so.

"Did you notice my white truck?" She tossed a tease.

"Not really," he volleyed back. Mostly he saw cardboard boxes packed around it, although not as many boxes as at his house.

He turned quickly before she moved out of his space. Somehow his hand made a gentle landing on her waist. She was gracefully tall and elegantly slender, a fact he'd missed when she wore her baggy postal shirt. Her single braid made her cheekbones more prominent and her brown eyes luminous. He was struck again by the shield that was her smile. He was struck again by her beauty, inside and out. He was struck again by the urge to kiss her.

"Mom?" Olivia stood in the living room, staring down the hall, unwittingly breaking the spell between them.

Mandy stepped back. Ben's hand fell away.

"Is Mom the name of your cat?" Ben closed and locked the garage door.

"Please don't joke about her," Mandy said in hushed tones.

Ben turned serious, more convinced that he'd found one of Mandy's secrets. "Is Mom armed?" Should he be more concerned?

"She doesn't need a gun to be dangerous," Mandy continued in that low voice. "And I'm feeling a little vulnerable right now since technically this is her house and we don't have permission to stay here."

That statement required a pause in the house search. His brain fit another piece of the puzzle that was Mandy in place. "You're breaking the law by staying here." That explained Olivia's hesitation during her defense of Mandy at the post office.

"I'm the estate trustee." Mandy gave him a gentle push in the direction of the hallway. "I pay the bills on this place for my mother."

"But you don't have permission to live here." Not a question. Mandy hadn't asked to stay. She'd shortcut protocol. "Why not?"

"Because," Mandy said, exhibiting her experience in raising a child by using a one-word argument. She pointed to the hallway as if that would end the discussion.

Ben let her win this battle, but only because there was a piece of fudge in his future and he was going to get straight answers out of her while he ate it.

He opened the first bedroom door. Books and notebooks were in a heap on the open closet floor. Three pairs of flip-flops and various crumpled items of clothing covered the carpet. The twin bed was neatly made with a frilly pink bedspread. Dozens of nail polish bottles stood huddled on top of a small dresser.

Olivia slipped past him, swooping up dirty clothes and kicking her flip-flops to the side. A teenager's idea of straightening up.

The Zapien sisters followed him to the next door in the hall.

Ben opened the second bedroom door. Another twin bed. Another small dresser. The room and closet were empty, but as clean as a hotel room awaiting a guest.

The Zapien sisters both blew out breaths.

Ben opened the last bedroom door. He knew without being told it was Mandy's room. It smelled like her, of paper and moonbeams. Her full-size bed hadn't been made. The teal flowered bedspread was rumpled. The pillow still had the impression from her head. Dirty postal uniforms were piled in a basket.

"I'm getting in the shower." Olivia grabbed some clothes and then disappeared into the bathroom.

"False alarm. Thank you." Mandy reached around Ben to close her bedroom door. "You can head on your merry way now."

"Not without the fudge you promised." His not-so-merry way had led him to her. He wasn't going anywhere without his reward. Turned out, he could be bought by fudge.

She stared up at him with dark eyes filled with regrets and secrets, and other things like weariness and worry and longing and loneliness.

Or maybe that was a reflection of what was in his eyes, a product of having worked nonstop 24/7 since he'd arrived in town.

Mandy left him in the hallway. "There's one last piece of fudge."

"That's a big piece," he said upon seeing it. "How about we share?"

He thought she'd refuse. Instead, Mandy led him to the back patio and invited him to sit on a wooden glider with her. The sun had set. The sky was darkening. The moon would be low, hidden behind her large tree.

She offered him a piece of fudge.

Ben took a small bite, expecting nothing much.

But like Mandy, it was much, much more than he anticipated. Before he knew what he'd done, he'd eaten it all. "This fudge should be outlawed." It was the right texture, the right sweetness, the right antidote for his sullen mood this evening. "I needed that."

She kicked the glider into motion. "You looked in need of a break when you came upon us. Rough night?"

"I'd rather talk about fudge. Or your high school fire experiences." Or...he had a long list of things he'd like to know about her.

"Why does it seem as if I'm always telling you things and getting nothing in return?" Her gentle smile teased.

"I told you my dirty underwear story," he pointed out.

"And I told you about Mr. Moon."

She had. He'd never look at the moon the same way again. "Tell you what. We'll swap. Story for story. Something we've never told anyone before." Too late, he realized he'd have to divulge a secret of his own. He checked his pager.

"I don't want your jokes." Mandy slumped down, resting her head on the back of the glider. "I want to know why you were upset tonight."

"And you'll tell me about your mother?" *What?* He'd meant to ask about the high school fire Granddad was upset about.

Mandy looked as surprised as he was by his question. "You can ask anyone in town about my mother."

"I don't want gossip." Ben made an encouraging motion with his hand. "I want the details."

Mandy kicked the glider into a stomach-dropping swing. "My mom was an only child and a daddy's girl. Wild and willful, my grandmother used to say." Mandy rolled her head to the side, seeking his gaze. "She got pregnant in high school and married my dad. They moved to Santa Rosa. Enter me. Enter divorce. Enter my return to Harmony Valley."

He ran the back of his hand down her bare arm, turning his palm over to cover her hand. "Those were stingy details."

"I don't usually talk about my mother." Her gaze dropped to their hands.

His fingers curled around hers. "I'm honored."

"My mother likes to have fun," Mandy began slowly. "She likes pretty things. She likes it when men spoil her with fun and pretty things. She was swiping right before there was an app for that."

Firefighting absentee father aside, Ben realized how lucky he'd been to have stable, happily married parents.

"When I was little, younger than Hannah, I used to think my mother was a princess. I never saw her without her hair done, makeup on and wearing pretty clothes." Mandy's gaze drifted toward the backyard. "I used to try to be pretty for her. I wore dresses and Grandma fixed my hair. But I was a gangly, awkward thing, not pretty enough to stop her from leaving."

Ben imagined Mandy as a little girl, sitting at her bedroom window and wishing on the moon. "That was her loss. She couldn't see how beautiful you were inside."

Mandy grinned at him. "You don't even realize you're doing it, do you?"

"Uh..." Ben retraced his last words. Too late, he realized his error. "Was the correct response something along the lines of how beautiful and princess-like you are outwardly? Sorry. I'm not a guy who tosses out easy compliments and smooth lines."

"I could tell." She leaned back, staring up at the porch ceiling. "It's okay. I'm getting used to it."

"Really?"

"Not really." She grinned again. "Just kidding. That was too good a setup to resist."

He acknowledged her good-natured dig with a nod, sensing she was ready to move on from the topic of her mother before he was. "Do you think you'll ever have a relationship with her?"

"No." A flat denial. Mandy kicked the glider into motion again. "When I was fourteen, Mom showed up with this beautiful baby girl. She was so tiny, so precious. I just knew that Mom couldn't leave Olivia. Here was a princess fit for a queen."

"But she left anyway."

"Of course. Mom needs to be worshipped." Mandy's smile was the one she used to hide her pain. "And no matter how perfect Olivia was, as a baby, she wasn't capable of worshipping at Mom's altar."

As a firefighter and first responder, Ben saw dysfunctional families all the time. But he never heard their stories.

"We'd moved to Santa Rosa after my grandmother died. Somehow, Mom found us a few years later. But it was almost better because she lived in the area, too, so she didn't arrive expecting to have room and board and royal service."

Ben squeezed Mandy's hand in the hopes that she'd continue.

And she did. "When Olivia was... I don't know. Thirteen? Which would mean I was twenty-seven. Mom wanted to take her out on New Year's Eve. *Out to party?* The nerve of her." Mandy shook a little, not quite a shiver, not quite an angry tremor. "And Olivia... She was dying to go with her. I knew how she felt. I knew what it was like to bask in what little attention Mom threw my way. But I couldn't let Olivia go." She looked into Ben's eyes with a regretful gaze. "And so, I gave my mother money to leave without her."

The glider had been well constructed. The wood creaked faintly with each pass.

"It was the right thing to do." Ben gave her hand another squeeze.

"Was it?" Mandy might have gently tried to pull her hand away.

Ben linked their fingers together. "It was."

"But Olivia was crushed. She cried on my shoulder until midnight, hopeful that Mom would come back and get her. I cried to the moon after she went to bed." Mandy glanced toward the tree and the moon they both knew was hidden behind it.

"And you haven't seen your mom since?" he asked softly.

Mandy shrugged. "She came for Grandpa's funeral. And she visited us again a few months after that. She caught us as we were going out to a doctor's appointment. Olivia latched on to her and wouldn't let her leave. That was the day they confirmed Olivia had cancer."

"Did she leave you in the doctor's office?" Her mother seemed the type. Ben was angry just thinking about how uncaring Mandy's mother was.

"No. Mom came home with us. She let me make her dinner. And after Olivia went to bed, she told me she couldn't bear to see her baby suffer. She told me..." Mandy wiped her cheek with her free hand. "...she told me how weak she was, and then she waited." Mandy swallowed. "She waited until I gave her money and told her not to come back."

"And Olivia assumed she'd been abandoned again."

Mandy turned pleading eyes his way, looking for forgiveness when it wasn't his to give. "Mom would've left regardless. For all I know, my grandmother could have been paying for her to leave when I was a kid."

The unspoken implication being if her grandmother had done it, Mandy's bribes wouldn't seem so bad.

"Would it have been better for Olivia if you'd paid her to stay?" He'd heard a strong support group made a huge difference in medical recoveries.

"She would've divided us." Mandy raised her chin, so certain. "Olivia and I are very close, and I believe our unity helped her win this battle."

And yet, Mandy hadn't told her sister the truth. "What if your mom shows up now? What if she tells Olivia the truth?"

"I'll stand by what I've done." But her lower lip trembled.

He brought Mandy closer on the glider, sending it swinging in all kinds of haphazard directions. "Or you could tell Olivia the truth *before* your mother ever gets here."

Mandy dropped her forehead to his shoulder. "Not everyone finds the truth as easy to tell as you do." Her breath wafted over his biceps. "Especially when considering telling the truth to a teenager who could do something dramatic like run away to be with her irresponsible mother."

"You're afraid the truth will put her in danger?" Ben passed a hand over Mandy's smooth, thick hair, letting his palm rest on her nape. "That she'll go off with your Mom?"

"I'm afraid the truth will make Olivia hate me." Mandy knocked her forehead gently against his shoulder a few times.

"You've done a great job raising her." Ben tilted Mandy's head up. "The truth has never made anyone hate me."

"Permanently, you mean?" Mandy scooted away from him, sitting in the other corner and crossing her arms. "It's your turn."

He missed the warmth of her body next to his.

"Ben." She poked his shoulder. "Don't renege."

Ben stared at Mandy, at her gentle smile. The first day they'd met, he'd imagined she never had a care. Now he knew better, and he could see the tension around her eyes despite that smile. "It's about Hannah."

"If you tell me she has cancer, I'm going to need a hanky."

Ben shook his head. "It's not that. She's my godchild and I'm her guardian. After months of searching, I've finally got a lead on the man who's supposed to be her father. I don't know if he knows Hannah exists. She's never met him. I had to hire a private investigator just to find him. And I don't know if he's really her father, because..." *Talk about truths making someone despise you.* "...I was Erica's best friend but I never met him."

Oh, that was a cop-out.

Mandy was still. Mannequin still. She didn't even push the glider with her foot. "I can't imagine turning a little girl over to a stranger is in any way healthy or safe for a child." Her hands rested on her thighs. They were the unadorned hands of a hardworking woman—no rings, no polish. "Are you going to do a background check? Are you going to meet him first and see what kind of man he is? What if Erica didn't want this guy to raise her child?"

"Those are all valid points, but..." And here, the cold hard truth of his past arm-wrestled its way out. "Maybe I'm not the man to raise her. My dad wasn't around a whole lot when I was growing up. What do I know about being a dad? And what if I'm just like my father, never there when she wants me to be because I'm on a shift."

Mandy dragged her foot, slowing the glider to a stop. "You think you'd be a bad father because of your long hours and dedication to the job?"

He grunted.

"Hannah dotes on you." Mandy leaned forward. "You think you've had no training as a parent? Everything I learned about raising Olivia, I learned from the post office. And everything you need, you learned from being a firefighter."

"Do tell." Ben stretched his arm across the back of the glider.

Mandy shifted closer, snuggling closer still when his arm drew her near. "Raising kids utilizes the same skill sets you need to be a firefighter. You can't do everything at once, and kids don't need everything at once. So, you prioritize the biggest fire." She kicked the glider back into action. "After Olivia's diagnosis, I felt overwhelmed. But I made a list, including ideas of what I thought was best for Olivia and what Olivia wanted to do. And then I worked through the list. I made appointments with experts. We got answers. And then Olivia and I talked through everything and sought treatment. Her job was to stay positive. Mine was to make sure we were always moving forward."

She hadn't convinced Ben he'd be a good father. But one thing Mandy had said stuck in his mind. "You asked Olivia?"

"Absolutely. No matter your age, it's the not knowing that'll drive you crazy. It's like being stuck in slow-moving traffic with no idea how long it'll take to reach your destination. You feel helpless and then you feel overwhelmed and then…" Mandy leaned back, so caught up in the conversation she seemed unaware she rested her head on his shoulder again, unaware her smile fairly glowed. "And, well… You know what I mean."

He did.

Ben brushed a lock of hair behind her ear and let his palm rest on her cheek.

She dragged her foot, which sent the glider twisting recklessly, like a corkscrew rollercoaster in the dark.

Ben was losing his balance. He was free-falling. He rested his thumb on her lips to steady himself. Or maybe to reassure himself this wasn't a dream.

"Ben?" Mandy whispered against his thumb, sounding unsure.

Ben was suddenly very sure. That he wanted to get to know her better. That he wanted to take her to dinner. That he—

Ben closed the distance between them and pressed his lips to hers, letting the glider add to the momentum of the moment—the kiss, the discovery, the knowing that this was right. His hands moved to the curve of her neck and the strength of her shoulder. Her skin was soft. And she tasted of salsa, and something he couldn't quite name, not with the glider making his stomach do flip-flops and his brain short-circuited by the unexpected rightness of this kiss.

This kiss... It was a first. His first kiss on a glider. His first kiss in Harmony Valley. The first time he'd kissed Mandy. It felt the way a first kiss should be.

He drew back and stared into her dark eyes, into her unsmiling face. "Lori Caldwell who?"

Mandy flopped back in the corner of the glider as if she couldn't get away from him fast enough. She opened her mouth to speak, but Olivia beat her to it.

"I probably wasn't supposed to witness that." Olivia opened the slider screen door, and Mandy fled through it, sending the glider on a crazier ride than that kiss. "And Ben, note to self," Olivia continued. "The first words out of your mouth after kissing a girl shouldn't be the name of some other girl."

She shut the slider. And locked it.

Chapter Thirteen

Mandy should have known that Ben would be waiting for coffee at four twenty the next morning.

She should've known her heart would swoon and flutter over him in his uniform backlit by bakery lights with a soundtrack provided by chipper birds in the town square.

She still couldn't quite reconcile him kissing her. They'd just been talking. And yes, he was gorgeous, and it was a bit exciting to have all that gorgeousness directed her way, but no way had she been reading the signs of a kiss. He'd leaped over the friendship guidepost and kissed her.

Sad to say, it was an excellent kiss, too. The man did not disappoint in that department.

This morning, Mandy was determined to keep her distance. "In case I didn't say it yesterday, I'm not civil before my first cup of coffee." Especially when the man who'd kissed her so tenderly had pulled back afterward, gazed into her eyes and murmured another woman's name. "There will be no talking about last night."

"What will you do if instead of *us* talking, only I do?" He was in command mode, standing tall and looking her directly in the eye.

Was it fair that the man's intensity made her insides tango?

Mandy rejected him with a swipe of her hand. "If you talk about last night, I'll go to work without coffee." She bared her teeth in what felt nothing like a smile and watched Tracy scurry around the bakery getting it ready to open. If Mandy was lucky, she'd open early.

"I had an interesting night," Ben said, earning Mandy's glare. "I was part of a midnight kidnapping."

Mandy's glare morphed into openmouthed surprise. Even the serenading birds went silent.

She'd expected an apology-filled monologue, which she'd reject. What kind of an example would she be to Olivia if she forgave him such a transgression? Besides, forgiveness implied there'd be more kisses.

"This kidnapping..." he continued.

Mandy suspected Ben of a lot of things, including being passionate about his work and being annoyingly honest. But kidnapping? "I suppose nothing about you should surprise me."

He grinned at her as if that kiss last night meant something. "Midnight kidnapping is a term we use for a specific type of call."

Mandy didn't want to be curious. She sighed. "While I wait for my coffee, I have time for you to explain." She sat on the wrought iron chair and thrust her hands into her windbreaker pockets. "But only about the kidnapping."

He took a step closer, blue eyes magnetizing hers. "There are calls where we can't rouse a breathing patient. Protocol is to let the ambulance take them to the hospital. And sometimes when the patient wakes up in a place that isn't their home or their bed..."

"They feel as if they've been kidnapped." Mandy scraped her heel across the pavement, hating that he was being charming as he let her in on a secret of his profession. Hating that she liked that he was being charming and educating her on the firefighting life. Hating the sound of his deep, soothing voice and that he'd managed to take a few more steps in her direction.

Had he no shame?

Have I?

"It's a little disconcerting for everyone involved when something *unexpected* happens." Make no mistake. They weren't talking about 911 calls anymore. His grin didn't apologize. It found humor.

In their kiss!

Mandy slapped her hands on her thighs and stood.

An arm's reach away, Ben cleared his throat and toned down his grin from triumphant to merely charming. "Your sister looked good yesterday."

He was playing the family card? Two could play at that game. Mandy turned to face the bakery door. "Your dad's color was better yesterday, too."

"He was rested." Ben wasn't to be baited. He turned the same direction that she was, somehow coming closer to her. "And Dad did eucalyptus breathing treatments yesterday. Who knows what he'll try today?"

"Some of those natural therapies work wonders," Mandy said before thinking better of it. It was the natural therapies that had gotten her into trouble financially, because insurance didn't think they were justified.

They stood shoulder to shoulder, nearly touching.

"It's the little things that make a difference, isn't it?" Ben ran a hand through that dark as midnight hair. "Lori Caldwell tried to suck my face in the eighth grade. The experience scarred me." He didn't turn. He didn't look at her, but his fingers found hers. "And you, Mandy Zapien, are no Lori Caldwell."

Mandy's heart did the swoony, fluttery thing. "I would've bet money you couldn't earn my forgiveness."

"Honesty is a double-edged sword," he said simply.

Mandy was muted by the tender way Ben held her hand, the warmth of his shoulder and the mind-boggling possibility that Ben might want to kiss her again. That he might want to go out to dinner sometime or come over and watch a movie. His mother would gloat and Olivia would grin and—

Mandy put the brakes on the runaway relationship train.

Friends. Relationships began with friendship. Where had they left off last night? Er...before that kiss. "You'll give Hannah a good home." The way he worked a conversation to mend fences and diffuse tension, how could he not?

"About that..." Ben glanced down at her with the apologetic face she'd expected to see first thing this morning. "I mean, she's great. But after sleeping on it, I realized she'd be better off elsewhere."

The sharp pain of her mother's leaving sliced Mandy's insides. She extricated her hand from his and put some space between them. "You're giving her up?"

He flinched. "Try to understand. I don't have a nine-to-five job like you do. I'm gone twenty-four, forty-eight or seventy-two hours at a time."

Tracy opened the door. "Morning, peeps. Coffee's ready."

Mandy held up a hand that shook when Ben would have gone inside. "You make it sound as if there's never been a fireman who's a single parent. You make it sound as if Hannah is disposable, like a cat you take home from a shelter and then decide you don't want and give back." Mandy knew all too well how that felt.

"I didn't ask for her," he said carefully.

"But you don't even know..." Her voice was shaking now, too.

And Tracy was holding open the door, listening.

Mandy lowered the volume to a whisper. "You don't even know what kind of man her biological father is. I thought you wanted to do what was right."

"I said I wanted to do what was best for Hannah." Ben wasn't looking at Mandy. He couldn't see how disappointed she was in him.

Tracy backed into the bakery with a follow-me gesture. "Hot cinnamon twists. I know you want one."

Mandy did, but she also wanted to hear what Ben had to say. "We'll be there in a minute." She stood in Ben's way. "Don't break her heart." Her palm pressed over her own. "At least wait until you've met this guy. Last night you were open to the possibility of keeping her. What happened between then and now?" She gasped and took another step back. He'd complimented her on how she raised Olivia. "Were you thinking that we...that I... Did you kiss me because you were looking for someone to help you raise Hannah?"

"No." He grimaced. "I kissed you because I wanted to. I...I *needed* to."

Five minutes ago, his admission would've had Mandy floating on air. "What changed?"

"While I was talking to you last night, it became clear to me," he said slowly. "Here in town, I have a support system, but once I leave—"

"Leave? You just got here."

"I want to investigate fires." Ben pushed past her. "And I can't do that here." He tossed some bills on the counter. "You said something about cinnamon twists, Tracy."

"Fresh from the oven," she chirped, as cheerful as those darn birds in the town square. "How many?"

"One." Ben's face was a cold blank mask. "And black coffee. To go."

Mandy ordered a black coffee, too, and hurried out the door behind Ben without a cinnamon anything. "You're brushing Hannah off because you wanted to pursue a different career?" Mandy would never choose her dreams over the fate of a child. "What would Erica say?"

"She'd tell me to go for it because I'm not Hannah's father." He stared across the street to where he'd parked the fire truck over several spaces. "If I was Hannah's father, she would've put my name on that birth certificate. Erica was honest."

Disappointed at his attitude, Mandy hung on to her smile for dear life. "I can't be with someone who puts their needs over that of a child in their care."

"Understood." Ben handed her the bag with the cinnamon twist. "Try not to start any fires today."

"Why are you and my grandpas firefighters?" Hannah sat at the firehouse kitchen table. She had a box of new crayons and a firefighter-themed coloring book.

"Because we like rescuing people and keeping them safe, kind of like the way you like helping animals." Ben sat at the table with her with his laptop out. He was checking prices and availability of equipment and turnout gear with the hopes of suiting up several volunteer firemen someday. But his attention kept drifting to Mandy. To her passionate defense of Hannah. Her caring smile. The accusation in her eyes that he was a disappointment. The declaration that she couldn't be with him.

"Why don't you have a fire dog?" Hannah turned the coloring book so Ben could see the Dalmatian riding shotgun in a fire truck. "It says right here. Every fireman needs a dog."

"Before we can get a dog," Ben said, allowing a small smile, "we have to have the proper equipment to fight fires and stay safe. We need the essentials."

"A dog is...what you said." She grinned, looking a lot like her mother right before Erica used to say, "*I told you so.*" Hannah turned the book back around.

"A dog comes after helmets, turnout gear and oxygen masks." He clicked on the next website. "After trucks and hoses and radios."

Hannah pushed her rectangular glasses up her nose and glanced around. "You've got all that."

"We're adding firefighters. They'll need gear, too, including radios and pagers." Shoot. He hadn't thought of pagers. He added them to his list.

Hannah colored the fire truck green with broad strokes that went far over the line. "There's more to being a fireman than helping people."

"You're right. You have to buy stuff, manage inventory, screen applications..." Shoot. He needed to print some applications for the meeting tonight.

"No," Hannah said in her ultrapatient voice. "I mean, you do more than rescue people. The lady at the bakery said she feels safer after you 'spected her. And a man in front of the restaurant said the sun was shining because you'd put out a fire." She looked up at him with Libby-blue eyes.

Ben's heart clenched. How could he deny she was his?

"What did that man mean?"

Ben needed more than a moment to compose himself.

By that time, Hannah was back to coloring.

"It means we were lucky." Ben was lucky to have spent this time with her. He took her small hand in his. "Han, do you ever think about John Smith? Your father, I mean. You won't see us...me as often when you go live with him."

"I think John Smith should come live here. That way I won't have to move again. Granny Vanessa just learned how to make macaroni and cheese the right way. And Grandpa Keith just learned how to read Goodnight Moon."

"And me?" He hardly dared ask. "What did I learn how to do?"

Her voice dropped to a whisper. "You learned how to be the best godfather ever."

"I haven't seen that raccoon of yours." Utley sat in a webbed folding chair on the post office's loading dock. His shirt today was neon yellow with hula girls.

"Good riddance." Mandy balanced on an old wood ladder, painting the wall where the fire had been, wishing she could just as easily paint over Ben's objections to keep Hannah.

The plumber had come and gone. The van filled with supplies from the mail hub in Santa Rosa had come and gone. The mail truck with the day's mail had come and gone. A trend, this coming and going from her life. Take Ben, for example.

Don't think of Ben.

Unfortunately, that was all she was thinking about.

"He'll be back." Utley turned his face to the sun. "Pests always come back."

It took Mandy a moment to realize Utley wasn't talking about Ben.

"Shh," she said. "Riley might be listening and thinking we want him back. Don't jinx us."

"We're already jinxed." Olivia shoved mail into post office boxes.

"We? Us? That's the first time you've included me." Utley sounded miffed.

A ruckus down the road drew their attention. Hannah rode her pink bike toward them, towing a rattling, red wagon behind her.

"Hey," Utley said when she rode into the driveway and stopped. "Who are you?"

"I'm Hannah Thompson." She blinked at him from behind her serious glasses. "And I'm going to be a veterinarian." Her eyebrows pinched. "Or a librarian. I love animals and books."

"Hey, Hannah." Olivia waved. "I'll see you this afternoon."

"Okay." Hannah tucked her flyaway hair behind her ears.

Hannah was adorable. How could Ben even think about giving her up? And for what? A job?

Mandy wanted to shake some sense into him.

Utley's jaw worked as he tried to stay serious. "Well, Hannah Thompson, future vet and bookworm, what can we do for you?"

Hannah set her kickstand and got off her bike. "Grandpa Keith told Granny Vanessa that you had a raccoon problem, and then Ben told Grandpa Keith that Mandy should shoot the raccoon." She turned spectacled eyes their way, taking them in. "I'm glad you don't have guns out. I was worried you might shoot the raccoon before I could come to the rescue." She wrestled the cage from the wagon to the ground with a clatter and then surveyed the grounds. "Where did you see the critter last?"

"Riley loved the hedges." Mandy set the brush down on top of the paint can. "You aren't going to try to trap him."

"It won't hurt." Hannah dragged the wire cage across the asphalt. The sound made the red-winged blackbirds in the nearby trees take flight. "I got this from Great-Grandpa Felix. I'm good at catching animals."

"He might have moved on." Olivia shut and locked the mailboxes. "We haven't seen him."

"Are you sure Riley wasn't a girl?" Hannah stopped mere feet from Riley's hedge. Her face was red from exertion. "If she was a girl, she could have gone somewhere to have kittens." Hannah shaded her eyes and looked around. "There's a house back there. Does anyone live there?"

"No." Mandy said, gathering her wallet and phone for the mail run.

"That's where I'll look." Hannah took some marshmallows from her pink shoe bag and put them in the trap. "Empty houses are where wild animals go."

"She's got a point," Utley said. "Someone should tear that house down before that raccoon eats wires over there and burns the place."

"Riley, the arsonist." Olivia began putting things away and closing the rolling window above the customer service desk because Mandy had decided it didn't make sense to be open for business while she delivered mail.

"Raccoons don't start fires," Hannah said staunchly.

"I was joking." Olivia locked the window.

"Let's not joke about fire." Mandy returned to the mail room and folded the ladder, storing it against the wall. She breathed a sigh of relief. Organization was everything. Ben couldn't fault the post office now.

Don't think about Ben.

"We're closing up, Utley," Mandy said.

The old man heaved himself up and moved slowly toward the stairs. "I was needing a smoke anyway."

Mandy folded his chair and put it inside by the ladder.

Hannah shoved her way into the bushes, dragging the cage behind her.

"Are you going to the volunteer fire department meeting tonight?" Olivia examined her nails before looking up at Mandy. "You should go and show Ben that kiss meant nothing."

Mandy was afraid that kiss meant everything.

"I'm not going." Mandy didn't want to have a discussion about Ben, especially not in front of Hannah. "Shouldn't you call Hannah's grandmother and make sure she knows where she is?"

"Why?" Olivia retrieved her purse from its hook by the office door.

"Because it's the adult thing to do."

"Oh, is shirking your civic duty adult, as well?" Olivia sauntered toward the stairs and said in a put-upon voice, "Hannah, does your granny know where you are?"

The new fire alarms shrieked. Outside, the bell clanged.

Mandy ran for the extinguisher. And then the sprinklers came on.

Utley and Olivia managed to make it to the parking lot, dry as toast.

Mandy stood in the middle of the mail room, drenched and searching for a fire.

In the distance, the whine of a fire truck's siren built.

Hannah came around the corner from where Riley used to hang out, pushed her glasses up her nose and said, "*Sorry*."

"Turn it off," Mandy cried, racing for the steps, bolting down them and around the corner. "Whatever you did, we need to turn it off." Quickly, before Ben showed up.

Mandy was still pushing buttons and turning valves every which way on the fire control panel when the fire truck pulled into the parking lot, lights and sirens blazing.

Ben took in Mandy's position by the box, and her dripping state with a shake of his head. "Looks like faulty wiring to me."

"Faulty? But..." Mandy bit back an accusation toward Hannah. She wasn't sure Hannah had tripped anything, and she knew firsthand how it felt to be accused of something you didn't do. Admitting defeat, Mandy came out from behind the bushes. "Can you fix it?"

"Let me see." Ben leaned in, his long arms reaching the control panel without him having to wade into the shrubbery. A moment later, the water stopped and the alarms ceased. He went over to Hannah and knelt in front of her. "Han, I've been searching for you everywhere. You need to tell Granny Vanessa where you're going."

Hannah made a huffing noise, hands on her slim hips. "I told her this morning. There were baby frogs to be relocated. Iggy needed to be fed. And a raccoon saved."

"She thought you meant in the backyard."

"Ben," Hannah said in a voice that spoke of patience hard-won. "The only living thing in our backyard is a cricket."

Mandy hurried to the mail room, waving to Keith, who was on the phone, presumably with his wife. She stopped at the top of the stairs to wring out her shirt and her hair.

"Han, we talked about this," Ben said. "No disappearing."

"I told her." Hannah sounded like she was going to cry.

The post office was flooded. Mandy's hopes were crushed. All that hard work...

She turned away, unable to face it. Olivia was taking pictures with her cell phone and Utley had walked to the street to have a smoke.

"Okay, listen," Ben said to Hannah. "I have a department radio. It's like a cell phone, see?" He held it out to the girl.

"It's not like a cell phone." Hannah's chin jutted mutinously. "It's big and bulky."

Ben ignored her complaint and bent over to show her. "Push this button to talk." He pressed a button on the side and spoke into the radio. "Hello, Grandpa Keith. I found Hannah."

"Copy that," came a staticky reply.

Hannah's eyes widened.

"You can listen to Grandpa and I talk to each other." He handed her the radio. "All I ask is that you call me on that and tell me where you are."

"Like...all the time?"

He nodded. "Every time you ride to a new place, peanut."

Hannah cradled the radio in two hands. "Mom used to have a radio like this."

Ben swung Hannah into his arms. His gaze met Mandy's. "And now you have one, too."

How could he give that little girl up without a fight? Mandy almost shed a tear.

But Mandy had no time for a breakdown. Luckily, they'd closed up before the sprinklers came on. Her supplies were saved. The mail was either in post office boxes or the Jeep. But her laptop and the computer they used at the service window were most likely ruined. It was another setback she didn't need.

"Olivia, can you mop?"

"You're going to need more than a mop. And I can't help you. My shift with Hannah starts in twenty minutes."

Mandy gritted her teeth. She knew better than to rely on anyone.

There had to be a silver lining here somewhere.

Or...this was rock bottom.

She was wrong.

The fire alarm went off again.

Chapter Fourteen

"I want to go down by the river." Hannah skipped ahead of Olivia with blond ponytails that bounced on the shoulders of her pink T-shirt.

It was Olivia's first day as the girl's babysitter. She'd painted teddy bears on her fingernails in honor of the occasion. Not that Hannah had appreciated her art. She'd told Olivia they needed to get out of the house so Granny Vanessa could nap. And then she'd dragged her outside into the summer heat.

Olivia hadn't had a chance to tell Vanessa about Ben's *faux pas* last night with Mandy. She didn't want to talk about Ben and Mandy kissing in front of The Youngster. Said child might have lost Olivia her post office job, which wasn't much of a loss. After the fire alarm and sprinklers went off a second time, Ben had declared the building unsafe for operation. He'd gotten on the phone and tried to talk to Mandy's boss. Meanwhile, Mandy got on the phone and tried to get Perry the Electrician to return.

Hannah continued skipping. She had blond ponytails that shouldn't be bouncing because Hannah wasn't a bouncy girl. She bounced anyway.

"We can go to the river," Olivia promised. "But first I want to check out the winery."

Hannah stopped skipping and turned around. "What's a winery?"

"A place where they make wine." A place where the dude worked.

Someone had bought stamps earlier today and she recognized the logo on the front of their shirt. It was the same as the one on the dude's. Olivia wanted a second chance with the dude. And Hannah was the perfect excuse to wander onto winery property without looking like a lovesick teenager.

"Are there animals at this place?"

With Olivia's luck, no. "Let's go see."

"Okay." Hannah skipped ahead, turning toward the town square.

"Hey, this way is quicker." Olivia pointed to the alley behind El Rosal.

"I have to make my rounds." The little girl kept skipping.

It was the first inkling Olivia had that she might not be in charge.

They checked on a family of doves. They pet obese cats and friendly dogs. They sat on a rock in a field in silence waiting to see what kind of creatures might show themselves. They wound their way through the town, never in a straight line, until Olivia smiled with grim determination and thought about the benefits of working for the post office. It seemed to be beating babysitting. The nail polish bottles in her purse rattled in agreement.

Finally, their path came close to the winery, and Olivia charged down the gravel driveway toward her man.

"Oh, it's a farm," Hannah said, skipping past her, a marathon runner in training. "A barn and a house. And look. Chickens."

There was a big red barn, and a two-story white house with dormer windows. And sadly, chickens. A few people sat on the patio drinking wine. Olivia felt sophisticated just watching them being sophisticated.

Hannah fell to her knees on the dirt near a big brown chicken and began to make clucking noises. The chicken strutted closer, circling Hannah as if taking her measure.

"Hey, mail girl!" The dude had come out of the house. He waved at her. He was still tall, still cute and—*bonus!*—had a clean shirt on. "What are you doing here?"

Olivia's legs felt as if she'd been dancing all night. She was afraid she might reach the dude and collapse at his feet. "I'm babysitting." *Lame! Lame! Say something else.* "And you have chickens." *Gah. That was worse!*

Crossing the parking lot toward her, the dude chuckled as if he found Olivia both charming and amusing, which made Olivia's legs stop shaking so much. "I have some packs of chicken feed for the tourists." He tossed her a small burlap bag with a drawstring.

Hannah's brown chicken ran toward Olivia, pecking the ground around her feet, closer and closer until Olivia thought she might peck her pink toenails.

"Olivia," Hannah said in an aggravated voice. "Feed her!"

Olivia managed to open the bag and shake some feed on the ground, backing away and smiling the way Mandy did when she wasn't happy but didn't want anyone to know. How sad was it that Mandy had wanted to be an astronomer and ended up working at the post office? How sad was it that the dude was turning back to the guests on the patio?

The bag was empty. The chicken moved closer to the patio with the wine drinkers. The dude went back inside the farmhouse.

"Let's go," Hannah said, dragging Olivia by the hand. "There are other animals that need me."

Mission accomplished. Olivia went willingly.

"What's wrong with you?" Hannah tugged harder.

"I'm going to marry that man," Olivia said dreamily.

"You are?" Hannah slowed down, apparently a bit of a romantic. "What's his name?"

"I have no idea."

The country duet blaring on the radio was old-school. They crooned about love and twanged about their problems and blamed each other for their homely looking kids. Mandy could almost laugh.

"We thought you could use some help."

Standing in a large puddle and feeling as if she was only pushing water around with her mop, Mandy walked out of her office to see who could possibly want to help clean up the fire-alarm flood at the post office. Olivia had taken off, claiming she had to babysit. Ben had left, but not before notifying Mandy's supervisor that she'd failed a fire inspection.

It was Keith. He stood in the parking lot at the edge of the loading dock in his blue navy fire uniform. Only his head and shoulders were visible at the floor level. His face was slightly flushed, and his breathing was a little uneven.

There was more than bad fish impacting his health. She hoped those meds he received would help him breathe easier.

"I'm afraid this is a lost cause." Mandy didn't want to admit it out loud, but there it was. The mail was safe, but the rest...

This was an epic fail. Other failures, other losses, came tumbling back.

She'd been unable to make her mother love her. She'd been unable to help Grandma beat cancer. She'd been unable to talk sense into Grandpa about whom he left the house to. And now? This. She'd done nothing wonderful here.

"I wasn't sure how bad the damage was, so we brought a bit of everything and everyone." Ben's mother appeared at the stairs holding an armful of towels.

Mandy walked into the middle of the mail room, her feet making a splash with every step. "That might not be enough."

Agnes came around the post office corner. "I brought a clothesline. You'd be amazed at how quickly papers dry when they hang from a clothespin. Had a roof leak once. Dripped all over my tax return."

Mildred sat on her walker behind Agnes. "And I brought chocolate chip cookies. Chocolate makes everything better."

"Which is why I brought a thermos of hot chocolate," Rose said, completing the presence of the town councilwomen.

Eunice appeared behind them with another armload of towels. "If I would've known we were making an entrance, I would've prepared a witty remark."

Others reported in. People Mandy barely knew or had only met once on her route.

"You're here to help me?" Touched, Mandy's eyes welled with tears.

"It's what we do in Harmony Valley," Agnes said. "We pull together."

"If you don't mind—" Keith cleared his throat "—I'll organize the troops."

"By all means," Mandy said.

It seemed like a band of elves had descended upon the post office. A clothesline was hung in her office and papers pinned to it. Vanessa submerged Mandy's laptop in a large plastic tub filled with rice, claiming it worked with cell phones and was worth a try. Counters were dried. Floors, too. Her listing office chair was thrown in the dumpster. Another appeared in its place, donated by Eunice, who claimed to never sit at a desk. Every drawer and every cupboard was opened and inspected for water damage.

Hours later, Mandy thanked them all with a hug. They'd forever be her angels.

Finally, the only ones left were Keith and Vanessa. The three of them lugged five-gallon construction buckets filled with wet towels to the parking lot.

"I talked to your supervisor," Keith said in a hitching voice. He leaned on the side of the truck while Mandy and Vanessa dumped wet towels in the bed. "He said it might take time for the place to be rewired, but he was relieved to hear it wasn't as bad as some people feared." He exchanged a glance with his wife and then checked his pager.

"Stop." Vanessa gently swatted his hand away from the device. "Firemen always look at their pagers when they want to leave."

Mandy frowned. Hadn't Ben snuck a look at his pager when he was with her?

"Correction." Keith laid his hand on his wife's shoulder and then ran his palm down her arm to cup her elbow, just as Ben had done with Mandy. "We check our pagers before important time. It's a karma thing. You check your pager, and because you did, it won't go off during the important stuff."

A likely story.

Vanessa seemed to buy it. She kissed her husband's cheek.

Mandy hefted the last of the towels from her construction bucket into the back of Keith's pickup, mumbling, "That sounds like the tale of someone's lucky shorts."

"Did you…?" Vanessa dropped her wet towels back in her bucket. "Did my son tell you about his lucky shorts? He never tells anyone about that."

"Don't tell me it's true." Mandy dumped the excess water on the shrubs lining the parking lot. "I mean, that Ben's dirty shorts turned him into an all-star pitcher."

"That's all he told you?" Vanessa was staring at Mandy like a policeman stares at a suspected felon. "He didn't say anything about his shorts and...*us*?"

"No."

"Do you mind...?" Vanessa appeared torn. "I think you could be important to him. Ben hasn't shown any interest in anyone in so long. Could we tell you more of the story?"

Mandy began to protest. What good would Vanessa's tale do? Ben didn't see the world the way she did.

"It's not a long story. But it might help you understand our son." Keith reached for Vanessa's hand. "I was a gung-ho fireman in my youth. Worked every shift I could as a fireman and an EMT."

Mandy was a reluctant audience, fully expecting to be told too much information at any moment.

"Keith picked up extra shifts so I could stay home with the boys," Vanessa said proudly. "We have two sons. Now, Ben. He's our oldest. He's always been taller than average, and he had so many growth spurts he wasn't always the most coordinated player on the field."

"He was horrible at sports," Keith said gruffly. "It was torture to watch him play."

Vanessa tsked. "He got better."

"With his lucky shorts?" Mandy ventured a guess.

"Exactly." Vanessa nodded. "But our younger son, Mike, was a natural athlete. For a while, there was talk about him earning a college scholarship in baseball. Imagine how thrilled we were. College is so expensive."

"And he could have gone on to the pros. So one year I took time off to take Mike to travel ball tournaments and exhibitions." Keith closed the tailgate with a resounding bang. Instead of turning, he held on to the metal and kept his back to the women.

"While they were away, Ben's coordination fell in sync with his size," Vanessa said in hushed tones, as if imparting a much-guarded family secret. "Keith never saw him pitch. Ben was devastated."

Poor Ben.

"Sometimes you don't realize you're favoring one child over another until it's too late." Keith gave Mandy a sad smile. "Come on, Vanessa. We've taken up enough of this young lady's time." He dug his keys from his pocket, got in the truck, and let the two women have a moment.

"I know Ben loves his father," Vanessa said quietly. "But because of the choices we made, Ben believes firemen can't be good dads. He's got fire in his blood, and he's determined to stay single until he retires...or the right woman comes along to prove him wrong."

Vanessa looked at Mandy as if she believed she was that woman.

Chapter Fifteen

Ben expected men to show up at the first volunteer firefighter session.

The crowd wore perfume.

Ben bet Keith was to blame. His father claimed he wasn't feeling well enough to attend. More likely he was too chicken to face the music of six females staring at Ben's every move. There were five elderly women in the crowd, including one with a walker. A redhead about the same age as Mandy sat in the front row, checking out Ben's...well, Ben's everything.

He was surprised Mandy hadn't shown up.

She'd be an asset in this crowd. Although she was probably busy cleaning up the post office. Ben hadn't been able to help her. He had too much of his father's paperwork to get caught up on.

He'd set out folding chairs for the meeting in the common room and had made twenty copies of the application. Because of the arguments he'd had with Mandy—*two in one day*—he'd been looking forward to this. His stress level needed this.

He couldn't just call off the meeting, not with the possibility of at least one recruit. He tried to assess the redhead's arm strength without seeming to check her out.

She smiled, clearly thinking he was checking her out.

Ben looked away and cleared his throat. "Is everyone here for the volunteer firefighter program?"

As one, the women nodded.

"I'm going to read a list of requirements." Ben held up a sheet of paper and read the first requirement. "At least eighteen years of age."

The elderly ladies giggled, one of which was Eunice.

The redhead nodded. "I'm legal." She'd worn a black skirt, white blouse and heels to a firefighter meeting?

Spirits sinking, Ben read, "Must hold a valid California driver's license."

The lady in the walker slouched.

Ben read, "Must be able to lift fifty pounds."

"Just once?" the redhead in the front row asked, a wrinkle in her otherwise smooth brow.

"It's not a one-time test." He tried not to look at the only woman under the age of forty in the room. "Some of our equipment can weigh a lot. The SCBA equipment…" At their blank looks, he translated, "The self-contained breathing apparatus, which is the oxygen tank and mask. That alone weighs nearly fifty pounds."

The redhead stared at a spot on the back wall.

A miniature woman with very short gray hair raised her hand. "Actually, three of us are here representing the town council." She introduced herself as Agnes, the woman with the walker as Mildred and a willowy woman with her white hair in a bun as Rose. "We won't be trying out for one of your firefighter positions."

That was a relief.

"And we had time to kill before bingo," added Mildred. With her round curls, round face and round glasses, she had a striking resemblance to Mrs. Claus. "So Eunice and Carol had to come along."

That explained why five elderly women had shown up.

The redhead took advantage of the interruption in Ben's program. "I might not be cut out to be a volunteer firefighter, but I can provide refreshments." She didn't bat her eyes like Eunice, but she worked them up and down his uniform. "Say eight o'clock tonight at El Rosal's bar?"

Ben's face felt hot.

"I didn't hear what she said." Mildred raised her voice. "What did you say, dear?"

"She asked him out," Rose shouted.

"And what did he say?" Mildred shouted back.

"He said thanks, but no thanks." Ben softened his rejection with a smile. "I'm on duty." For the first time since coming to Harmony Valley, he was glad he was working 24/7.

"Some other time." The redhead left with a clack of heels, leaving the elderly contingent twittering in her wake.

It was official. This was a disaster.

"You poor dear." Agnes stood. "Did no one tell you that Emma Jackson and Becca Harris went into labor earlier today? Half the town and nearly everyone of firefighting age is at the hospital in Santa Rosa."

"Best reschedule." Rose nodded her head.

"Great advice." Ben was relieved he might have a volunteer program after all.

"We really need to be going." Mildred banged her walker into place. "We can't be late for bingo."

The elderly women filed out. Ben began folding chairs and planning the next meeting. He'd need to do some one-on-one recruiting this time. Ask around. Network. The town council seemed to be plugged in.

Mandy walked up the driveway. She wore blue jeans and a green tank top that showed the wiry definition of her slender arms.

Ben had never been so happy to see a muscular woman in his life.

"Am I early?" She lingered at the garage door, taking in the folded chairs. "Your dad said to come at seven thirty."

If his father wasn't dead, Ben was going to make sure he died a slow, unpleasant death. "You don't have to volunteer." But he sure needed her.

"I do." She sighed. "Agnes called me just now. Olivia dared me to show, kind of like you did." Her gaze bounced off his. "And I'm kind of a sucker for taking on responsibilities when I already have my plate full."

"I appreciate that, especially given the events and discussions of the past twenty-four hours."

"I can get past the kiss. And I can get past you not helping me clean up after the sprinklers went off." She crossed her arms over her chest and flashed her secret weapon, that smile. "But it's going to be tough to overlook you telling my boss that the post office was unsafe. He wants to shut it down. Permanently. It took your dad calling him and me begging him for thirty minutes to convince him we can go on."

"It's just the mail. Your life is more important than any bill someone is expecting in their mailbox. Which, I might add, would burn if you don't upgrade all the electrical in that building."

"You had no right. Given time, we would have passed." Her voice. So calm. She was trying hard not to break any eggs.

"I had every right. It's my job to protect people. You, Olivia, Utley, even Hannah hangs out there. I can't let any of you get hurt."

"We won't get hurt," Mandy said, looking away. "We're moving processing and sorting to a substation in Cloverdale until the issue is resolved."

"That's fantastic." She wasn't smiling. Why wasn't she smiling? "What's the big deal?"

"The big deal is that I've been demoted and bumped down a pay grade until my boss decides it's worth it to reopen here. If he decides to reopen here." She set her chin stubbornly. "You had no right."

"I had every right." He grabbed her shoulders. "Hannah's mother died in a fire that started because of faulty wiring. It was a building being renovated. An old warehouse they were converting into lofts. The owner fought every inspection with the same argument you're making—it's good enough. They took the city to court twice because they wanted to preserve the original plastered walls. The company in charge of the renovation had a good track record. But the owner was impatient, stubborn. And for what? A unique feature in their sales brochure?" He shook his head. "It burned to the ground, killing two firefighters. So if you think fire safety can be shrugged away... If you think I've inconvenienced you, think about Hannah and what she lost."

He pulled her closer. "Think about what would happen to Olivia if you were trapped inside that precious post office of yours. Think about those left behind."

Mandy held on to his shirt, gripping the fire-resistant material. "You're right. It's just... I can't afford the pay cut. I can't afford to move out of that house." She shuddered. "I can't afford the truck to break down. I can't afford to help Olivia pay for cosmetology school. And at this rate, at my interest, I'll be paying Olivia's medical bills until she's thirty."

"Your life sucks." Ben held Mandy away from him so he could look at her face and make sure she wasn't crying. "But you can't complain, because my life isn't so great either at the moment. Want to fill out an application?"

She nodded.

A sleek Tesla parked in front of the firehouse while Mandy was filling out paperwork.

"If you're here for the volunteer firefighter meeting," Ben said to the newcomer, hoping this was one of the dot-com millionaires who lived in town, "come on in."

"I'm not here for the meeting." The newcomer was tall, blond and wore a suit. Charcoal gray. Red patterned tie. A haircut so crisp it looked as if he'd just walked out of the barbershop. The shine on his black leather shoes matched the shine on his black Tesla. He removed his fancy sunglasses, which had probably cost more than Ben's first car. "At least, I'm not here for that meeting. I'm John Smith."

The air seemed too thick to breathe. The station lights too bright. This was John Smith? Erica's long-lost boyfriend? Hannah's dad?

So much for Ben's theory that the guy was a deadbeat and a loser.

He could still be a disappointment.

Ben hoped for Hannah's sake he wasn't.

"I'm looking for Ben Libby. Something about a bequeath from Erica Thompson's estate?" John didn't stop walking until he was within handshaking distance.

Ben wiped his suddenly sweaty palms on his pant leg before offering his hand. "I'm Ben." He introduced Mandy, who sat behind him filling out her paperwork.

She put her pen down and watched the two men.

"So... Erica." John assessed the station with a sharp, blue-eyed glance. "I was very sorry to hear about her passing."

Ben wanted to ask how sorry. Heartbroken-love-of-his-life sorry? Two-ships-that-passed-in-the-night sorry? Hoping-to-get-some-dough sorry?

Mandy beat him to the interrogation punch. "How did you two meet?"

"At Lake Merritt." John had a million-dollar snow-white smile. "My niece was having a birthday party. Erica brought someone else's kid. I guess they couldn't get off their shift. She was something. A force, you know?"

Ben nodded. He knew.

What wasn't clear was what she'd seen in John.

Hannah's father gave a wry half laugh. "Erica told me my tie clip could feed a family on the south side of Oakland for a month."

"You wore a tie to a kid's birthday party?" Mandy softened her question with a half smile, as if she and John shared a joke. "On a weekend?"

Ben was grateful one of them could still smile.

"I came from a breakfast meeting." He widened his stance and lowered his voice, going into presentation mode, still flashing all those pearly whites. "I'm in international finance. In my line of work, it pays to look like I'm used to handling large sums of money, no matter what day it is."

Ben cleared his throat. "Did you date Erica long? I only ask because...I've known her for more than a decade and—"

"She didn't mention me." John's smile lowered in wattage. Fewer teeth. More human. "We dated about a year. On and off. Mostly off." He rubbed his forehead, toning his delivery down even further. "Did I leave something at her place? It can't be all that important after all these years." He fingered his tie clip.

Ben fought back a shouting swell of anger. Anger at Erica for not telling John she was pregnant. Anger at John for disappearing from Erica's life. Anger at himself because he was far from convinced that John was good father material. "Erica had a daughter. She's seven. And..." The anger clogged his throat. "...y our name is on the birth certificate."

John dropped a step back. "And you want money from me. The girl needs child support?"

"No." Fury fisted Ben's hands, hardened his voice. "She needs her father."

John's eyes narrowed. "I should explain why Erica and I didn't work out."

"Please do," Ben said, body still coiled to punch something...someone.

Mandy came to stand next to him. She touched his clenched fingers, and a miracle occurred. They loosened. Hers slipped between them.

John noticed. He rolled his shoulders and attempted a smile. "Look. I spend three weeks of every month out of the country. My job consumes me." The smile came back full force, attempting to sell his perfectness. "It has to. If I lose focus, I lose my clients' money, which means corporate layoffs, reduced advertising budgets, cross-business downturns at economy-impacting levels." He paused to let his importance sink in. "I live and breathe my work. If I had a wife or kids, I couldn't do what I do."

Truth cut at Ben's insides with a poisonous double edge. With a few minor tweaks, John's reasons for staying single and not taking on the role of Hannah's dad sounded a lot like Ben's reasons for staying single and not taking on the role of Hannah's dad. Didn't make Ben like him any better.

John backed toward his car. "I'm sorry. But I'm not your guy."

Mandy squeezed Ben's hand. She was probably ecstatic that John was rejecting Hannah.

"She looks like you," Ben blurted. "Blond hair. Blue eyes. Tall for her age." He didn't say she had a heart, whereas John didn't seem to.

A flash of white teeth. A pat to his smooth blond hair. And John shook his head. "I can't accept she's mine based on an entry on her birth certificate. You understand."

Oh, Ben understood, all right. He understood that John was a selfish egotistical fool. "You'll take a DNA test. We already sent Hannah's in. If they don't match, you're off the hook." He was letting John off easy. "In the meantime, maybe you should think about what being a dad means to a little girl who's lost her mother."

John stopped smiling and spun away.

Chapter Sixteen

"Can you believe that guy?" Ben was still worked up about John's appearance twenty minutes after the guy left. He paced the fire station. "He asked about money! And he said he can't be Hannah's dad because he's too busy making money!"

"I heard." Mandy had been patiently listening to Ben's tirade, waiting for him to come out and say John was unacceptable, and that he'd battle to keep Hannah. Not that John seemed willing to put up much of a fight.

"John acted like he influenced the rise and fall of foreign countries." Ben rounded the fire engine and stomped the length on the other side. "He acted like that was more important than Hannah. Can you believe it?"

Ben didn't expect her to answer. He paced. He ranted. He blew off more steam.

Mandy sat on the front bumper of the fire truck, willing to give him five more minutes of support before she left.

Ben came around from the side, and she knew the moment she saw his face that the hard edge of truth had finally hit him. The rage was gone. He looked drained.

"Tell me he's not me." Ben sank onto the bumper next to her.

"He might be a little you." A gentle tease encased in truth.

Ben dropped his head into his hands and groaned.

"He's dedicated to his career. He's a perfectionist." She rubbed Ben's back. "And he's scared of being a dad."

Ben groaned again. But he didn't argue. "Thank you for staying." He lifted his head and his tortured gaze.

"I think you'll find staying is harder than leaving." She hadn't enjoyed bearing witness to the exchange. "But I couldn't leave. You promised me a pager."

Ben blinked. Focused on her face. Shook his head. "I'm not changing my mind about Hannah, so it's back to business."

"Yes." She removed her hand from his back. "I won't lie. I was hopeful you'd change your mind, for Hannah's sake. And maybe a little for my own. I can't be with someone who won't fight for a child in their care because..." She almost lost her nerve. "Because that would mean he wouldn't fight for me."

They stood, neither willing to compromise.

And inside, Mandy's heart seemed to be breaking.

"It is what it is," Ben said in a defeated voice. He led her to the common area and rummaged in a cupboard until he found a pager and a charger. "On a positive note, you didn't break any eggs when you broke up with me."

Oh, eggs had cracked. She just wasn't going to tell him. "For the record, there was no us to break. It was just a kiss."

"Me and Mr. Moon." He held her gaze too long. "We beg to differ."

Olivia sat outside Giordano's waiting for Mandy's lunch order when *he* appeared at the corner.

He. The dude.

He walked with a long, easy stride. He wore blue jeans and another stained T-shirt with the winery's logo on it. And he looked...dreamy.

Olivia pretended to check her cell phone, watching the dude walk toward her from the corner of her eye.

"Hey, mail girl."

He's talking to me?

Don't blow it. Don't blow it. Don't blow it.

Olivia's insides turned as she did. "Hi." *My name's Olivia. What's yours?* She tried to smile even though she couldn't get the words out.

"I'm here to pick up lunch for the office." He flashed her a wide grin. "I'm Ryan." He offered to shake her hand as she introduced herself. His hand swallowed hers. "Nice seeing you again, mail girl."

She had a nickname. Olivia wanted to squeal. Unless...he'd forgotten her name already. "Hope your lunch is ready."

Hope your lunch is ready?

She was such a dork.

The restaurant door behind her closed. Olivia wanted to run away. She stayed put.

"Where's that sister of yours?" Utley had snuck up on her from the other end of the street. He put a sandaled foot in the gutter and leaned forward on his other foot.

"Mandy should be here any minute. She's driving up from Cloverdale with the mail." Giordano's was having a lunch special, and Olivia had offered to treat Mandy to lunch with her paycheck. Mandy was heartbroken over Ben, not that she'd admit it. And after everything her sister had done for her, Olivia wanted to make Mandy feel loved.

"The post office never got shut down when I worked there." Utley sounded like he needed to gargle.

Olivia cleared her throat and stared at her phone. Utley was like the Grumpster. He intimidated her. She glanced up.

He was still standing there.

"Okay, bye," Olivia said. She was getting a high rating on the *lame-o* scale today. She looked back down at her phone.

Thankfully, Utley shuffled off.

The door opened again. Olivia turned to say goodbye to Ryan.

He sat down next to her.

Next. To. Me.

In a blink, Olivia had a wedding dress picked out. Baby names. Christmas traditions. And...and everything.

"I added a pizza to my order." Ryan rubbed his hands on his jeans. "They don't always have pizza."

Olivia stared at him with her mouth open. He'd sat next to her. He wanted to talk. She was speechless. Ryan was gazing across Main Street at Martin's Bakery. She was staring at his long dark hair and wondering what it would feel like if she touched it.

Say something. Say anything!

"Your hair is longer than mine." *Not that.* Olivia slumped, but there was nothing to slump behind.

Ryan laughed.

Olivia swiveled around to look at him to see what joke she'd missed.

His brown eyes sparkled like ice-cold root beer. "Every August we winemakers grow our hair long."

She forgot about being lame. "You're a winemaker?"

He bumped her shoulder the way Mandy sometimes bumped her shoulder. "Don't sound so disappointed, mail girl."

"I'm not disappointed, I..." She had to get a grip. "Okay, I'm disappointed. There's no one my age around here. I thought you were in college."

He drew back and studied her. "Are you in college?"

"No." She felt her cheeks heat and hoped she didn't look like a tomato. "I'm going to cosmetology school soon." Just as soon as she turned eighteen and collected her inheritance from the Grumpster.

"Did you just graduate high school? In June?"

She nodded. "I didn't walk. I took the test." She rushed on. "I missed a lot of school because..." *Don't tell him!*

But Ryan knew. He took in her short hair and slightly puffy cheeks. "*Oh.*" His grin slipped just enough for her to notice. "You're okay now, though."

"Yes," she said firmly, with a smile, like Mandy always did.

"My mom has had cancer three times. Each time was harder than the last." The way Ryan said it, he didn't believe she'd survive a fourth round.

A shiver ran up Olivia's spine. "I'm sorry," she choked out, standing because the door to Giordano's had opened and the woman who'd taken her order was looking at her, bag in hand. "I'm sorry," she said again.

But she wasn't only sorry that his mother was sick. Her sentiment applied to herself as well.

Because no matter what Dr. Abadie and Mandy said, Olivia was going to die from cancer.

Cancer didn't strike once. It came again and again.

Until you were dead.

"Food." Mandy collapsed into a kitchen chair. "Thanks for the treat. I don't have time to do more than nibble."

"You just got here." The sandwich wrapper from Olivia's lunch was crumpled on top of the tile-topped kitchen table next to a wadded napkin and a soda can. The teen was bent over the table painting white skulls and crossbones on her black nails.

"Now that I'm just a mail carrier, I have to report in before lunch, after lunch, at break and when I'm done delivering the mail."

"Did they put a GPS tracker on you, too?" Olivia blew on her nails.

"I'm lucky to still have a job. Taking the Harmony Valley position was a risk." A stupid, sentimental risk. They were worse off than before. The commute to Cloverdale was going to require a lot of gas.

"You got demoted and I got laid off. It was a stupid move." Olivia was rarely so harsh, so obviously itching for a fight. "Speaking of which, are we moving back to Santa Rosa? Or is your mistake permanent?"

"Did something happen today? Are you feeling okay?" Had Olivia had another nosebleed? Was she having stomach pains? Headaches? Unable to concentrate?

Olivia opened a bottle of clear-coat polish. "This is as good as I get."

There was drama in the air. "Shouldn't you be going next door to babysit?"

"I'm thinking of calling in sick."

The urge to break some eggs rose up unexpectedly.

Mandy lost her appetite. "Olivia, that's irresponsible. You're not sick."

"But I could be. I wouldn't know." She stoppered the polish and met Mandy's inquisitive gaze. "That guy I met at the post office? Ryan? His mother had cancer three times."

Here we go again.

"You aren't going to get cancer again." *Knock on wood.*

"Don't lie to me!" Olivia slapped her palms on the tabletop. "I can take the truth. I'm an adult." And then she contradicted that statement by bolting out of the kitchen and running down the hallway.

Maybe it was the demand for the truth. Maybe it was the way nothing had been going right for Mandy. For once, she forgot about eggs and patience and smiles, and followed Olivia, practically shouting, "You may be eighteen soon, but that doesn't make you an adult. Adults are responsible and reliable. They don't call in sick when they're not."

"I can't be reliable if I can't rely on my health. When cancer comes back—"

"*If! If! If!*" Mandy couldn't believe she was shouting or that she didn't want to stop.

"I'm not going to cosmetology school. Why learn something new when I'm just going to die young?" Olivia was calm. Icy calm.

Mandy was mad. Raging mad. "I'm so glad you've thought this through. While you're waiting to die, you can prepare for the big earthquake to hit. It's got to happen before you croak. After all, your doctor said you'd live to be a grandmother and geologists predict the Big One will strike at any moment."

Olivia started to put her hands on her hips and then must have thought better of it—heaven forbid, she ruin a wet nail. She raised her hands instead, almost as if she was being held up. "I would've been better off with Mom."

"And I would've been better off if I'd have let her take you. You would've had at least one baby by now and probably been hooked on drugs or alcohol—*or dead*—but at least one of us would be happy." Mandy grabbed her mailbag and headed for the door. "Maybe this birthday you'll get your wish and Mom will show up."

As soon as Mandy slammed the door, she was slammed with regret. She knew better than to lose her temper, but she had no time to apologize. She clocked in by scanning a letter destined for Ben and marched onward.

And she kept slogging along, replaying the argument in her head until she reached Agnes's house where the diminutive woman was waiting for her.

Agnes hugged her. "Congratulations on being Harmony Valley's first female firefighter. My mother used to tell me stories about the protests women made for the vote. Your grandmother would be proud."

Mandy didn't think they'd have been proud of her outburst today. She thanked Agnes halfheartedly and kept walking. She had to avoid delays today since it was her first day not being in charge.

A few minutes later, it was Eunice who awaited her. She wore a brown velvet tracksuit that complemented the purplish tint to her gray hair. "Please tell me your sweet young sister is opening a nail salon here."

"I can't tell you a thing." The pager at Mandy's belt vibrated. She checked the readout. The address was only a few blocks away. She was needed by the fire department. Her legs felt as sturdy as a scarecrow's. "My first call."

"Is it a fire?" Eunice asked.

"I don't know." Mandy hurried off, mailbag banging at her hip. She called her supervisor and left him a message, not caring that she'd be in trouble. She was needed.

The fire engine siren filled the air. The Libbys were on their way, too.

Mandy ran the rest of the way.

Ben pulled up just as Mandy reached the address on her pager. She'd worked up a sweat.

"Thanks for coming." Ben climbed out and unlocked compartments in the truck. "The first aid and medical kits are here. You may need to unlock them someday if Dad or I are busy."

Keith appeared at the front fender of the truck. "Got a call about a man complaining he's dizzy." He led her to the front door. "The first hour after an incident is called the Golden Hour. Most people who receive the right care in those critical sixty minutes survive." Keith knocked on the door. "Fire department." When there was no answer, he tried to open the door. "It's locked." He pounded on the door this time and yelled, "Fire department!" The effort had him gasping as he tried to refill his lungs.

"Are you okay?" Mandy took hold of his arm.

"Fine," Keith wheezed.

"There's a lockbox." Ben set his gear down and hurried to a box mounted next to the mailbox. He rifled through his key ring, selected one and then inserted the key into the box. He took a key from the hook inside and handed it to his father. "Some people pay for these so we don't have to break their door down when they call 911," Ben explained.

Keith opened the door and looked at Mandy. "Stay behind us." And then he went in calling, "Hello? Fire department."

Ben passed her with the med kits. "You never know what state of mind people are in, especially when they called but the door is locked."

"Great," Mandy murmured.

Her legs were more unstable than they'd been when she'd been paged. Who knew rescuing people could be dangerous?

Instead of a gunman, they found an old man lying in his bed in a back room. He was slack-jawed, his stare vacant. Mandy had seen death and near death. This man—*this stranger*—he didn't seem to be far from death's door. She felt sick. She'd assumed when she volunteered that she'd be going on fires, not bearing witness to someone's passing.

Ben began to take the man's vitals while Keith talked to him.

"What's your name, sir?"

The old man mumbled something unintelligible.

"Adam Franklin," Mandy said, feeling useful for the first time. That usefulness made it bearable to stay. "I've been delivering his mail."

"Adam," Keith said without missing a beat. "When was the last time you drank something?"

Using his thumb and forefinger, Ben lifted a bit of skin from Adam's forearm and then released it. The skin was slow resuming its shape. "Dehydration."

"Adam," Keith said in a booming voice. "Have you been sick? Throwing up? Diarrhea?"

Adam gave the barest of nods.

"Starting an IV." Ben rummaged through his boxes.

Keith got on the radio with dispatch and requested an ambulance.

"What can I do?" Mandy asked.

"Clear a path for the gurney from the front door through here." Ben spoke quietly. "Don't ask my dad to lift or move anything heavy. If you need help, ask me."

Forty-five minutes later, Mandy helped Ben carry the medical kits to the fire truck while Keith walked next to Adam's gurney to the ambulance. The intake of fluids through the IV had helped Adam immensely. He was able to communicate in short sentences, but he was still too weak to be left alone.

"Are you disappointed this didn't turn into a kidnapping?" Smiling, Ben stroked her arm from shoulder to elbow. "I'm joking. We joke afterward to release the tension. You did good in there, but you look like you're about to faint."

She didn't faint. She babbled. "I've seen sickness. I've seen death. But only with people I know. I delivered this man's mail, but I'd never met him. And then I'm in his bedroom and trying to help keep him alive in some miniscule way."

"The job can be surreal," Ben admitted. "But it's rewarding knowing you helped someone, isn't it?" His gaze probed for understanding.

She managed a smile and a nod. "You were incredibly focused in there."

He began putting away the med kits. "I have to be."

"And yet, you took a moment to give me words of encouragement and care for your dad." She leaned in and kissed his cheek, because he'd been kind. "Thank you. And now, I've got to deliver the mail."

"Practice putting on your turnout gear." Granddad walked among the fire trainees like a general before a major battle, chest puffed out, platitudes dropping like spent gun shells.

The atmosphere was more Halloween than fire academy.

Ben wasn't complaining. The Harmony Valley Fire Department was about to get a huge boost in body count.

Two days after his recruitment meeting netted him only Mandy as a volunteer, Ben had held a second meeting. This time, seven men showed up. Three volunteers, including Mandy, had medical certification. And now they were having their first official training session.

Ben had begged, borrowed and bartered for used gear. Boots in four different sizes. Coats, gloves and pants in two different sizes. Helmets, masks, oxygen tanks.

Technically, Ben was in charge of training. Dad was at home trying out a new breathing treatment and resting. Granddad had shown up with a crate full of kittens. He took charge of showing the recruits how to dress while Ben readied the few self-contained breathing apparatus sets he'd scrimmaged.

"Some of you are going to wash out." Granddad was on his fourth pass of the evening. "That's just the way it is." He scowled toward the corner where Mandy and Joe Torino were joking and helping Will Jackson with his gear.

Ben had wanted to scowl a few times himself. Four of the volunteers had grown up with Mandy. Ben envied their easy camaraderie. Since the wiring failure at the post office, Ben had barely seen her. Mandy left long before Martin's Bakery opened up. She had a thirty-minute drive to Cloverdale, where she sorted and picked up mail, then drove back and delivered the mail in Harmony Valley. She didn't go out to tell secrets to the moon. And the number of emergency calls had decreased. She'd accompanied him and Dad on only two medical runs.

As for brushfires? They'd had none.

Granddad continued to pontificate. "There are those who like to set fires—"

"It was an accident," Mandy said for about the tenth time with a sideways glance at Ben.

"—and those who like to put fires out." Granddad raised his voice. "Just like there are dog people and there are cat people. Did everyone have a chance to hold a kitten?"

"Yes!" the entire room chorused.

Will, who was one of the winery owners and a childhood friend of Mandy's, came to stand next to Granddad for inspection. He had blond all-American good looks and didn't flaunt it like John. The new dad (a boy!) was a take-charge, likable guy, despite being a millionaire.

"Now this…" Granddad clapped Will on the back. "This is a man who puts out fires and is a cat person." Granddad slipped a half glance Mandy's way. "A couple more times putting on this suit and you'll be ready for your SCBA equipment."

"I'd like to clear the air," Will said in a loud voice.

"Excellent." Granddad sent another dark glance Mandy and Joe's way. "And if we lose a few recruits after your speech, so be it."

After being given the floor, Will didn't waste any time. "I'm sorry, but…I started the fire at the high school, not Joe or Mandy. We were flicking matches and—"

"Now he wants to be a martyr." Joe ran the Torino Family Garage on the outskirts of town. Where Will was poster-boy fair, Joe was lost-boys dark. Joe was a workhorse, openly thrilled to live a boyhood dream of being a fireman.

"No." Granddad clutched Will's arm. "You can't mean it." He looked to the sheriff, but Nate just shrugged.

"I'm afraid I do mean it." Will looked serious, but Ben had already learned that Will often looked serious.

"It was an accident," Mandy repeated.

"In all fairness—" Joe came forward to shake Will's hand "—I'm not sure whose match started it."

"But…" Granddad was absolutely floored. "Joe took the blame."

"I shouldn't have let him." Will looked like a weight had been lifted from his shoulders. "But I thought it'd ruin my chance at Stanford."

"And Mandy's at the post office," Joe pointed out.

Granddad's eyes narrowed. "And the fourth? The janitor saw four of you."

The three match-flingers went silent.

"That's not our story to tell." Joe nodded at Mandy.

Ben was struck by the loyalty of the three childhood friends. Most secrets didn't stay secrets in a small community.

Of course, most secrets weren't kept by Mandy.

Chapter Seventeen

The steak and shrimp fajitas were from El Rosal.

The cake was chocolate and from Martin's Bakery.

Olivia had made it to age eighteen.

She felt no different. Her face was still too round, her fingers too fat. She still felt like she was fighting for her life, analyzing every twinge, every nosebleed, every ring in her ears.

It was hard to hear anything above the music in El Rosal.

"There's only twenty dollars in this card." Olivia glanced at Mandy. They were having a late dinner because it took Mandy forever to deliver mail. Olivia didn't know why. The town wasn't that big and there were more vacant houses than occupied ones.

"Happy birthday." In addition to still being in her postal uniform, Mandy wore one of her detached smiles, the kind that drove Olivia insane. When she smiled like that, nothing got to her.

Perversely, Olivia liked it when she got under Mandy's skin. She felt closer to her when they argued. They were real with each other when Mandy lost her stupid smile and shouted at her.

"Is there another card?" Olivia asked, although she already suspected the truth. "From the Grumpster?"

Mandy shook her head.

Olivia scowled.

"Let's have cake." Mandy's eyes were too bright.

Olivia frowned, hoping Mandy didn't start crying. On those rare occasions when Mandy cried, Olivia bawled.

"*I. Don't. Want. Cake.*" Olivia was being a big, dried-out piece of dog poo, but she'd been waiting for nearly two years for her inheritance. And now... And now...

Olivia pulled herself together the same way she'd pulled herself together after every bad reaction she had to her treatment...

Mandy squeezed her hand. Olivia squeezed back.

This was her birthday. There would not be tears. "The Grumpster said he left me something, Mandy. He mentioned a four-letter word—*bank*. He told me it'd help me achieve my dreams." She didn't remember his exact words, but he'd said something like that.

Without letting go of Olivia's hand, Mandy reached into her purse and produced a small blue jewelry box. The kind of blue box people in the movies got when they shopped at Tiffany's.

A tear slid down Mandy's cheek. Olivia didn't think there was a Tiffany's diamond in the box. Or a check big enough to pay for cosmetology school.

She freed her hand, wiped her eyes and opened the box.

Blood rushed in her ears, drowning out the music. "It's Grandma's engagement ring." Her brass engagement ring.

Olivia swallowed. The sounds of the restaurant returned.

Mandy sniffed. "She always said—"

"You don't need anything but love to be happy." Olivia felt sick. "The Grumpster left me a brass ring." Not money for school. Not even a gift card for Starbucks.

"He didn't know you'd be sick." Mandy's smile said they had to grin and bear it. That Olivia had to suck up life's disappointments and deal with it. "He didn't know we'd be in debt. He might have done things differently if he had."

Anger shook Olivia's limbs the way it would if the Big One had arrived. "This is why Mom left all the time." Olivia's temper rose. "Because the Grumpster was a jerk."

Mandy shook her head, but her smile wobbled, and her gaze collapsed to the small cake on the table between them.

"He was. He'd yell. He'd yell and he'd need you." The feeling that she was a swelling, growing piece of dog poo was hard for anyone to ignore now. Olivia was shouting to be heard above the music. "The Grumpster only needed you. He had no use for me."

"You're remembering Grandpa when he was old and sick." Only one side of Mandy's face held on to that smile. "Can't you remember him how he was before?"

The past was a blurry black hole where chemo had stuffed Olivia's memories. The good ones anyway. She recalled some of the bad. "I don't want to remember. I don't want to remember when he came home from work and stood in the hallway while you wiped Grandma's butt and cleaned her bedpan. I don't want to remember how he went out the door to work whistling when you had just come home from a shift and slept in bed next to Grandma because she didn't feel good. How can you say Mom didn't leave because of that? She didn't want to be a slave to illness or to them!"

"That's enough." Mandy stood, digging into her wallet, and tossing bills on the table along with a few tears. "You think taking care of someone you love is a chore? It's not. It's a privilege." Mandy stuffed her wallet back in her purse and snapped it shut. "You think cancer just appeared in you overnight? It didn't. Dementia is the same way. It creeps up, feeding on your insecurities, your need for independence, your fear of death." Mandy wiped the back of her hand over one cheek. She was crying, not smiling.

For once, Olivia didn't feel close to her sister when she wept.

But Mandy wasn't done. "You, of all people, should understand how a body can betray you. How you lose control even when you don't want to, how fear makes you want to cry or scream or just sit and do nothing. You have no right to judge our grandparents. No right at all!"

Olivia heard Mandy's words and resented them for making sense. She was hurt and she was alive, and life was supposed to be a bowl of ripe red cherries. But it wasn't and someone had to be to blame. Why couldn't it be Mandy?

Olivia choked on a sob. She didn't want that for Mandy. But after all she'd gone through—the fear, the pain, the humiliation—she deserved something didn't she?

Mandy ran out of the restaurant, which had grown quiet. Even the music, usually loud and cheerful, had faded into a slow, mournful song.

People stared. People whispered. People waited for someone to come along and shovel the big pile of poo that was Olivia out the door.

Clutching the box with brass ring, Olivia scrambled out of her chair and ran after her sister. Embarrassed, hurt, angry, she caught up to Mandy on the other side of the town square.

"Why did Grandpa hate you so much, Mandy? When he died, he gave you nothing. Not even this stupid brass ring."

"He didn't hate me. He knew I could handle the responsibility." Mandy alternated between walking and running, sobbing and gasping for breath. "I can't talk to you right now."

Mandy was crying. Well, too darn bad. Olivia was crying, too.

"I can be responsible," Olivia said.

"You weren't. For years." Mandy spit out the words with uncharacteristic heat. "Grandma cleaned your room and your clothes. Grandpa made sure you did your homework. Even now, you can't make dinner when it's your turn."

Olivia was beginning to see how the world and her beloved sister saw her. And she didn't like it.

She followed Mandy home in silence, wiping away her tears, fairly sure she didn't deserve to cry.

Happy birthday to me.

"My girls!"

Mandy froze. One hand on the key in the lock, one foot inside the house.

Not today. Not today.

But really, her wish was that she didn't have to see her mother any day.

Reflexively, Mandy reached behind her for Olivia and drew her inside. "Mom, what a surprise."

Olivia's expression when she saw Mom leaked the emotions Mandy was all too familiar with—surprise, apprehension and the yearning to be loved.

Teri Zapien sat on the blue-and-tan plaid couch wearing a gauzy blue sundress and wedges that were out of style. Her black hair was too black. Her widow's peak more pronounced than when Mandy had last seen her. But the smile…the spider-weaving-a-web smile was the same. "I guess there's no need for you girls to knock since you seem to have a key."

"It's only temporary until we get back on our feet." Mandy wished she'd had time to change out of her uniform before dinner or had had the energy to comb her hair into a neat braid and add a little color to her face. What she hadn't done made her vulnerable, like a soldier going into a gunfight without a Kevlar vest. "What brings you to town?"

"It's my baby's birthday." Mom's toxic smile crept toward Olivia.

Mandy felt a burst of uncharacteristic rebellion. "You missed the last one. And more than half of my birthdays."

Mom used a lot of eyeliner. When she narrowed her eyes, they looked like dark, dangerous slits. "Mandy, you didn't die without me."

Olivia made a strangled noise.

The urge to protect Olivia had Mandy's fingers convulsing around her sister's.

Normally, this was where Mandy sent Olivia on an errand or asked Mom to look at something in the kitchen. But she'd babied Olivia the same way Grandpa had babied their mother. Maybe it was time her baby sister experienced life as a grown-up in Mom's world.

Maybe it was time the truth came out.

"No, I didn't die without you." Mandy forced herself to meet Mom's dark gaze, to meet her challenge with one of her own. "I got stronger every time you left, while you seemed to stay the same. I got stronger because your parents taught me how to be kind and loving, something you rejected." Mandy let go of Olivia's hand. "I got stronger taking care of Olivia. My sweet, brave little sister who deserves better than you."

Mom smoothed the skirt of her dress, penciled eyebrows raised as if daring Mandy to continue.

Mandy obliged. "And Olivia needed me to be brave when you weren't around. When she skinned her knees. When her first boyfriend broke her heart. And when the doctor pumped enough chemicals in her to kill cancer. *Or kill her.*" That's what it had felt like. "And Olivia came through and became the talented, beautiful person you see here."

Olivia stared at Mandy as if she'd never been given praise before.

"No, Mother. Your leaving didn't kill me. No, Mother. I do not wish my childhood was any different. You gave me to the best people on the planet to raise me. And no, Mother. I don't care that Grandpa left this house to you, because he left me the keys and the money to keep it up. And do you know why? Because he knew you can't do much more than shop and date men who'll never love you. And frankly, you don't deserve to be called Mom."

"Are you finished?" Teri asked in a tone that felt like the spider closing in on the trapped fly.

"No, *Teri.*" Mandy lifted her chin, refusing to be cowed. "Grandpa's money is almost gone. You'll either have to pay the upkeep yourself or sell this house."

"We'll see." Teri indicated her children should sit.

Mandy didn't want to sit, but she had no choice. She chose Grandpa's recliner. Olivia perched on the arm.

Teri leaned forward, smiling at Olivia. "Did you ever wonder why I didn't come to visit you while you were sick, sweet thing?"

Here it comes.

Mandy sat very still.

Mandy could've told Olivia to go to her room. She could've offered to pay the house utilities from her own salary. She chose to let the truth come out and hope Olivia could forgive her.

Teri may have been heartless, but she wasn't completely stupid. She recognized Mandy's decision to see this through with a brisk nod. "Sweet thing, I wanted to be by your side, I really did. But Mandy wanted me to stay away." Teri paused, taking measure of her audience like a huckster did with a carnival crowd.

Olivia looked at Mandy, a question in her eyes.

Mandy's pulse was chugging like a mail truck engine going up a grade, but she was committed to face this wreck head-on. Quietly, with as much dignity as she could muster.

"You wanted to visit?" Olivia sounded small and weak and in need of a protector.

Mandy wanted to pull her sister into her lap.

Teri nodded.

"Then..." Olivia glanced at Mandy one more time. "Why didn't you?"

Mandy held her breath.

"Because your sister paid me." Mom smiled. It was a satisfied, happy smile. The smile of a spider that had drained the fly.

"Is that true?" Olivia drew back, as if being near Mandy made her sick.

"Yes." Mandy was losing Olivia. And she had only herself to blame.

"You lied to me about this and the inheritance?" Olivia stood, fists clenched and voice loud as she transitioned to full-drama mode.

"Yes."

The spider pounced. "What inheritance?"

"I hate you," Olivia said to Mandy.

"What inheritance?" Teri repeated.

"I hate you both!" Olivia ran to her room and slammed the door.

"I thought that went well." Mandy stood, willing her legs to stay beneath her.

"What inheritance?"

Mandy retreated to her bedroom and closed, but didn't slam, the door.

"It came." Ben's mother met him at the door with the smell of spaghetti and the wave of a white envelope. "The DNA results."

It was late. Ben had been submitting paperwork to the state for his volunteers and emailing information to his recruits about upcoming training. He expected dinner, quiet and bed. He'd hoped for a night without an emergency call. And now this.

Ben couldn't seem to move his legs.

"Go on." Mom waved it near his face. "Open it."

Ben held the envelope on its edges, as if it had been dusted with anthrax and might kill him. He checked his name and address. He checked the return name and address. How could such a small thing be such an incredibly big deal?

He felt numb. Novocain numb. The kind of floaty numb that you knew would eventually give way to a sharp, unpleasant pain.

"Ben." Mom clamped her fingers around the top of the envelope and tried to take it away.

Ben held on. "I need to be alone."

That wasn't true. He needed to talk to Mandy. Barring that, he'd settle for a heart-to-heart with the moon.

Ben went into the backyard without eating anything. The moon was building back up to full strength. The sky was the clearest it had been in weeks. The cricket chirped. Ben had no idea how long he waited for Mandy, but he finally had enough waiting. He stuffed the envelope in his back pocket and walked to the end of the yard.

The cricket stopped chirping. The leaves in the tree above him rustled. In the distance, a small dog barked.

Harmony Valley was peaceful. It was a good place to raise a kid.

So why did the idea eat him up inside?

A window at Mandy's house slid open. It was either Olivia's room or Mandy's.

Ben was willing to bet it was Mandy's. He entered her yard and went to stand near the dark window that was hers.

"If I hadn't seen you coming, I would've been creeped out," Mandy whispered, her silhouette barely visible behind the mesh screen.

"You were looking for me?" He turned around. Yep, she could see him standing in his yard from her window.

The cricket picked up where it'd left off.

"I was trying to see the moon," Mandy said unconvincingly.

Ben grinned. "You were looking for me."

"You can tell yourself that if it makes you feel better." She was grinning, too.

Ben could hear it in her voice. He moved closer, leaning his shoulder against the stucco wall. "Why are we whispering? Is Olivia asleep?"

"My mother blew in tonight. Many eggs were broken, mostly by me. I'm not sure Olivia will ever talk to me again." There was a catch in her voice, as if she'd been crying and might cry again.

He wanted to hold her. "Olivia found out how you paid mommy dearest to stay away."

"Yep."

Ben wished he'd been there for her. "Didn't you point out that mommy dearest took the bribe money?"

"I was hoping Olivia would come to that conclusion on her own." Mandy sighed. It was the sigh she made when her cares got too heavy. "I wish I could see Mr. Moon. I didn't want to go outside and wake anybody."

"You're doing fine telling your secrets to me." He could listen to her secrets all night.

Inside her room the ceiling fan whirred, and Mandy was alone. In the backyard the cricket did his nightly serenade, and Ben was alone.

We should be together.

There was just the little issue of her requirements in a man.

Ben glanced back the way he came.

"Again," Mandy whispered, "I spill my guts and you give me nothing."

Ben wanted to give her things, things she'd rejected, like a chance to own his heart. But he knew she appreciated secrets. He withdrew the envelope from his back pocket. "I got a letter today."

"Yeah, Einstein. I delivered it."

Ben held it up. "I haven't opened it yet."

"The plot thickens." She waited for him to explain.

He hoped no eggs would be broken. "I wasn't entirely honest with you the other night on the glider."

"If you tell me that envelope contains a copy of your marriage license, I might have to do you bodily harm." She was only half joking.

The time for jokes had passed. "Hannah and I took a DNA test. And here are the results."

"Uh... I thought Erica was your friend?"

"She was. There's just this one time—"

"Spare me the details. Having been kissed by you once, I can relate to Erica's decision." She sighed, in exasperation this time. "That sounded harsh."

"I deserve it. I didn't tell you the truth." He washed a hand over his face.

"This is a big thing for you." Her voice lightened. "You didn't tell me the whole truth."

"Not proud of that."

"But...once you know the results, it'll influence what you decide about fighting for Hannah." There was no mistaking the hope in her voice.

Ben had always considered himself a decisive man. He wished this decision was out of his hands. He'd invited John to come by tomorrow in the hope that he wouldn't need the envelope. "Let's say I'm her biological father. John would be relieved."

"Let's say you're not." Leave it to Mandy to cut right to the chase. "Clearly, John doesn't want her."

"But he can provide for Hannah better than I can. She won't have to worry about cars or college tuition."

"She'll be raised by nannies three weeks of every month. Are you okay with that?" By her tone, she wasn't.

And in truth...he wasn't either.

Mandy wasn't letting him off the hook easily. "More to the point, do you think Erica would be okay with that?"

"Erica lost her vote when she named John the father and me her godfather and guardian." Ben had known Mandy's position on this issue. Why was he getting defensive? "Look, I know I should open up my heart and embrace the idea of being Hannah's father, but I can't."

"Why not?" Mandy didn't give him the chance to answer. "And if you say it's because your dad was a fireman and sucked at raising kids, I'm going to call you on that. You turned out okay. Honest to a fault maybe, but okay."

"That doesn't mean I didn't get hurt growing up," he said petulantly, belatedly realizing that his childhood had been a fairy tale compared with hers.

"It doesn't mean you didn't get over it either. Give yourself time to get used to the idea. You'll do the right thing for both you and Hannah."

"How do you know?" How could she know when he didn't?

"Because you're unable to live with a lie. Not for long. And not to yourself."

"I'm selling the house, Mandy," Mom announced the next morning. She'd risen uncharacteristically early, hogged the bathroom and emerged not looking age appropriate. Her heels were too high. Her bodice too low. And her makeup? Too much. "There's nothing you can do about it."

Mandy said nothing, which pissed Olivia off, because Olivia had heard everyone getting up early and had arisen at the hour of the dead—*4 a.m.*—so as not to miss anything.

Mandy saying nothing was unusual. She always had something to say. Except last night when she hadn't defended herself.

Olivia burned with frustration.

"You can send me the check when it sells," Mom continued. "In the meantime, I'm leaving. I'll pack up a few things. Mementos and such." When Mandy didn't rise to the bait, Mom turned to Olivia. "Why don't you come with me, sweet thing? You can do my nails. I can see Mandy doesn't let you do her nails."

Olivia stopped breathing. Her head felt light. Mom had never asked her to go before. Well, she'd invited Olivia, but Mandy had paid her to leave Olivia behind.

She'd always imagined Mom went to a special place, a place where there were no rules and everyone dressed in pretty clothes, although...Mom's clothes weren't as pretty as they used to be.

"Don't go." Mandy stared at Olivia as if she couldn't believe she'd spoken. "Don't go and I'll..." Mandy cast her gaze around the kitchen, at what little they had, at her postal uniform. "I'll get you a loan for cosmetology school."

"Get her a loan?" Mom laughed and broadened her smile. Her smile wasn't like Mandy's. It was too hard and too bright, like a shiny fake penny. "Olivia shouldn't have to make the payments. She's had cancer. She deserves everything she wants."

Now we're talking.

Olivia had survived cancer. She did deserve the good things in life because she'd experienced the bad.

"Responsible adults pay their own way in life." Mandy rinsed her coffee cup in the sink.

That was the best Mandy could do?

Olivia huffed. It wasn't good enough.

"Pack up what you need, sweet thing. We'll leave around nine."

"I can't stop you, Olivia." Mandy hesitated at the sink. "You're eighteen. But you'll always have a home with me."

Mom snorted. "She'll probably charge you rent."

Chapter Eighteen

"There's no reason for this meeting," Ben's mother said in a hushed voice around noon the day after the DNA results had arrived. "You could be her real father. Erica made you her godfather and guardian for a reason. Open the envelope."

Hannah was in the backyard poking beneath the bushes in case any new critters had come to stay. Dad was outside on the front porch waiting for John to arrive.

"This is for the best," Ben said, glancing at his pager. He had double knots of tension in his chest. "I wasn't listed on Hannah's birth certificate for a reason."

"He's here," Dad announced in a smooth voice, coming in from the front porch. He'd spent the morning with his eucalyptus breathing treatment. "Can you believe it? He drove a chick magnet vehicle to meet his daughter for the first time. He's too flashy. I don't like him."

Mom called Hannah inside. Her fine blond hair had already escaped the braids over her ears. Her cheek and one knee were dirt-smudged. And her pink blouse had a stain at the hem.

"Ben?" Mom looked from Hannah to him. "Should we change?"

"No." Let him see who Hannah really was. "It's okay." Ben took Hannah's hand. "There's someone I want you to meet."

Typical Hannah. She grew quiet and watchful when in new situations or with new people.

They stepped onto the front porch.

John had driven the Tesla and was wearing a suit again. He came up the walk carrying a bouquet of pink roses and a small baby doll. "Are you Hannah?"

Han nodded solemnly.

John probably closed a lot of deals with that smile. He'd need more than a smile to win over Hannah.

Ben was supposed to want John to win over Hannah. Less than a minute in and he found himself rooting against him.

"These are for you." John held out the roses and the doll, uncharacteristically unpolished both in action and his choice of gifts.

Hannah heaved a weary sigh, the one she reserved for meddlesome, disappointing adults. She accepted the flowers first. "Spiders love roses." She craned her neck to stare up at John. "Because bugs love roses and spiders eat bugs."

John looked perplexed, which eased at least one knot of tension in Ben's chest.

"I'll put these in water." Mom whisked the flowers away.

John handed the doll to Hannah.

It was her turn to look perplexed. "Why are you giving me this?"

"Little girls love dolls," John said, sounding less confident than he appeared.

"This little girl doesn't love dolls." Dad gestured to the door. "Come inside. Must be hot in that suit of yours."

Hannah gave her gift a thorough examination on her way inside. "She doesn't do anything." She dropped the doll on the coffee table.

Ben began to breathe easier.

Mom set a vase with the roses on the hearth. "It's not what the doll does, it's how you play with her. You can pretend to be her mother or her older sister." She fussed with Hannah's hair.

Hannah heaved another sigh and sat on the couch.

"So, you like more interactive toys." John unbuttoned his jacket and sat in Ben's father's lounger, eliciting a frown from Dad. "What about video games?"

"*No*," the Libbys chorused.

"She's seven," Ben said, feeling the need to add, "Too young for video games, tablets or cell phones." In case John had other ideas.

John had tried gifts. And potential gifts. He resorted to his fallback—that smile. "What do you like, Hannah? I'll get you whatever you want."

Mom gave Ben a look that said: *Open that letter and get rid of this guy.*

"I like..." Hannah swiped at her nose with the back of her hand. "Animals. Reptiles. Bugs. I have an infirmary. Do you want to see?"

"Yes."

"What I like you can't buy." Hannah pulled away from Mom's hair repair and ran to the garage door. "Come on." When all the adults had joined her in the garage, Hannah said, "These are all the animals I've rescued."

John's brow wrinkled. "Do people drop them off?"

"Oh, no," Dad said with unrestrained glee. "She finds them. All over town."

"She has a tendency to wander off if left unattended," Mom said, not at all apologetically.

Ben felt a rush of love for his parents.

"I go mostly when Granny naps," Hannah said, defending herself. "But I'm supposed to leave a note. Granny doesn't mind me rescuing anything—*except snakes*—as long as she knows where I am."

John looked as if his most promising financial deal had gone sour.

"I don't think he likes snakes either." Hannah turned to Ben. "Who's your friend?"

In the rush to the door and the nerves, they'd forgotten to introduce Hannah to her father.

John took the Libby hesitation as a sign that he should introduce himself. He put out his hand the way he'd done when he and Ben had met. "I'm John Smith."

His statement hung in the air, along with his hand.

And then Hannah screamed.

Everyone flinched—the Libbys, John and the animals in the cages.

And then Hannah stopped screaming and ran.

Mom's car rattled and made more noise than an MRI machine.

And it wasn't just vibrating. It was trashed, filled with cigarette butts, empty fast-food bags and...was that a pair of panties?

Ew.

Olivia's jaw clenched and she tried to relax because they hadn't even left Harmony Valley yet and it was afternoon.

Mom had wanted to swing by an old friend's house, leaving Olivia in the car for an hour. Then she'd driven through the back alleys downtown and dumpster-dived. Olivia had refused to get out of the car. Mom had stuffed a bag of pastries she found behind the bakery under her seat and tossed a pair of men's sneakers in the back. And then she'd gone back to the house because she said she forgot something, only Olivia was convinced Mom just felt like she needed to scrounge more stuff. She came out with an armful of clothing and a bag of canned food.

This was feeling less and less like a trip to a special place and more like a bad mistake.

But Olivia wasn't ready to give up. This was supposed to be an in-your-face payback to Mandy. She'd paid Mom for years to stay away.

Mom chose me.

Olivia was going to see something Mandy never had—Mom's house.

Mom hit a pothole, and the car nearly shimmied off the road.

"Are you sure this car is safe?" Olivia clutched the loose door handle.

"Would I be driving it if it wasn't?" Mom's mouth curled up in a half sneer. "How quickly you try to bite the hand that feeds you."

Mandy hadn't fed Olivia anything. "I'm a teenager. I speak my mind." Although technically, she was an adult now.

"I'm not taking you along to listen to whatever fluff is on your mind. I want to know what your inheritance is."

"My what?"

"Don't play dumb." Mom took her eyes off the road and put them on Olivia. It was the eyes that brought the memories steamrolling through Olivia's head, flattening the chemo-brain barricade for good.

"Those sweaters are hideous." Mom had sulked on the couch one Christmas morning wearing a burgundy silk halter top.

"We love these sweaters." Mandy had hugged Olivia tighter to her side, her smile like a shield. They wore matching sweaters Grandma had made. They were soft and snuggly, like a hug.

"It's a family tradition," Grandpa said, smiling benevolently at Olivia, who'd smiled back.

Great. Knitting was a family tradition? Olivia was going to have to learn how to knit.

Mom hit another pothole.

Another memory leaped to the forefront of Olivia's mind.

"Why don't you two act your age?" Mom had said to Grandma and Grandpa as they danced around their kitchen on New Year's Eve.

Grandma had been wearing a sparkly cocktail dress and heels, and Grandpa wore a suit. Grandma had made the girls wear their best dresses. They played big band records loud enough to rattle the windows, and danced like it was their last night on the planet.

"We love it." Mandy spun Olivia around like the ballerina on her music box.

"You could love it, too," Grandpa said. "It's a family tradition."

Olivia laughed and kept spinning, vaguely aware of the tension, but happy to be surrounded by love.

Great. Another family tradition. Olivia was going to have to learn how to dance.

The dashboard rattled as Mom accelerated.

Another memory crept in, one not as cheerful.

"Where did she put your wallet, Dad?" Mom had whispered to Grandpa as he lay in a hospital bed.

Olivia had been twelve and had been sleeping in the window seat.

Mom turned, as if sensing Olivia was awake. "You know where Grandpa keeps his coffee money, don't you, sweet thing?"

Mandy had appeared in the doorway in her postal uniform, looking tired after a long shift. She took in Olivia's expression, and the predatory way their mother had been leaning over the hospital bed. "Olivia, can you tell the nurse Grandpa wants pudding?"

Olivia had run to the nurse's station and waited there until Mom left, tucking bills into her wallet as she walked toward the elevator.

Mom hit another bump, making the dashboard rattle up a storm.

"Why did you take Mandy's money?" Olivia demanded, turning in her seat.

Mom's sharp laugh grated on Olivia's nerves. "I'm your mother. I don't have to answer to you."

"Did you spend it on drugs or beer or…or…some stupid guy?"

Mom ignored her question. "Let me borrow your cell phone."

"Why?"

"Because I left mine at home." She grabbed Olivia's purse and dragged it into her lap, rooting around until she came up with the phone. She drove and dialed at the same time.

Even Olivia, who'd never taken her driver's test, knew that was illegal.

"Hey, Jerry. It's me." Mom balanced Olivia's phone between her shoulder and chin, steering with her knee, while she opened Olivia's wallet. "I've missed you, too. Look, I've got some money." She stuffed the bills in her bra and tossed Olivia's purse back at her. "How about we go out tonight? And then…" Mom laughed. "I know, right?"

Olivia's stomach churned. She'd made a terrible mistake.

Great. I'm going to have to apologize to Mandy.

All Olivia's life, she'd let someone else deal with her mother, pretending not to know what a selfish loser she was. She'd let Mandy do all the dirty work, holding the uncomfortable conversations, paying Mom and her slimy negativity to vacate the premises. So what if Mandy had done it without telling her? Mandy had done the right thing. Olivia had been a baby, a child, a scared invalid.

But not anymore.

Olivia dug in her purse until she found Grandma's brass ring. She slipped it on her finger, not caring that the bronze clashed with the orange-and-yellow ombré shading she'd put on her nails. Just this morning, she'd been thinking how awesome it looked, just like candy corn. Which just went to show what a baby she was.

But not anymore.

"No more," Olivia said out loud. She wouldn't be the weak link in Mandy's life.

She met Teri's gaze—*Teri*, not Mom.

Mandy was right about that, too. Teri hadn't earned the title.

"I'm alive," Olivia said. "No thanks to you." She had Mandy to thank for that.

Olivia thought of Mandy's ugly work uniform and thick boots. Mandy could have left Olivia at any time. She could have put her kid sister in a foster home and gone on with her life, graduated from college, worked for NASA. Mandy gave up everything for her. "I'm alive because Mandy had the guts to stay. She raised me. She took care of Grandma when the cancer came back, and she took care of Grandpa when his mind gave out." Olivia drew a deep breath, fighting tears and wishing Mandy's hand held hers now. The ring would have to do. "But she will not take care of you. Not anymore. I won't let her."

Teri had hung up the phone and put it in her bra with Olivia's money. "In case you weren't listening to our early-morning conversation, sweet thing, I told Mandy to sell the house. We're parting ways." Teri gave her the half smirk again. "But you and I... We're just beginning. We're going to party, and you will tell me about your inheritance."

Olivia recoiled against the door. She'd bet the guys Teri partied with weren't as cool or as nice as Ryan.

The stop sign at the highway loomed ahead. Once they turned toward Cloverdale on the two-lane, there'd be no more stopping. There'd be no getting away.

"Pull over," Olivia said. "And give me my phone."

Teri cackled. "Regrets? So soon?"

Olivia's stomach spun. She had one last card to play. "Pull over. I'm going to puke."

Teri jerked the wheel and pulled onto the dirt shoulder.

Olivia grabbed her purse, threw the door open and made a run for it.

Chapter Nineteen

Olivia was gone.

Mandy felt as cracked and broken as the eggs she'd hurled at her this week.

She'd driven to Cloverdale for the mail and then back at speeding-ticket speed, hoping to find Olivia at home.

She wasn't.

Mandy had wandered through the house unable to stop replaying the hurt on Olivia's face when she'd realized Mandy had lied to her.

She'd stood in Olivia's room, looking at the things she left behind. Gym shoes. Her sweatshirt. Would she have a warm place to sleep at night?

Mandy's breath stuck in her throat.

She should have paid Teri off again. She should have protected her baby sister, insisting she stay even if she was eighteen. She should have...

It was too late to change anything.

Mandy sought refuge in the master bedroom. She looked out the window, but Ben wasn't in his backyard. He'd become her rock without her realizing it. She hoped he did the right thing with Hannah, not just for Hannah's sake, but because their relationship might grow if he did. She opened her grandmother's scarf drawer. Those poor scarves hadn't been taken out and admired in years. Grandma had a scarf for every season and holiday. Mandy shook each one out and laid them on the bed like a patchwork quilt.

At the bottom of the drawer was a thick manila envelope. She took out the contents and began reading.

Oh, my word.

Mandy sank onto the bed. Thirty minutes later, she locked up the house to deliver the mail, replaying more than the events of the past twenty-four hours. Grandpa's last wishes weren't his official last wishes.

Utley blocked her path on the sidewalk. His shirt today was sky blue and decorated with brown surfboards. "I've been looking for you. This time of day, you should be southwest of the town square."

"Is Dave paying you to keep tabs on me?" She wouldn't put it past her autocratic supervisor.

"I don't know who Dave is. All I know is—"

"I'll make up time in the next half hour." Based on the amount of mail she had in her bag, she'd be fine. What she didn't have time for was Utley's censure.

Utley didn't budge his Birkenstocks from the sidewalk. She had to take to the street to get around him.

"If I were postmaster," Utley called after her, "the station would never have been closed down."

"Don't bet on it," Mandy mumbled, thinking of Ben.

She'd perfected the fast walk through years of delivering mail. The day was hot and muggy, clouds gathering as if promising rain. Mandy wasn't fooled. It rarely rained this time of year. She made good time for several houses and quickly worked up a sweat. She'd be back on schedule soon.

About the fourth house from the corner, she ran into trouble. She'd just power walked to the metal mailbox hanging near the door of a pretty blue Craftsman house when a spindly voice from inside called out, "Who's there?"

"Mandy, your mail carrier."

Hannah rode her pink bike past, as if Granny Vanessa was hot on her tail.

"Hannah?" For a moment, Mandy was torn between the elderly woman inside the house and the little girl with messy pigtails flying behind her. "Hannah? Did you leave a note for your grandmother?"

"Hello?" the spindly voice called again. "Is anyone there?"

Mandy couldn't take the chance that the woman inside was in trouble. She turned back to the door once more. "It's Mandy. Your mail carrier. Do you need help?"

"Can you bring me my mail?"

"Of course." Mandy retrieved the mail she'd just dropped, watching Hannah stop at the corner house and peer into the bushes before riding off.

No one lived in that house. The windows were boarded up and a truck sat in the driveway with cobwebs in the wheel wells. She hoped Hannah didn't poke around there often.

Mandy glanced at the name on the mail and stepped inside. "Hello, Viola. Here's your mail."

An elderly woman with bright red pin curls sat on a blue velvet couch. Her walker was out of reach on the other side of a TV tray. "Thank you. Can you get me a glass of water?"

Mandy put the mail on the tray and hurried into the kitchen, returning a moment later with a glass of water.

"And some crackers," Viola said. "They're in the cupboard to the right of the refrigerator."

Mandy hurried to oblige.

"And my knitting. It's in a bag in the corner."

"Viola, I've got to be going." Utley was probably waiting on the sidewalk, and he'd be right to nag this time.

Viola stared at her with glazed, dilated brown eyes. "No one comes to see me anymore."

"I tell you what." Mandy backed to the door. "I'll come by tomorrow." And she'd ask Agnes to look in on her, too.

"Oh, how sweet." Viola's brow clouded. "I'm sorry. Who are you?"

"I deliver your mail." Mandy closed the screen firmly before turning around, expecting to see Utley, but the street was empty.

Something popped at the corner house. Smoke rose from the old truck in the driveway. And then there was flame.

Mandy ran across the road and dialed 911.

There was nothing like the adrenaline rush of a rig running with lights and sirens, especially after the debacle with John and Hannah.

Ben had tried calling Hannah on the radio after John left, but she hadn't answered. And then the call had come in about the fire.

Ben maneuvered the rig around a tight corner. It was a vehicle fire, all right. The truck was fully ablaze, and a crowd had gathered across the street, including Mandy.

"Let's give it a cocktail mix," Dad said, indicating he wanted to add chemical suppressant to the water.

"I'm taking that plug." Ben pointed to the fire hydrant in front of the house. He put the engine in Park, leaving the lights flashing. Heat from the fire reached him as soon as his boots hit the ground. He grabbed a connector hose and a wrench and ran to the fireplug.

"I called it in." Mandy appeared at his side, still carrying her mailbag. "What do you need me to do?"

Mental note: *Train volunteers on how to draw water from fire hydrants.*

"Put on the turnout gear from the rear seat. Put on everything, including the SCBA. I repeat. Everything, including the mask." Vehicle fires were toxic. "Ask the chief if you have any questions." In short order, Ben removed the valve and attached the hose to the hydrant, glancing back to make sure Dad had the other end hooked up to the truck.

Dad gave him a thumbs-up.

Mandy was adjusting her gloves. Her face was pale behind the mask. First fires did that to a person. Although it wasn't exactly her first fire. He loved that she faced challenges head-on. He loved that she was on a scene with him. The fact that he was using the L-word in the midst of a call should have been alarming. Instead, in the midst of the chaos, he felt at peace.

Nate and Joe joined them, opening the back of the cab for their turnout gear.

"We don't carry enough water in the pumper truck to put out big fires," Dad was saying to Mandy. All SCBA made the wearer's breath sound like a scuba diver on a fast walk. But it also distorted voices. Dad's deep voice sounded a bit like the air-labored supervillain Darth Vader. "And the water from the hydrant doesn't have enough pressure to fight a fire. So we suck it into our tank where it's pressurized and primed."

"What can I do?" she asked.

"Stand back from the hoses, listen and watch," Dad ordered. "Best way to learn."

Ben strapped the oxygen tank to his back, put on his SCBA and checked the air pressure. He unwound the hose and positioned himself on the lawn, waiting until the sheriff and Joe had their masks on. "Joe, steady the hose behind me. Dad, give me the juice."

Foamy water designed to saturate and suppress chemical flames shot from the hose with an intensity that would've challenged Ben's balance if he hadn't been ready for it.

The fire went down easy. Water and toxic residue were on the lawn and driveway, trickling down to the gutter. Ben signaled for the water to be cut, but he stayed on the lawn on watch in case the fire decided a resurrection was in order.

Several minutes later, Dad called it and they commenced cleanup. Ben and Joe were sprayed down with clean water by the fire chief so nothing toxic clung to their gear. The rest of the crew had been a safe distance back.

Mandy removed her mask and voiced what had been on Ben's mind the entire time. "How on earth did this junker catch fire?"

Ben exchanged a glance with his father. "Did you see anyone around before the fire began?"

She shook her head. "Hannah rode past and Utley rode me about being behind schedule, which is a daily occurrence for him. And then I went into Viola's house and when I came out—"

"*Poof*," Ben said with a small smile.

"Cars don't just spontaneously combust." Joe's mask hung tight on his chin. The mechanic had the right gung-ho attitude but needed more instruction on how to don his gear.

Ben loosened Joe's mask straps.

"It can be as simple as lighting a bag of potato chips on fire and leaving it on the seat." Dad was only slightly wheezy, but he sat on the engine's bumper, looking pale from exertion. "Or if someone put a lit firecracker down the gas tank, it would've exploded."

"I heard a pop." Mandy put her mask and helmet in the backseat of the fire truck and began removing her turnout gear.

A car backfired.

Ben's head came up. His gaze found a car at the end of the street. A gray car headed to the next corner. He pointed. "Whose car is that?"

"Utley's." Joe shook his head. "I keep telling him to bring it in for a tune-up."

"Utley." Ben turned to Mandy. "He hangs around the post office, drives a gray car and has a tin of matches he said he didn't want to let go to waste."

"You can't mean..." Mandy looked from the burned-out car to the empty street corner. "He's an old man."

"Yeah," Joe seconded. "He's old."

"Arson doesn't discriminate based on age," Dad said with the air of authority. "Wouldn't you agree, Sheriff?"

Nate nodded.

"He was my grandfather's friend." Mandy's hand crept to her throat.

"You told me he was supposed to have been postmaster someday. You said he's been on your case about post office management. He sounds frustrated." Ben looked to Nate for support. "Plausible?"

The sheriff nodded, a man of few words.

"Utley's a tall, old guy." Dad got to his feet. "He could have cut that high wire in the post office. Or put the wrong wattage bulb in the light fixture."

"Or messed with the fire control box," Ben added.

"I'll bring him in for questioning." Nate shed his turnout gear.

"Smoke," Agnes shouted from across the street.

Ben had forgotten they had an audience.

The group of firefighters turned back to the vehicle.

"Not there." Agnes pointed to the sky. "Look over the rooftops."

Black smoke billowed above the houses.

"Hannah!" Olivia barely had enough air to call to the little girl.

After escaping Teri, she'd run to the river without looking back. She'd followed it for what seemed like forever until she'd spotted Hannah standing in the field behind the post office. The one with knee-high grass and an old spooky house.

"What are you doing in this field alone?" Olivia demanded. In truth, she was so very, very glad to find anyone she knew that she nearly hugged the girl.

But Olivia was an adult now. She had to watch out for Hannah, protect her from bad influences, like Teri. Olivia did a slow turn, looking in all directions. Thankfully, there was no sign of Teri.

I escaped.

Olivia started to shake.

She'd escaped with her purse and wallet but no money and no cell phone.

No cell phone. All her contacts…All her *life.* Not cool.

"I'm going to report her to the sheriff," Olivia vowed, walking on shaky legs. "Hey, you still haven't said what you're doing."

"I'm looking for Iggy." Hannah stood still, poking the grass with a stick as if trying to flush something out. She wore her pink shoe bag over a pink T-shirt.

Olivia was going to have to tell Vanessa enough pink already. "Is Iggy a raccoon like Riley? Or a mouse?"

"Iggy eats mice."

Olivia did a little high-stepping dance and almost dropped her purse. "Get out of this field right now."

"Why?"

"Well, duh." Olivia couldn't stop moving. She'd gone out of the frying pan and was in the fire. "Iggy is a snake."

"So?" Hannah pushed her glasses up her nose.

"So? Snakes bite." Olivia grabbed Hannah's little arm and shook it. "Come on." But her foot landed in a gopher hole, and she fell.

On the ground. *Where there were snakes!*

"Stop screaming," Hannah said in that put-out voice of hers.

Olivia scrambled to her feet, sniffing and tasting metallic fear in her mouth.

"Your nose is bleeding," Hannah said.

Fear spread through Olivia like wildfire, leaving her weak-kneed. She wiped her nose. Sure enough, her hand came away streaked with blood. "I need a doctor." And Mandy. She pinched her nose.

"You need to sit down." Hannah took possession of Olivia's free hand and led her to a large granite rock. It was gray with black speckles and as large as the Grumpster's chair in their living room. "Sit here." Hannah dug in her pink bag.

"Do you have a phone?" Olivia said in a nasally voice. "I need to call Mandy." Her voice sounded younger than Hannah's.

Two nosebleeds. There'd be doctors and tests and pokes. And underlying it all would be the fear: *was cancer back?*

"She can't come get you." Hannah handed Olivia a clean tissue. It was folded and flat, as if it'd been smashed in her pink shoe bag a long time. "She's working. I saw her delivering mail." For once, there was a glint of interest in the girl's eyes. "Why do you need her? Where're your mom and dad?"

"My mom is...gone." *Good riddance.* "And I've never met my dad. All I have is Mandy."

"My mom is gone, too. To heaven," Hannah whispered, staring at the ground. She sat on the rock close to Olivia and snuggled closer. She was a hot and sweaty kid, but she was an improvement over Teri.

Still, Olivia hoped the next words out of Hannah's mouth weren't going to be that her mom had died of cancer.

"All I have is Ben," Hannah continued to whisper. "And Granny Vanessa and Grandpa Keith and Great-Grandpa Felix. And my grandparents in Sacramento."

"That's a lot of people." More than Olivia had.

"But none of them are my mom."

That was a sentiment Olivia understood.

The sun beat down on them, but it wasn't so hot that the birds and the frogs were silent.

Something moved in the grass nearby.

"We're safe here," Olivia said, more for herself than Hannah. The kid was something of a pro when it came to animals.

Hannah hadn't moved on from the last part of the conversation. "Moms kiss it and make it better."

"That's what Mandy does for me." But no matter how fiercely Mandy hugged Olivia, she couldn't guarantee cancer was gone forever. Olivia pinched her nose harder. "I hope I'm not dying."

"You don't look sick." Hannah giggled. "And your sister said you weren't dying. She said it was just hot and dry here."

Olivia liked that idea a lot better than thinking the cancer was back.

Hannah gazed up at her. "Do you try to be good for Mandy?"

"Not all the time." She was an irresponsible, selfish princess. She had no idea why Mandy had put up with her for so long.

Hannah nodded. "Mandy must love you a lot."

Olivia bit her lip and looked at the tree line. Would Mandy still love her a lot when she showed up at home? "Ben must love you a lot, too."

Hannah shrugged and returned her attention to the ground. "I try to be good for him, but he keeps saying I have to go back to my dad, no matter how much I want to stay with Ben."

"Ben doesn't want you?" That couldn't be. Hannah was a good kid. Sure, she was a pain in the butt, but if Ben didn't want her, what did that say about Mandy wanting Olivia?

"Ben introduced me to my dad today." Hannah's voice was super-small now. "I thought Ben was going to send me away. Right then." She slid off the rock. "There you are, Iggy." Hannah picked up a gray snake with a kink in its tail. She hadn't been staring morosely at the ground. She'd been looking for the snake!

Olivia bit back a scream.

Okay, it was a baby snake. And it was kind of cool the way the snake wrapped around Hannah's arm, but creepy, too.

A thought occurred to her. Olivia released her nose and drew her feet up. "Are you running away?"

Hannah blinked up at Olivia as if the idea had never occurred to her. "Should I?"

"You're jumping to conclusions about Utley." Mandy wasn't one to get carsick, but the thought of Utley being a felon combined with the lumbering motion of the fire truck was making her head hurt. Although it could have been from wearing the heavy firefighting gear.

"We're not starting a witch hunt." Ben cut a corner a little too tight. One of the tires bounced up the curb. "He'll get questioned...or caught in the act of starting a fire."

"You should train me to drive," Joe said from the seat across from Mandy. He had his head out the window like a dog enjoying a car ride.

"Vanessa, don't worry." Keith was on the phone with his wife. "Hannah will turn up. She always does." He hung up. "I hope that girl turns up soon."

That girl. Even though Mandy knew they meant Hannah, she worried about Olivia.

Her temples began to pound.

"There it is." Ben took the next turn slower.

The fire came into view. Dry grass that had once been a front lawn was burning.

"That house is empty." Mandy leaned forward, trying to be sure. Yep. "I've never delivered mail there."

"Wear your masks." Ben parked in front of the fire. "No telling what he started this fire with."

"Utley set this fire to slow us down." Keith coughed. "It's an arson tactic."

"Why would he do that?" Joe was lapping this up. He'd missed his calling when he chose to be a mechanic.

"So he can get away." Ben leaped to the ground, setting his mask in place.

"Come on." Mandy climbed out more carefully, carrying her mask. "He's a lonely old man with nowhere to go."

"He's an arsonist," Ben said firmly, helping her put on her mask. "He's looking for an outlet, and now he knows we know it's him. He'll be setting fires all the way out of town."

"How do you know that?" Mandy demanded as Nate pulled up behind them in his truck.

"I don't have time to argue." Ben led her toward a fire hydrant. "I'm going to show you how to attach a hose to a plug. Joe, you're going to take the hose."

Joe jogged over to them. "Is it inappropriate to high-five? I'm going to knock down a fire." He practically squealed like a girl.

"I alerted the phone tree." Nate joined them. "Everyone in town is on the lookout for fires."

And then the work began in earnest.

Ben showed Mandy how to remove the fire hydrant cover and connect the hose. She struggled for leverage with the wrench but managed to get the job done.

"Let's hear it for Harmony Valley Fire." Joe was giddier than Mandy had ever seen him. "I'm ready for the water." When it came, the rattle and pressure in the hose almost knocked him to his knees.

Nate and Mandy helped keep him upright.

Mandy's phone rang in her back pocket, which was beneath her fireman's pants and her coat. She removed her gloves and dug for it. The name on the display filled her with relief. "Olivia? I've been so worried. Where are you?"

"I have no idea where Olivia is." Teri sounded put out. "She jumped out of the car."

"*She what?*"

"You heard me. I must not be a total reject as a mother, because I thought you should know."

The phone went dead.

Chapter Twenty

"Okay, you talked me out of running away but…" Hannah tilted her head. "Hey. Do you hear that?"

"Sounds like kittens." Olivia was hungry and thirsty, growing tired of arguing with a little girl who didn't listen to reason. It was only when she'd pointed out to Hannah that she'd be leaving the animals in the infirmary if she ran away that Hannah had relented.

"It's coming from that old house." Hannah put Iggy in the shade of the rock and skipped toward the white two-story.

"We're not going inside." Olivia caught Hannah's shoulder before she'd gone too far. "That's trespassing."

Hannah shrugged out of Olivia's hold. "Are you afraid of snakes *and* kittens?"

"No." Olivia was afraid of houses that had peeled paint, broken windows and looked like a set for a horror film.

Hannah tapped her cheek in a fake gesture of deep thought. "My great-granddad Felix might keep me if I rescue some kittens." When Olivia continued to balk, Hannah made the ultimate proposal. "If you go in there with me, I'll let you do my nails."

"At your house?" Olivia added, because she wasn't totally irresponsible.

"Deal." Hannah gave a big nod.

Olivia hitched her purse higher on her shoulder and followed Hannah to the house and up the front porch steps. The boards creaked and the mewing stopped, as did Hannah. She held a finger to her lips.

They stood listening long enough to give Olivia cold feet about going inside. "This is creepy. Anyone could be in that house." A murderer. A pervert. Witches.

The mewing resumed.

Hannah opened the front door with the familiarity of someone who lived there, not a kid who didn't belong. And she didn't hesitate. She led. She led Olivia to the interior stairs. "This way."

The stair treads groaned beneath their feet as if threatening to disintegrate, in which case they'd probably fall through to the basement where the vampires were sleeping.

At the top of the stairs, Hannah pushed a door open. The hinges sounded like the laugh of the knife-wielding psycho in the last horror movie Olivia had watched with Mandy.

The kittens quieted.

There was something wrong here, something Olivia couldn't quite put her finger on. And it wasn't her overactive imagination.

Hannah made a beeline to the closet and opened the door. "Just what I thought. Mama isn't here."

Olivia came closer. The room smelled like a backed-up toilet. The kittens squirmed on a pink sweatshirt, kind of like the one that Hannah had worn one day last week and... "Those are baby raccoons."

"Yes. About a week old."

Olivia frowned. "You've been here before."

"Yes, but Riley chased me away." Hannah dropped to her knees by the babies. "She's not a very good mom."

"That's it. Time to go home and get a manicure." Olivia had been bamboozled twice in one day. Worse, the second time, she'd been bamboozled by a kid less than half her age. "Is that why you wanted to trap Riley? Because of the babies? You're planning a reunion."

"Yes. We're going to put the babies in your purse and then in the trap at the post office. Riley will go in the cage and they'll be together always."

"Those things aren't going in my bag. This is Michael Kors." She may have bought it used online, but it was still designer. "Put those stinky things in your bag."

"It's too small. If Riley gets trapped and I don't know about it, she's going to be taken away without her babies."

That was on Hannah, who'd put the trap there in the first place.

"Sometimes moms and kids aren't meant to be together," Olivia said sharply.

"Moms should never, ever, ever leave their kids." Hannah crossed her arms over her chest and…

Were those tears in her eyes?

Too late, Olivia remembered that Hannah's mom was dead, and Ben had tried to give her away to some stranger.

Something growled behind them.

Olivia whirled around.

Great. Riley wasn't such a bad mother after all.

"You've got skills, boy," Granddad said to Joe while they cleaned up after the third front-lawn fire where he'd joined the fire brigade.

"Thanks, Mr. Libby." Joe had a knack with the hose. His love of method and precision might have been a reason he was a good mechanic. After all, he'd gotten the fire engine running. "I'm really sorry about the high school fire. My wife says I was a troubled youth." The fact that Joe grinned when he admitted this last fact didn't cancel the sincerity of his apology.

Ben was grateful Granddad was in a magnanimous mood. So far, the trouble Utley had caused with his fiery breadcrumbs had been small. That didn't change the fact that his handful of available volunteers—*Mandy, Nate and Joe*—were green and every new situation was a teaching moment. Of course, Nate had left on a manhunt for Utley. Two of the other five volunteers were away at business meetings. Two, including Will, had accompanied their wives to Cloverdale for their newborns' first checkup. One was down with food poisoning.

If nothing else, the day was teaching Ben that he needed a larger number of volunteers.

Dad sat in the engine's shotgun seat with the door propped open. His eyes were small, and his mouth pinched. His skin color had been better earlier in the day as had his temper. The fire chief was at his physical limit, and he was extremely unhappy to have reached it.

Ben stood on the sidewalk beneath him. "It's time to call Cloverdale Fire for reinforcements."

"We can handle these—" *wheeze-gasp* "—small fires." *Wheeze-gasp.* "Great training." *Pant-pant.* "For recruits."

The trouble with Dad wanting to be on top of things and in control was that Utley had fallen over the edge and was out of control. "We can handle it until Utley sets something bigger ablaze. With the sheriff and half the town looking for him, he's got to be getting desperate." The sheriff had mobilized their elderly audience into canvassing the area, looking for Utley and more fires. Ben leaned in closer, lowering his voice. "Swallow your pride, Dad. Make the call."

He must really have been struggling to breathe, because he took a hit from his inhaler and then a long drink of water. "Not yet."

"Yeah, it's always fun until someone gets hurt." Ben stomped back to the business of doing the fire chief's job. The engine had to be ready to move when the sheriff's call came in about the next fire.

"You're making good on things now," Granddad was saying gruffly to Joe. "At the next one, hit the edge of the fire closest to the building first rather than beginning at the sidewalk."

"Save the asset first." Joe nodded. "Gotcha."

"You okay?" Ben asked Mandy, who'd just finished sealing the fire hydrant cover in place.

She'd been quiet since they'd argued over Utley's innocence. Her ponytails were frizzed from the humidity created by dousing fire with water. Her face and gloves were streaked with grease from wrestling with fire hydrants. She didn't smile. She didn't look determined.

She didn't look at me.

Mandy stared at the horizon. "How can you be here when Hannah is missing? Olivia left with my mother this morning. And then ran away from her this afternoon. I want these fires to end. I want to know that my baby sister is safe. I want to apologize for the broken eggs. I want to know..." She flinched, her expression cracking like one of her emotional eggs. "...that no matter what, we'll always have each other."

"I'm compartmentalizing." Ben touched her shoulder too briefly. He'd prefer to gather her in his arms. "And I'm able to do it because of who Hannah is. She plays it safe. She's capable and responsible."

Mandy flinched at his word choice. "She's seven. You've already rescued her once from the river."

"My mom is searching for her. Nate told his team to look for her, too." Ben couldn't afford to think about Hannah now. "That kid has more street smarts than I did at her age. She spends hours with those animals at the infirmary. She's not clingy. I give her space."

"Seven year-olds don't want space. They want love. And they need lots of it." Mandy's gaze trapped his. "I've seen the lights on at the fire station late at night. You spend time away from her on purpose because you don't want to care too much. You can't commit to being her father because you don't want to break her heart. You can't even acknowledge that you were born to lead because leading a fire crew would be like heading a family. And heaven forbid you put yourself out on a limb where people might be disappointed in you."

Mandy's words sent a shaft of ice through Ben's chest.

But it changed nothing now.

Later... Later, it might break him.

The raccoon wouldn't let them out the door. Riley had them trapped in a corner.

The afternoon sun beat through one of the only unbroken windows in the house. It felt like an oven and smelled like a litter box.

"Don't worry," Hannah said with false bravado, clinging to Olivia's hand. "It's hot and she needs food and water."

"Our bodies are made up of about fifty percent water." Why couldn't chemo brain have taken that fact from her?

Hannah tilted her head and asked softly, "Do you think she knows that?"

Riley bared her teeth.

"Yes," Olivia said.

Hannah pushed her glasses up her nose. "Then we should be still and quiet."

Easier said than done when Olivia wanted to run screaming from the room. But she kept breathing deeply and standing still. If nothing else, cancer had taught her to be immobile when she was afraid. But cancer hadn't taken her voice, and that raccoon wasn't going to either. "I can't believe you wanted to save that thing."

"Even *things* need saving." There was a wistful quality to Hannah's voice. "That's what my mom used to say."

Her dead mom.

That's what this was about. All Hannah's passion for animal rescue.

Olivia channeled Mandy's calm and compassion. She put her arm around Hannah and drew her close. The kid was hotter than a space heater and comforting her made Olivia want to cry.

How had Mandy done it all those years?

Oh, yeah. Her smile and her humor. "When we get out of here, brat, I'm asking your grandmother for a raise."

Hannah leaned into her the way Olivia used to lean on Mandy. "Forget it. Your job is done. John Smith will take me away." Hannah looked up at her with tear-filled eyes. "But he doesn't like animals or snakes."

"He's a jerk." Like Ben, who didn't want Hannah. "I could learn to like snakes."

"Really? You're brave." Hannah returned her attention to the mama she'd misplaced her mommy issues on.

Riley the Raccoon paced and curled her lip at them.

A gray car sped up the driveway toward them, kicking up dust.

"It's Utley." Olivia had never been so happy to see the crotchety old man. She banged on the window and shouted, "Hey! Hey, up here!"

Riley's snarling increased. She crept forward on those creepy little clawed finger-paws.

"Shh!" Hannah shook Olivia's arm. "You're upsetting her."

Olivia stopped yelling. After a moment, Riley stopped growling. Didn't change anything. They were still hot. The room was still stinky. And they were still trapped.

Utley stood nearly beneath them at the front steps. He held a glass bottle with a piece of white cloth stuffed in the top.

"What is he doing?" Olivia was afraid she knew. She'd seen enough teen dystopia movies to recognize a Molotov cocktail. Her insides shook with the need for a bathroom.

Utley tucked the bottle under his arm and took out a matchbook. He lit a match, held it to the cloth and then tossed it toward the front door. The bottle thudded on the porch, making Riley growl and whirl, dividing her anger between the bedroom door and the two girls.

"No!" Olivia banged on the glass.

Utley glanced up but almost immediately looked back at the porch. He disappeared beneath the roof of the porch. Hopefully this was all some big joke and he was going to climb the stairs and save them.

Whoosh-boom!

The house shook.

Riley backed up from them and growled louder.

"What happened?" Hannah wrapped her arms around Olivia's waist. "I'm scared."

"It's Utley. He's the arsonist Ben's been looking for. We have to get out of here." Olivia could swear she smelled smoke. And there was no sign of the old man. "Come on." Olivia took Hannah's hand, grappling the rising panic inside. She hadn't survived cancer to be cremated because of some crazy old dude and a cranky critter. She moved to the door, dragging Hannah along with her.

Or she would have if Hannah hadn't dragged her sneakered heels. "I'm not leaving without Riley." She bit her lip, glancing at the closet. "Or at least not without Riley's babies."

"No. We have to leave. Now." Olivia tugged harder, but Hannah's hot sweaty hand slipped from her grip.

"Don't let them die," Hannah pleaded.

Something crackled downstairs.

Olivia was willing to bet it wasn't Utley's feet cracking boards on his way up to rescue them.

"I smell smoke, Hannah. And I hear fire." Olivia edged along the wall toward the door, hoping that Hannah would come to her senses and follow. As she moved, Riley backed into the closet, crouching over her litter. Shoot. She should have tried moving this way earlier. "Come on, Han. If we don't leave now, we're going to be toast."

"Not without the babies." Hannah's chin thrust out. "Ben will come for me."

Olivia's jaw might have dropped on the floor. "Don't be stupid. Ben doesn't know where you are. No one knows where we are." The truth of her words sank in. Olivia fell back against the wall, needing support. "I wish I had my cell phone." She wished she'd never agreed to leave Harmony Valley with Teri.

"Hey. I have my radio!" Hannah dug in her pink shoe bag.

The smoke in the stairwell was thickening. The sound of a crackling fire was getting louder.

Olivia pushed herself up and went to the door. She couldn't believe her eyes. The fire was leaping up the stairwell. Its heat burned her skin.

How had it grown so fast?

She slammed the door and ran to the window, trying to pry it open.

Riley did no more than grumble, gathering her babies beneath her. She knew Olivia's efforts were futile.

They were already dead.

The radios Ben and Keith wore squawked.

The two men scrambled for the handhelds.

"Help!" A little girl's voice came through the small speaker. "Ben! Grandpa! There's a fire. We're trapped!"

Ben climbed on the fire truck bumper and scanned the horizon.

Mandy had the strangest feeling, as if the world had slowed and suddenly tipped on the opposite axis. "She said *we*."

We as in she and Vanessa? Or we as in she and Olivia?

Keith took the lead on the radio. "Hannah, who's with you?"

"Olivia and..." The rest of her answer was garbled until two words broke through. "...post office."

"No." Mandy succumbed to the weight of the heavy turnout gear, falling forward as she reached for a cleat attached to the side of the truck. She hung on to the sun-warmed metal and managed to stay on her feet. All Ben's dire predictions about the post office being unsafe were coming true. "No."

"I see smoke south of here. By the post office." Ben rushed around to the driver's seat. "Everybody in!"

Joe hopped in a seat behind Ben. Felix moved toward his own truck.

Mandy couldn't seem to let go of the cleat. The post office. Grandpa's legacy. Olivia. She'd be left with nothing that mattered.

"Nobody's dead yet." Keith helped her into the truck, despite struggling to draw a breath. "First rule of emergency responders. Remain calm." His phone rang as Mandy was strapping herself in. "Yes, Nate. Go ahead."

Whatever Nate said, it wasn't good. Keith called his father back, told him something and pointed east. The post office was to the south.

Mandy sat in her seat, cold and helpless, despite the heat and the heavy fire gear. For all she cared, the post office could burn. It was her sister's safety that mattered most.

Images of her flitted through her head. Olivia wearing a Dalmatian costume for Halloween when she was a toddler. Olivia baking cookies from scratch with Grandma. Olivia in a pretty yellow cocktail dress going to her eighth-grade Promotion Dance. Olivia with an IV in her arm, her face paper white, her eyes half-closed against the pain.

"Hurry. Please hurry," Mandy said to Ben.

"There's another lawn fire on Woodson," Keith said when Ben had the truck moving. He sucked on his inhaler and then sucked down water. "Dad and Nate can put it out with house hoses. Cloverdale Fire is on the way to the post office."

Chapter Twenty-One

T he post office wasn't on fire.

Ben couldn't work up enough saliva to make a good news–bad news joke about that, because in the field beyond the post office a gray car sat in front of a flaming two-story farmhouse. Six-foot flames shot out of the front door and first-story windows. Thick black smoke hung like a damning raincloud over the roof. The house was at least seventy years old. The wood would be dry. Fast fuel. Fast heat.

Fast heart. Ben's blood was pumping double time.

"Second story," Dad wheezed. "Right window. Two live ones." His eagle eyes had spotted the girls through the tree line.

"There's a driveway to the right." Joe pointed. "Turn here. Turn here."

Ben did, careening over a curb to make the tight turn. "ETA on Cloverdale?"

"Twenty-five." Dad got on the radio and updated the fire's coordinates.

"They're waving. They're alive." Mandy sounded as if she'd expected the worst. She didn't realize the worst was yet to come. Second-story rescues during a fully engaged fire were unpredictable.

Ben wanted to floor it. He couldn't. He had to take the engine off road.

"Whoa, big guy," Joe said when Ben sent the engine off the gravel driveway. "The house is that-away."

"We've got to come in sideways." Ben hated that he had to slow down even more over the rough terrain. "Utley's car is in the way and we need the ladder."

"Where is Utley?" Mandy asked.

"Body on the porch," Dad said, sucking in breaths like each one would be his last. "I'm in the bucket."

"We all appreciate your heroics." Ben shot his father a glance he hoped showed the man he wasn't being sarcastic. "You work the ladder. I'll go."

Dad nodded, looking almost relieved.

"Gear on first." Ben slowed even more to bring the truck around. "We have time to get the girls." He hoped. "What we don't have time for is rescuing rescuers. Clear?"

"Clear," Joe said from behind him.

Ben glanced back at Mandy. "It's gear on first or you stay in the truck."

"Clear." Mandy had tears in her eyes.

Ben began making plans. "I need Joe and Mandy to get Utley's body off the porch and to safety, administer CPR if he needs life-saving measures. Other aid can wait for Cloverdale." Neither one of them answered him. They were probably thinking Utley didn't deserve saving, certainly not if it was at the expense of rescuing the girls. "Mandy, connect the hose and work the gauges like the chief showed you. Joe, send water in the front door and toward any stairs in case we need them." Ben doubted the stairs still existed. The house wasn't going to be saved. The flames were too high. Their goal would be to keep it from spreading to the field or the trees or to anywhere else in town. But new recruits needed small goals. And the work would keep Mandy from panicking.

Ben parked the engine close enough to fight the fire and far enough away that if the house collapsed it wouldn't fall on the truck. The girls were hanging out of the window waving, shirts pulled up over their noses and mouths. The heat was intense. Smoke stung Ben's nose and eyes.

"Ben!" Hannah's face was streaked with tears. She held the radio in one hand and the neck of her T-shirt in the other.

"We're coming," Ben called up to her. "Hold on."

"Mandy!" Olivia's eyes were huge. She clenched the strap of her purse. "I'm sorry."

"It's okay." Mandy was trying to smile. Ben doubted the girls would see how hard it was for her to do so. "Ben's coming to get you with the ladder."

The crew suited up fast. While Dad set down the legs to stabilize the engine, Ben double-checked Joe's and Mandy's pressure gauges on their air tanks and sent them to the porch. Amazingly, the fire was still contained inside the house walls. The porch and an unmoving Utley weren't burning. While they carried Utley to the far side of the truck where he'd be shielded from the fire, Ben and his father mounted the engine from the rear.

Dad bent over the ladder controls, breathing heavily but not moving anything.

"Hurry," Hannah yelled. She began to cough.

Ben patted his old man on the back and tried to keep his tone light, fearing subtlety would be lost behind the distortion of the mask. "Do you remember how to make this thing go?"

Dad glared at him. Sweat dripped down his forehead. "I'm not dead yet." He raised the ladder slowly and swiveled it toward the girls.

Utley lay unmoving on the dry grass.

Ben spared a glance to Mandy, who'd connected her end of the hose to the engine and was priming the pump. "Is he alive?"

"He shouldn't be," Mandy snapped back. She paused and glanced up at Ben, her heart apparent in her eyes even behind her breathing apparatus. "You're going to save them?"

He gave her a thumbs-up. "And then you and I are going to talk about the future for us and those two girls up there."

She nodded. Her response wasn't eloquent, but it gave him hope.

Dad bumped Ben's chest with the back of his hand. "Go."

Ben hesitated, staring up. A ladder. His feet could slip. He could fall. He never had before. But the girls…

Ben cleared his head. This was his most important rescue. He couldn't let anything distract him.

"You're the best man for the job," Dad said in his wheezy voice. "Bring our girls home."

The Libby living room was full that night.

Full of life. Full of joy. Full of family.

And full of the smell of eucalyptus.

Ben's chest nearly burst with happiness.

Dad reclined in his chair breathing through his oxygen mask watching something on his phone with earbuds in. Mom passed around a tray of cookies she'd baked. Ben sat on the couch with Hannah in the crook of one arm and Mandy in the crook of the other. Olivia was snuggled up to her sister. The events of the day had drawn them together.

Home.

That's what it felt like. Ben drew Hannah and Mandy closer.

Family.

The actual rescue had been uneventful. Ben went up the ladder and helped the girls down. They'd been taken to the hospital as a precaution but were released with a clean bill of health.

The house hadn't survived, but with the help of Cloverdale Fire they were able to contain the fire so that it didn't spread farther.

And Utley? He'd been taken away for psychiatric evaluation. He'd survived the ordeal with nothing more than a bump on his head. Maybe a concussion.

Surprisingly, Dad had confessed to the mayor that his health wasn't 100 percent and offered to step down. The mayor had turned to Ben and asked his opinion.

Ben didn't have to think twice about his answer. "As long as he knows his physical limits, he's an asset. We need his experience and steady hand to help with the volunteers."

Dad had hugged him and whispered, "You'll be the next fire chief of Harmony Valley."

Ben knew it was true. He'd learned to appreciate small-town living. He'd never give this life up to be a fire investigator.

"We're going to need a bigger couch." Mom handed Olivia a chocolate chip cookie.

"Don't plan on me." Olivia sat up straight. "I'm going to cosmetology school."

"Yes, you are," Mandy said firmly, her head resting on Ben's shoulder.

Olivia's chin went up. "And you're not going to pay my way."

"No, I'm not." Mandy's happiness reverberated through her voice and seeped into Ben's chest like a gentle caress. "But I can cosign your loan."

"What about all the..." Olivia lowered her voice. "...debt?"

"Well," Mandy said slowly. "I found our grandparents' will today. It's signed and notarized and leaves the house to us, not Mom." She'd shown Ben the will earlier, wanting a second opinion. He'd recommended she consult a lawyer.

"But Grandpa gave you his will." Olivia frowned. "I saw it."

"He gave us a handwritten note. Never notarized." Mandy didn't smile. The sting of what they'd been through the past two years was still too fresh. Once they sold the house, they'd be able to pay off Olivia's medical debts, but they probably wouldn't have enough to pay for her schooling. "I went to see a retired lawyer in town while you were napping to be sure. He said since Grandpa had been diagnosed with dementia, anything he wrote without validation by two different lawyers is void."

"Can we check on the raccoon trap later?" Hannah piped up.

"Not tonight." Ben gently tugged one of her blond braids. The last thing he wanted to do in the dark was to tangle with a raccoon.

"Are you still worried about Riley?" Olivia tossed her hands about. "She trapped us in that house and then as soon as I got the window open she abandoned her babies!"

"She was scared," Hannah said staunchly, unwilling to back down.

"We were all scared," Olivia went on, relishing the stage. "I didn't jump out the window and leave you there, did I?"

"No, you didn't." Hannah studied her fingernails. They were painted green, and if she lined up her fingers just right a gray snake slithered his way from left to right. "And you saved Riley's babies, too."

"You owe me a purse," Olivia grumbled. "I've got to save for a new cell phone."

"How about another cookie." Mom was enjoying the company and the girls.

Ben cleared his throat. It was time. "I called John Smith before dinner."

Hannah leaped out of her seat, preparing to bolt, tears gathering in her blue eyes. "Why?"

"I told him he wasn't your father." Ben held out his arms. "Because I am. And dads have first dibs."

Hannah squealed and ran to him.

"I couldn't let you go, peanut. I love you that much." Ben squeezed her tight. It would take some paperwork to make it legal, and the much-relieved John had offered to start a college fund for Hannah, so maybe all the angst was worth it.

His mother came to stand beside him. "Ben, did you open—?"

"No." He took out a folded envelope from his back pocket and showed her it was still sealed. He went to the fireplace, took a match from the mantel, lit the envelope, and tossed it in the grate. "I knew the answer in my heart all the time."

The smiles from the women in his life made everything worthwhile. Made home worthwhile. Dad removed his earphones. "What's the hubbub?"

"Hannah is ours." Mom sat in his lap and kissed him. And then she squinted at his screen. "Hey, that's Ben on the mound."

At Ben's questioning look, Dad defended himself. "Since Mom converted our VHS tapes to digital, I've been watching you and those lucky shorts pitch." His voice turned gruff. "You had skill, son."

Ben didn't think his dad could have given him any better gift.

"You should have told me!" Mom flung her arms around Dad's neck and bussed his lips.

"I wanna see." Hannah climbed into their laps. "I'm Team Libby."

"Grandpa Keith keeps us guessing, doesn't he, Hannah?" Mom held the phone so that she, Hannah and Dad could all watch. "But we love him anyway."

"Copy that." Ben crooked his finger at Mandy. Only one thing could make this day more complete. "Come with me."

"Where?" Mandy stood. She wore blue jeans and a navy blue T-shirt with the Harmony Valley Fire logo. It'd been a gift from Granddad at dinner. She was a long, tall drink of water, and Ben was a thirsty man.

"We have a date with Mr. Moon." Ben took Mandy's hand and led her outside into the moonlight. He sat on the wooden picnic table and drew her to sit on the bench between his legs so she could look at the moon.

Mandy draped her arms over his knees. "What a day. And now it's just you and me and Mr. Moon."

"You were a trooper on those fires." He massaged her shoulders. "You didn't panic. You took orders and you got the job done."

"I have a good fire captain."

"Really? Tell me about him."

She chuckled, the sound mixing with cricket song. "He's strong and loyal."

"Don't forget honest to a fault."

"I wouldn't say his honesty is a fault." She turned, moving to sit on the bench so she was facing him. "But he's also patient and kind. Maybe he's too handsome and confident for his own good."

"You can never be too handsome or confident." Ben threaded the fingers of one hand through hers. "He sounds like a man the smartest, hardest-working, prettiest woman in town can have a future with."

Mandy nodded, her gaze warm and accepting. "I think he knows a thing or two about raising kids. Not that he couldn't learn more." She slid her free hand around his neck and drew him closer. "Some might even call him a keeper."

Ben knew she wanted a kiss, and he was more than happy to oblige.

Just not yet.

"I have something for you," Ben said when their lips were nearly touching.

"I certainly hope so." She grinned.

Ben pulled back.

Mandy's smile fell. "Ben?" She sounded unsure.

Ben had never been more sure of something in his life.

He took a ring from his pocket and slipped it on her finger. "It's an old family heirloom."

Mandy stared at the brass—*her grandmother's engagement ring*—and then lifted tear-filled eyes to his.

"I know we haven't known each other long." His palm cupped her soft cheek. "But when you find someone who makes you happy, and keeps you grounded, and understands the importance of telling secrets to Mr. Moon, you need to make a statement. About the future, about love and about kisses."

Before he knew what hit him, Mandy was kissing him. And maybe crying a little but smiling through it.

The sliding door opened behind them.

"That's not how we told you to do it," Olivia shouted, jolting the couple apart. "Tell me this isn't going to be the way you do things because that was—"

"Perfect," Mandy said, drawing Ben back to her. "*Honestly*, you were perfect."

Epilogue

Someone turned off Mandy's country music in the Harmony Valley post office.

Mandy stopped sorting mail, turned, and was immediately enveloped in a hug from Olivia.

"I passed!" Olivia hugged and bounced and laughed, her enthusiasm contagious. "I passed! I passed! I passed!"

Mandy let herself be carried along with Olivia from one end of the post office boxes to the other. It felt wonderful to celebrate the positive with her sister.

Finally, the bouncing and spinning stopped, and Mandy held Olivia at arm's length. "Congratulations!"

"I passed all sections – hair, skin, make-up." Olivia hadn't set out with such high expectations. But in talking to Brit, who operated the local hair salon, she'd realized it was short-sighted to only be able to work in one field.

Olivia was glowing with joy and pride. Closing in on Thanksgiving, her body had recovered from its fight against cancer. Her hair was shoulder-length and her features deceptively delicate.

What had been the worst day in Mandy's life – when Olivia left with Teri and then was trapped in a burning building – had been a turning point for her sister. Since that day, Olivia hadn't let small setbacks derail her confidence in herself or her hope for a healthy future.

Something clattered outside the lobby.

Mandy and Olivia went to the customer service window just as Hannah came rushing inside the lobby. Her bike had fallen over outside.

"Look what I found!" Hannah held a small gray kitten aloft before tucking the little ball of fluff into the crook of her neck. "Can I keep him?"

"Do you think that kitty will get along with the bird with the broken wing you rescued last week?" Olivia teased. "Or the baby frogs you found from the week before?"

"Yes." Hannah thrust out her chin, blond braids predictably askew. "Because you're going to help me, Olivia."

Olivia grinned. "Only if you let me cut and style your hair for Thanksgiving."

Hannah seemed to consider that a moment. "Okay. What should we call him?"

"Ben," Mandy said, smiling as she turned her grandmother's brass ring on her finger.

"We can't name this kitty Ben." Hannah giggled. "We already have a Ben."

"No." Mandy pointed. "Ben is here. Our honey."

"*Our honey*?" Olivia rolled her eyes, but the truth was that she loved Ben, too. She tried to boss him around, especially when it came to romantic gestures toward Mandy. "Ben is *your* honey. I have my sights on Ryan."

Ben entered the lobby, looking handsome in his firefighter uniform. "Hey, all my girls are here."

"I passed all my tests!" Olivia ran out to meet Ben in the lobby, destroying her comment about Ben being *Mandy's* honey as she threw herself into his arms. She doted on Ben nearly as much as Hanna did.

"That's great, Olivia." Ben twirled her around.

"And I found a kitten." Hannah came forward when Ben set Olivia down. "Can we keep him, Dad?"

Dad. Ben still got teary when called that.

Ben's gaze caught Mandy's. He beckoned her to join them in the lobby. "Do I ever have a choice if we keep an animal or not?"

"Nope." Hannah pushed her glasses up her nose and leaned against Ben's leg.

"Not really," Hannah added, hooking her arm through his.

Mandy entered the lobby, taking in her little family and feeling an overwhelming sense of love. For her sister, who was growing into an independent woman. For little Hannah, who never met a stranger, whether human or from the animal kingdom. And for Ben, whose honesty and unexpected love was giving Mandy a safe place from which to grow.

"I think I'm too soft on you girls. You always get your way." Ben's blue eyes sparkled with mischief. "And that's why I'm here to propose a vacation. The second weekend in June. After school's out. We're going to drive to Lake Tahoe and get married."

"Married?" Mandy's loving smile turned into a grin.

Ben shrugged. "You couldn't seem to settle on a date or a place, so…"

"San Francisco would be swankier," Olivia began her usual argument.

"No. I want to go somewhere where there are animals who need me," Hannah added her usual argument.

"And I don't really care as long as we're together," Mandy finished off, sounding something like a broken record. She closed the distance between them—*all of them*—and gathered her family close. "Ladies, I think we're going to have to let Ben take ownership of the wedding decision and live with whatever he decides."

"How romantic," Ben murmured.

"And honest," Mandy pointed out.

Somehow, Mandy and Ben managed to ease Olivia and Hannah to either side of them. Ben's arms settled around Mandy's waist and hers around his neck. From the look in Ben's eye, Mandy was about to be kissed. She'd never tire of kissing Ben.

"But only this one thing, right?" Olivia asked.

"Yeah," Hannah seconded. "Don't make it a habit, Dad."

"I wouldn't dream of it," Ben murmured, lowering his lips to Mandy's. And then he stopped, his lips a finger's breadth away from Mandy's. "Except…I would like something more for the family," Ben said, that mischievous smile making another appearance. "More boys. I need them on my side." And then he kissed Mandy.

While Olivia and Hannah made it clear they'd much rather expand their family with girls.

The End

If you enjoyed this installment of Love in Harmony Valley, I'm writing a bonus story for Olivia and Ryan, which you can read in installments at: https://BookHip.com/TKVNGGR

Downloading the scene will add you to Melinda's email newsletter list, which you can unsubscribe from at any time. No harm, no foul. But stay subscribed if you want more of their story.

Otherwise, read on for a sneak peek at the next book in the series: *Redemption in a Small Town.*

A Small Town Redemption
Excerpt: Chapter One

"What's the emergency?" Sheriff Nate Landry, fresh from chasing chickens at Clara Barra's house, took a seat on a creaky wooden pew in the back of the church. "Spring Festival meltdown?"

"The emergency is next," Flynn Harris said in a hushed voice so as not to wake baby Ian in his arms.

Nate's entrance met with turned heads, warm smiles and nods of recognition. The Harmony Valley Town Council was in session, better attended than some small-town basketball games. The meetings were held in the historic, steepled church downtown, being led from folding tables and chairs set up on the pulpit. That was the way of life in the remote northeastern corner of Sonoma County—casual, a bit of making do and a bit impromptu.

Flynn managed to brush reddish-brown hair from his eyes with his shoulder without disrupting his newborn's sleep. "The emergency is Doris Schlotski."

At mention of the woman's name, a little black rain cloud formed above Nate. He hated that rain cloud.

As the only lawman in town, Nate prided himself on figuring out what made each resident tick. *Doris Schlotski*. She'd moved here four months ago and was a conundrum.

About three months ago, Nate had issued Doris citations for violating both the noise and pet ordinances. She bred Chihuahuas and her ten adult dogs barked 24/7. She'd argued that they were only small dogs and quieter than a neighbor's Saint Bernard, which to be fair was a true statement, but big, old Bernie only barked at the Amazon delivery truck.

A few weeks after that he'd issued Doris a citation for permanently parking her never-used fishing boat on the street. She'd argued that her driveway wasn't wide enough for both her car and the boat. Just last week, he'd pulled Doris over for speeding. She'd argued that the speed limit hadn't been updated in fifty years and was therefore invalid.

Nate was still trying to determine what made Doris tick, but he was done arguing. He bet Doris wasn't. He bet she was here to argue about speed limits or public right-of-way or pet regulations.

Ian squirmed, rolling his head until the blue puppy blanket dropped unnoticed from his head and over Flynn's arm.

The door behind them opened, bringing a nip of evening air. Harmony Valley was near enough to the Pacific Ocean to be cooled nightly by ocean breezes and thick fog.

Nate tucked the baby blanket snugly around the tufts of red-brown hair on Ian's head.

Footsteps and whispers from the newcomers were covered by Mayor Larry recording a quorum on a request to rezone some property in the south part of town. The pew behind them groaned as someone sat down. At the front of the church, heads turned to see who'd entered. Inquisitive stares neighbors followed.

Nate began to turn to see who had come in when Flynn nudged him and said, "Here we go."

"Next on the agenda..." Mayor Larry squinted at his notes through black rectangular reading glasses. "'Sheriff elections?'"

Abruptly, everyone faced forward, perhaps as shocked by the agenda item as Nate was.

The little black rain cloud above Nate's head thickened. Doris wasn't here to talk about speed limits or public right-of-way or pet regulations.

She's here to talk about me!

Nate leaned closer to Flynn, keeping his voice down. "We don't have sheriff elections." He'd come to Harmony Valley nearly three years ago because the town was plain and simple. He'd been hired, plain and simple. He'd renewed his contract, plain and simple. Less than two hundred residents lived in town, most of them pleasant, law-abiding, elderly. Plain and simple.

At least, until Doris had returned to the area, breathing fire.

Doris approached the speaker podium like she was going to bulldoze it. She was shaped like a fireplug—short, compact, the promise of energy behind every step. Her gray hair didn't dare curl or frizz, not even in the fog. Barely an inch long, it stood on end. She was a fireplug, all right. Only instead of spouting water, Doris spouted words. That woman could outdebate a presidential candidate.

Nate sucked back a grin. She hadn't been able to talk her way out of those citations.

Something bumped the back of Nate's pew just as Doris began to speak. "Mr. Mayor—"

Nate's grin slipped free by half, poking holes in his rain cloud.

Mr. Mayor?

Everyone called him Mayor Larry, at the mayor's request. The aging hippie and tie-dye business entrepreneur was unorthodox, from his long gray ponytail to his tie-dyed attire and his penchant for naked yoga down by the river, a practice folks respected and avoided.

Doris addressed those on the dais. "Madames Councilwomen—"

Nate's war to contain the grin became more challenging. The three councilwomen weren't into formalities either.

"Ladies and gentlemen," Doris continued in her high-pitched, grating voice. "We should be proud of many things in our community. The wonderful festivals we have. The resurgence of new businesses. And the low crime rate. But that isn't good enough."

Not good enough? The little black rain cloud sucked the oxygen from the old church.

"In this age of police misconduct, the people need a voice." Doris had a death grip on the podium.

Nate thought it might be his death she planned.

"Can't see," came a little voice from behind Nate.

That innocent voice. It broke through the cloud.

Clop-clump.

It sounded like the tyke stood on the next pew back.

"That better, Juju."

Doris wasn't only upsetting Nate. On the pulpit, the town council murmured and shifted in their seats. Those in pews in front of Nate exchanged significant glances and whispered commentary.

"The people have a voice, Doris." Councilwoman Agnes Villanova drew the microphone she shared with the other councilwomen closer. "Residents vote for representatives of our town. Your representatives then vote on issues of health, well-being and safety. Why, just this last year your town council hired two firefighters and renewed the sheriff's contract."

Short, spunky Agnes ran the town from her seat to the mayor's right. Next to her sat Rose Cascia. Rose looked like a retired ballerina with her thin frame and her crisp white chignon. She might have pulled off New York sophistication if she didn't tap-dance her way into rooms. At the end of the table sat Mildred Parsons. Mildred could barely see, despite her thick lenses. She was made of soft angles, from the snow-white curls in her short hair to her plump frame.

Nate loved those old ladies. They chased away his storm clouds.

"Beg pardon, Madame Councilwoman." The smirk in Doris's voice carried to the back of the church without her having to turn around. "But I was talking about removing a layer of politics from the process."

"A layer of politics?" Spritely Agnes had the heart of a saint and silver hair as short as Doris's, except Agnes's hair relaxed on her head. "Are you questioning our dedication to this town? Are you questioning our...ethics?"

The crowd murmured in disapproval. The mayor and town council had been serving for decades. They were wise. They were beloved. They always ran unopposed.

Nate drew a calming breath. Whatever agenda Doris had, the town council would thwart it.

"What I'm saying is clear enough that everyone in this room understands," Doris said with the pomp of the self-important. "Everyone but you!"

In the midst of horrified gasps, a small hand landed on Nate's shoulder.

"Hi." Hot breath gusted in Nate's ear.

Nate glanced over his shoulder into a pair of large gray eyes framed by a dark mop of hair. He'd never seen the toddler before, but the boy was cute and most likely the reason for the curious stares a few minutes ago.

Across the aisle, Old Man Takata beamed at the tyke and tapped the shoulder of his neighbor Snarky Sam, who owned the antiques/used goods store on Main Street. Sam's smiles were rare. And yet he gave the kid a toothy grin.

The little boy touched his forehead to Nate's and repeated, "Hi."

"Hey," Nate said softly, unable to resist returning the boy's impish smile. "Be careful."

Feminine hands curled around the boy's torso and drew him back. Nate began to twist around to see who the hands belonged to when Flynn spoke again, halting him. "Do you think Doris would be more respectful of you if you wore a uniform?" Even in a whisper, Flynn sounded like he was enjoying this more than Nate. Of course, Flynn wasn't the sheriff. He was part owner of a winery.

"I don't need a uniform," Nate whispered back, not enjoying this at all. He'd rather be chasing chickens. "I have a star on my truck and a badge in my pocket."

Doris wasn't the whispering type. In fact, she was practically shouting now. "I'm saying that we the people and only we the people should decide who serves our community. Otherwise, we'll be stuck with a sheriff—" without turning, Doris pointed behind her, toward Nate "—who badgers our residents, berates citizens for their lifestyle choices and bullies the elderly with citations and tickets they can't afford to pay!"

"Freaky," Flynn said louder, causing the baby to stir and loosen the blanket again. "It's like you and Doris are psychically connected. She knew exactly where you were sitting."

"She saw me come in." Nate could solve that mystery more easily than the one involving what made Doris so bitter. "She can't be this upset over tickets."

Doris held up a sheaf of papers. "I have here twenty signed reports from residents about Sheriff Landry's behavior."

Nate didn't think he'd given out twenty tickets in the past year.

"Twenty reports stating that Sheriff Landry gave them warnings rather than a citation with a fee attached. Whereas I..." Doris had worked herself into huff-and-puff mode. "Whereas I have received three citations in the past three months! I demand we let the people decide who protects us. I demand we fire the sheriff and hold an election!" She dropped the stack of papers on the podium like a rapper dropped a mic at the end of a show. Except she kept talking. "I demand—"

"In my defense—" Nate said to Flynn, tucking Ian's blue blanket more securely around his tiny shoulders "—the only way to handle Doris is to give her a ticket and drive away."

"Now, Doris..." Mayor Larry made a rare appearance in an argument. Normally, he delegated trouble to the town council so he could remain as neutral as Switzerland. "These are serious allegations. Please approach with your notes so we may look them over."

Clod-clump. Clod-clump.

The kid behind Nate was on the move again.

"Notes?" Doris snatched up the papers again, clutching them to her chest. "This is my evidence!"

Clod-clump. Clod-clump.

The noise was drawing attention.

The gray-haired residents of Harmony Valley had probably never done the wave at a sports stadium. But their heads turned in the same ripple effect to stare Nate's way, starting from the back of the church and moving forward. And as they looked past Nate, grins and coos rippled through the assembled—

The little hand returned to Nate's shoulder, followed by a hot-breathed, "Hi."

When Nate turned his head, he received another gentle forehead bump. "You're an awesome little dude." Nate ruffled the boy's hair.

The boy's gray eyes widened in delight. "I Duke." He tapped his skinny chest and grinned.

The majority of the assembled chuckled. The majority being over age sixty-five and being grandparents or great-grandparents who appreciated precocious children.

Behind Nate, someone emitted a heavy sigh. Feminine hands drew the toddler out of view once more.

"For years—" Doris half glanced behind her as if sensing she was losing her audience "—you four have ruled Harmony Valley. Well, no more! The people want to be heard. The people want a say. The people want to vote for a sheriff of our own choosing!"

Campaign for sheriff?

Nate sat back against the pew. He wasn't the hand-shaking, promise-making, run-for-office type.

"Now, Doris..." Mayor Larry hated discord and looked as if he was ready to break Robert's rules of order and escape out the back. He started again. "Now, Doris—"

"Don't you *now, Doris* me. I want action and I want it now!"

"She slipped up there," Flynn noted. "She said I."

"*The people...*" Doris quickly self-corrected. "*The people* want action now!"

"I'm going to remind the speaker," Mayor Larry said carefully. "That there is a review process written in the town bylaws—"

"By you." Doris scoffed.

The mayor tilted his head down and stared at Doris over the rim of his rectangular readers. "Written by the town council over seventy years ago."

"Hi!" Duke shouted, completely stealing the limelight and bringing some much-needed laughter to the proceedings.

Doris spun, so upset at being upstaged that her short hair seemed to tilt forward and take aim at the upstager.

The few residents not enamored of little Duke straightened and quieted like school children caught misbehaving. The rest kept on smiling and scrunching their faces in funny ways designed to encourage the boy, not calm him down. Duke really was a cute kid. Not even Doris was immune to his charms. Her expression seemed to soften.

"We should wrap this up so we can all meet that adorable young man in the back." Agnes spoke into the microphone. "These are all good points, Doris. Therefore..." Agnes waited until Doris faced her again. "I move we hold a sheriff's election as soon as possible. Say...this week, so as not to hinder our Spring Festival plans."

Voices disappeared beneath a rush of sound in Nate's ears, as if he was passing a semitruck on the highway with his windows down. His position was an inconvenience to the Spring Festival? His livelihood? His future?

The assembled were just as shocked as Nate. The church had fallen into a stunned silence. There wasn't so much as a peep from Doris or Duke.

During the lull, Agnes elbowed Rose.

"Uh..." Rose looked as confused as Nate felt.

Mildred, who had more than a slight resemblance to Mrs. Claus, pushed her thick lenses higher up her nose and sighed. "I suppose... I second?"

Anticipating peace, the mayor beamed at the council. "All in favor?"

All three town councilwomen said, "Aye."

"Motion passed." The mayor closed out the meeting.

"An election?" Nate's plain and simple world was suddenly not so plain and simple.

"Don't sweat it." Flynn stared down at Ian with a whole lotta love in his eyes. "You signed a new contract and you're the only qualified candidate in town. In a week, you'll win by a landslide."

Nate's future was out of his control. He didn't think he'd sleep for a week.

"I Duke." The little dude gripped Nate's shoulder.

The woman's hands drew him back.

"*Juju*," the boy scolded.

In the past eighteen months or so, there'd been an influx of younger residents to Harmony Valley and a baby boom. Nate turned more fully in his seat to see who held his new friend.

Familiar gray eyes collided with his.

The storm cloud returned. And flashed with lightning.

"Hello, Nate." Julie Smith put nearly three years of disdain and disappointment in those two words.

"Julie." Nate shot to his feet, steady as always, guarded as always. If Nate was the sheriff, he was off duty. He wore a brown checkered shirt and blue jeans, not a service uniform.

Duke was balanced on Julie's thighs, his small hard-soled sneakers digging in for purchase as he reached for Nate once more.

Couldn't Duke loathe Nate as much as I do?

Couldn't Nate look as if the past few years had been one big heartbreak?

No on both counts.

Duke's fingers flexed as he reached for Nate.

And Nate? It was annoying how good he looked. His black hair might have been in need of a trim and his chin shadowed with stubble, but his teeth hadn't fallen out, his broad shoulders weren't bullet ridden and, worst of all, he didn't look sleep deprived.

The mayor and town council were still on the pulpit surrounded by animated residents with loud voices. Chaos had arrived in Harmony Valley, just not the way Julie had envisioned it.

The man next to Nate came to his feet. He wore a wedding ring, held a swaddled newborn, had spit-up on the shoulder of his yellow polo and New Dad bags under his eyes.

Julie gave him a sympathetic smile. Duke despised naps and could be a restless sleeper at night. Not as restless as Julie lately, but still...

The man with the baby cleared his throat, shaking Nate out of tall, dark and stunned mode.

"Flynn," Nate said slowly. "This is Julie, my..."

And there it was. That awkwardness Julie had been waiting years for.

She pounced. "I'm the sister of Nate's ex-fiancée."

Flynn slid a questioning look Nate's way.

Her moment had arrived.

Julie stood, scooping Duke to her hip with her left arm. "Didn't Nate tell you he was engaged? He left my sister at the altar." That wasn't all he'd left, but Julie didn't want to waste all her ammunition on the first volley.

Flynn didn't look as shocked as she'd hoped. She blamed Nate. He inspired loyalty wherever he went. Even after being dumped, April had forbidden Julie to confront him. But that ban had been lifted.

Now it was open season on the sheriff.

Duke toppled forward, letting his full weight drop between Julie and Nate, unexpectedly shifting Julie's center of gravity. She slurped in air like it came through a clogged milk shake straw. The stitches beneath her right collarbone pulled sharply, tugging at nerves that quivered up and down her neck and shoulder.

Mom was right. The doctor was right. It is too soon.

And too late to back out now.

Julie drew on years of resentment, drew Duke back and drew down her chin against the pain. She was here for justice. She was here to make Nate suffer. Surely that wouldn't take long.

Nate hadn't been shamed by her announcement that he'd backed out of a wedding. He didn't scowl or frown. He didn't put his hands on his hips and try to stare Julie down. She'd forgotten he was a man of few words.

Julie was itching for words. Fighting words. "My sister, April, defeated cancer and the idea that it might return gave Nate cold feet." She glared at Nate, daring him to contradict her.

"Not exactly," Nate said in a gruff voice, not riled enough to fully engage in battle.

Julie drew a breath to continue her assault, only to be interrupted.

"What a pleasure to see a new babe in our neck of the woods." It was the miniature old lady from the town council, the one with the relaxed, pixie-cut silver hair. She bestowed Duke and Julie with a friendly smile, and then gave Nate the kind of smile grandmothers bestowed on favored grandkids, before turning that smile on Flynn. "Can the council borrow you?"

Flynn edged past Nate, who was staring at the ceiling as if searching for divine intervention.

Julie hoped April wasn't smiling down on him. Her younger sister had always been the forgiving type.

But not me.

Before Julie could resume their sparring match, an elderly woman with unnaturally black hair and a severe widow's peak stood behind Julie and ruffled Duke's hair. "Who is this adorable young man?"

"I Duke," Julie's nephew repeated, thrusting his shoulders back. He loved attention.

"More importantly, who are you?" A pale elderly woman wheeled an oxygen tank to Julie's pew and adjusted the cannula in her nose.

"Oh, heavens, no. That isn't the important question. The important question is are you here to stay?" This from a rotund gentleman waggling a smile and bushy white brows.

At least ten elderly folk clustered around Julie's pew, clogging the aisle. They leaned on walkers and canes and the pew itself, waiting for Julie's answer.

"Is this how we treat visitors to Harmony Valley?" Nate asked them in a voice infused with patience.

For a moment, no one answered. And then someone said, "Yes," which made the group laugh.

"Her name is Julie," Nate said, still in patience mode. "And you can ask her questions some other time. Now, does everyone have a ride home?"

They dutifully nodded and pointed to their rides, or volunteered to take others home.

Amid the subsequent shuffle toward the door, Julie studied Nate some more, trying to figure out how he won everyone over.

He had that ramrod-stiff posture that signified confidence and a history of military service. His black hair was parted to the side where a cowlick prevented the hair over his forehead from lying flat. His brown eyes were serious more often than not, and when others were grinning he only allowed a half smile. He was bottled up and wound tight, keeping his emotions close to his chest. Even after he'd met April.

Which was weird. Everyone had loved April. She handed out smiles the way sample ladies handed out free food at Costco. She'd been the kid least likely to get in a fight and most likely to shed tears over sappy television commercials. She'd grown up to be a kindergarten teacher, of course. And she'd taught dance and tumbling to little ones for the recreation department. She was the opposite of Nate, who'd been a sniper in the Middle East, and Julie, who was now a sniper on Sacramento's SWAT team.

Julie eased her aching shoulder back, ignoring the growing feeling of exhaustion. She nodded toward the podium. "Stirring up trouble, I see."

"Trouble always has a way of finding me," Nate said with a half-smile.

Julie's aim was off. Nothing was ruffling Nate. Nothing was satisfying her need for revenge. She'd have to hunker down for the long haul. She'd never been good at the long game, at chess or Monopoly. This time, the stakes were higher than bragging rights or a pile of paper money. This time, she had to be the patient one.

"Want Mama." Duke collapsed against Julie's shoulder, his forehead pile-driving into the only tender spot on her body.

Her sharp intake of breath caused Nate to dip his head and stare at her more closely. She smoothed her expression into her game face, determined that he only see what she wanted him to see—a strong woman who despised him.

"You got married." Nate's gaze was gentle.

She didn't want his gentleness. She wanted his anger. She wanted to argue and shout and have him argue and shout back. "You think I'm married because…"

A small crease appeared between Nate's brows, only for a moment. "Well.. .this little guy…"

A surge of satisfaction shored up sagging dreams of revenge. "You think a woman has to be married to have a child?"

The crease returned, deeper this time. "You're a cop. Female cops don't—"

"You're a police officer?" asked the woman who'd been putting up a stink at the podium. She'd stopped at Julie's pew. Doris didn't smile. She didn't coo over Duke. She eyed the pair like a cattle rancher at a bull auction.

Julie didn't put much stock in the woman's claims. Nate was many things, but he was a good cop. And Julie wasn't keen on being sized up. But she wasn't here to cause a ruckus about it either, so she said, "Yes, ma'am," and ground her teeth at the interruption in her attempted takedown of Nate the Unflappable.

The woman stored that information with a brisk nod, and then moved toward the door.

"Mama." Duke crooned softly.

Nate glanced around, perhaps catching on to where this was going, perhaps assessing how much privacy they had. Or how much they'd need.

The more public his humiliation, the better.

"I'm not married." Julie's smile felt triumphant. "And Duke isn't *my* child."

End of Excerpt: Chapter One

Grab your copy of A Small Town Redemption on Amazon or on ShopMe lindaCurtis.MyShopify.com.

About the Author

USA Today bestselling author Melinda Curtis has written and sold over 70 titles, mostly contemporary romance, but including two writing craft books. Working both traditionally and as an indie, Melinda writes sweet romance, women's fiction, and sweet romantic comedies. One of her romances – *Dandelion Wishes* – was made into a TV movie – *Love in Harmony Valley* – starring Amber Marshall. Melinda is married to her college sweetheart, has three children, and currently lives in Oregon. When she's not writing, Melinda enjoys brief stints of gardening (if it's sunny) or catches up on cleaning and laundry (begrudgingly), all done efficiently so she can get to her to-be-read pile and list of shows to binge.

Check out www.ShopMelindaCurtis.MyShopify.com for autographed books, bundles, and sales: ShopMelindaCurtis.MyShopify.com

Explore the other books in the Love in Harmony Valley series!

Other Sweet Books/Series by Melinda Curtis:

A Cowboy Worth Waiting For, Book 1 in the Cowboy Academy romance series

A Kiss is Just a Kiss, Book 1 in the Summer Kisses (Grandma Dotty) romcom series

Can't Hurry Love, Book 1 in the small town Sunshine Valley romcom series

Kissed by the Country Doc, Book 1 in the small town Mountain Monroe series

Her Alaskan Valentine's Day Matchmaker, Book 1 in the bearded, Alaskan Matchmaker series

A Son for the Mountain Firefighter, Book 1 in the emotional, action-packed Mountain Firefighter series

Christmas, Actually, Book 1 in the long-running Heartwarming Christmas Town series

Christmas at the Sleigh Café, a 1st person romcom from the Christmas Mountain series

Discover more titles and a reading guide at: https://www.melindacurtis.net

Happy reading!
Melinda Curtis

Made in the USA
Middletown, DE
27 March 2025

73342969R20140